THE
TORAH
CODES

EZRA BARANY

Dafkah Books

THE TORAH CODES

ISBN: 978-0-9832960-1-0

Printed in the United States of America

Published by:
Dafkah Books
Oakland, California
www.TheTorahCodes.com

Cover design by Heather Smith

Go to www.TheTorahCodes.com for bulk orders.

For You.

Prologue

Trinity College
Cambridge, England
November 5th, 1692

The candle's flame danced, performing a show of shadows in Isaac's room. A drop of hot wax cried down the candle until it joined the hardened pool of old wax coating the corner of the table.

Isaac reread the letter from his friend in the twisting light. His friend had asked some bold questions. Isaac thought how to respond. Someone was playing a lute in the college courtyard, no doubt a student. Isaac spooned a bite of the sack posset, and savored the mixture of sweetened cream, dry sherry, and spices. He set down the bowl designed for alchemy, yet filled with food, and took up his quill.

Dear Nicholas

Your questions are well placed. In truth, there are not answers to all of them. The Bible signifies one of the greatest treasures that ever was bestowed upon us, providing us with nothing less than all that fullness of knowledge of things past & to come.

The essence of the Bible is not the revelation of truths beyond human reason unto life eternal, but is a prophecy of human history. And having searched after knowledge in the prophetique scriptures, I shall one day communicate it for the benefit of others.

Isaac searched for the words. His eyes fell upon his hand held mirror. The mirror was cracked, but did its job. Isaac set down the quill and picked up the mirror. He studied his reflection, then pivoted the mirror to reflect the candle. When he faced the candle directly and looked at the candle's reflection in the mirror, he found the mirror to be parallel to the imaginary line made between him and the candle. In fact, no matter where he held the mirror, as long as he could see the candle's reflection, the mirror stayed parallel to the line connecting him and the candle.

Isaac placed the mirror down flat on the table and continued his letter.

People should not be discouraged by past failures to understand these writings. They are not about the past. They were written for future ages. When the time comes, their meaning will be revealed in their fulfillment.

The folly of interpreters has been, to foretell times and things by this Prophecy, as if God designed to make them Prophets. God delivered the Prophecies, not to gratify men's curiosity of the future, but so that after they were fulfilled they might be interpreted by the event, and His own Providence, not the Interpreters, be then manifested thereby to the world.

As to your question of the end of days, there will be an end. The fearful, and unbelieving, and the abominable, and murderers, and sorcerers, and idolaters, and all liars shall have their part in the lake which burneth. And it is only by the Creator's intervention and the presence of chosen individuals that the delay of this cataclysm is achieved.

The Prophecies reflect the true church. And by the true church, I

*do not mean all who call themselves
Christians, but a remnant, a few
scattered persons which God has
chosen.*

As Isaac paused in thought, a splotch of ink from his quill dropped onto the desk. He stared, fascinated at the way the edge of the drop rounded and reflected the flame. Isaac flicked a few more drops of ink into the same splotch and watched the tiny puddle grow. He saw the relationship between the growth of the ink's circumference and the growth of the ink's area. For a brief moment he calculated the mathematical relationship, and then returned to the letter.

*The world must contain not less
than thirty six selected men who
are granted the sight of the Hebrew
Goddess. They are the "Lamed Vav
Hasidim," the thirty six righteous.
It is for these few humble people that
God delays the final destruction.*

*Naturally, I hold much trust in
you to keep these words in your
confidence. Should my feelings be
made public, I would be expelled from
Trinity College. That is why I ask
that you destroy this letter.*

*Your most affectionate
and faithful friend,
Is. Newton*

Isaac set down the quill and finished the sack posset. The spoon scraped the bottom of the wooden bowl with a series of satisfying sound waves. Isaac licked his lips. He returned his attention to the mirror. The lute outside was still playing as Isaac examined the candle's reflection in the mirror. The way the light was able to choose the shortest path from the candle to the mirror to himself made Isaac stare with wonder.

Part 1

FIVE

Chapter 1

Oakland, CA
November 5th,
Present Day

Digging up a corpse buried underneath a busy sidewalk creates all sorts of problems. For one thing, you get on-lookers. People who aren't necessarily going to like what they see. For another, the killer could be watching. And who knows if he's the kind of killer with a one-time vendetta, or the kind of killer who makes a sport of killing as many people as possible in one fell swoop. But the biggest problem of all is that, if you're like me, and you value your personal space and privacy, you lose those valuables when you get an audience watching you dig.

So it was time to make a decision. Should I walk away and pretend the body wasn't there, or should I start digging like a madman?

And what if the body wasn't there?

My work had given me a pretty extensive computer programming assignment to do at home over the weekend. An assignment I wasn't eager to start, so on my way home that Friday afternoon I stopped at Piedmont

Avenue. Piedmont Avenue is like a piece of Paris in the middle of Oakland, a city known for its slums. Seriously. Smack in the middle of a tough town, you've got a street lined with chi-chi restaurants, a movie theater showing art films, and dessert specialty stores.

Normally, I'd steer clear from such a place, but that evening, I was looking for a distraction, and that distraction was right off the freeway.

Piedmont Avenue was busy as usual. There's something to be said about anonymity among masses.

"Excuse me, sir. Could I ask you a few questions for a survey?"

Whoa! Where did he come from?

This kid was dressed in a white button-up shirt, navy blue slacks, and a narrow tie around his neck that said, "I have the best fashion sense in nooses." His clean-shaven face and trim haircut matched the professional look of his clothes. Looked as if he just left church. To do a survey? Seemed unlikely.

Normally I'd tell him to find a lake to piss in, but today was different.

"Sure," I replied. "Anything to delay my work."

"Okay, great!" He introduced himself and asked for my name.

"Nathan."

"Do you live in an apartment, condo, or single family home?"

"None of the above. Duplex. My landlord lives in the other half."

"Ah! You're smart!" The kid smiled. "Getting the luxury of a house at the cost of renting. Okay, next question. What area do you live in, Nathan?"

"Oakland Hills."

"Wow! That's a real nice area!" The kid wrote on his clipboard. "Would you call yourself the head of the household?"

"I live alone. You figure it out."

"Ha, ha." He looked at his clipboard and made a mark. "Do you have any electrical equipment? TV? Stereo? That sort of thing?"

"Both of those, plus a laptop, and desktop."

The kid scribbled and asked "flat screen TV?"

"Nope. Regular."

"Great. Do you value the security that your home provides?"

"You have no idea," I replied.

"And do you feel safe at home?"

"Safe as cement."

"Excuse me?"

"No one steals cement," I explained.

"Great. I'll just check the box 'feels safe.' Now if someone were to try and break into your home, would you do whatever it takes to stop them?"

"Of course."

"And do you have an alarm system?"

"Don't need one. I figure, if a burglar wants to find a house to break into, why drive all the way into the Oakland Hills when he can find one closer to downtown?"

"Excellent! So I'll mark you down as not having one." The kid made a check on his clipboard. "Not many people know that crime has gone up 23% in the Oakland Hills."

Ah. Here came the pitch.

"I'm certain you wouldn't want to wake up one day to find your stereo, television, laptop and desktop taken by someone who broke into your home," he continued. "You said that you would do whatever it takes to prevent someone from breaking into your home. And knowing how much you value the safety and security of your home, surely an intelligent man like yourself understands that purchasing an alarm system for only $499 would be a small price to pay to protect yourself."

"Commitment and consistency."

"Uh…excuse me?"

"You're using a tactic Cialdini calls commitment and consistency."

"I don't…" The kid looked like he'd been slapped.

"You got me to commit to certain values, such as saying I would do whatever it takes to protect my home, and now you're relying on my desire to be consistent with what I've said. But I could design my own alarm system for a lot less money, and I'm not about to let a tactic like that take away my dignity. Lastly, if you think I'd give you my address when you know I don't have an alarm system, then it's going to take a lot more than a nice tie and clean haircut to look the kind of smart you're gonna need."

The poor kid turned white, stammered something resembling a thank you and walked away.

I steered myself into a store that premiered exotic ice cream flavors. I chose vanilla. The cashier was easy on the eyes. Problem was she had this nose ring. Made her face completely asymmetrical. To me, beauty was in the symmetry of things. Like in math. A bunch of really complicated math can be cancelled out if it's also on the other side of the equal sign.

Here's what I mean. Imagine walking into your bedroom and seeing a fire-breathing dragon on your bed. You got the force of gravity pulling the dragon down, but you've also got the bed's support force pushing him up. Since the forces are equal, they cancel out and the dragon doesn't move up or down. That sweet symmetry keeps him steady and now he doesn't have to worry about falling. He can just focus on burning you to a crisp.

So I'm not sure why the cashier decided to ruin all that symmetry by punching a hole in her nose and sticking a piece of metal in it.

The ice cream came in a dainty cup with a dainty plastic spoon, which was fine with me, because it would take longer to finish. But I prefer those flat, wooden spoons for my ice cream. It just tastes better. I've heard wine tasters use "wooden" to favorably describe wine. I've never heard them say, "Ah! Tastes like plastic."

Walking outside, I took cold bites in the chill of the winter air. A homeless man about thirty years old, not much younger than me, held out his hand and asked for change.

I set down the ice cream on the sidewalk, pulled out my checkbook, wrote him a check for $499, and handed it to him. A look of surprise and shock crossed his face. I picked the ice cream back up and went on my way.

It was just after 4 p.m. on Piedmont Avenue when I finished my ice cream. Leaving work so early was a perk of being a computer programmer. Usually, I don't even need to show up at the office. I just went to the meetings that happened once or twice a week, and the rest of the work I did at home.

I threw out the ice cream cup and spoon, and peered into the shop windows. All of the items for sale—the magazines and cigars, jewelry and scarves, the fashionable gowns and women's shoes—had only one purpose in mind. To help people, be they rich or poor, show off a wealthy lifestyle. I wasn't one of those people. Even though I could afford such a lifestyle, I kept my money.

I needed to walk around someone, so I had to step on the dirt of one of the tree plots that lined the street. As I stepped on the soft dirt, my heart grew cold. I nearly threw up. A body had been cut up and recently buried underneath the dirt. A man with dark hair, a pin-striped suit, a golden wedding ring on his finger. I knew this. I knew this like I knew my own name.

There was nothing to indicate such a thing. A million reasons could be given for why the dirt was soft. But I knew there was a body down there. And that I was next.

Chapter 2

People kept on walking by me like noth-ing had happened. The trees rustled their leaves. I looked for a place to sit and think. A redwood bench across from the theater stood out. I sat down to reason it out. When was the body put there? Obviously after hours, when no one was around to witness it.

But that was the wrong question.

The right question was, how did I know there was a man buried there? The dirt was soft. I told myself that wasn't enough. There had to be more. More evidence.

I couldn't come up with anything. I didn't see any hair, didn't see any fabric, and didn't see any finger with any ring. The only conclusion left was that this was one of my manic moments. I have bipolar disorder and sometimes my senses are so keen, I can see things that aren't really there. And when I do, I get a little paranoid.

Just to make sure, I did a control experiment. I stood, walked over to a different tree, and stepped on the dirt. It, too, felt soft. So no one was buried. It was all in my head.

My mother, rest her soul, used to explain to her friends, "Nathan has these episodes. They're like having a panic button that gets pushed." But it wasn't like that at all. It was more like having a square panel of panic buttons, one hundred long by one hundred wide. Apparently, my chopped-up-and-buried-dark-haired-guy-wearing-a-pin-striped-suit-and-gold-wedding-ring panic button got pushed.

On the drive home I was pretty shaken up about my dead body delusion, and certainly not ready to take on this project my boss had assigned to me. I put all my attention on the road, hoping that would calm me.

The road curved more and more the higher into the Oakland Hills I went. I kept the window rolled down to feel the cold air hit my face. Further up the road, housing became less dense and trees became the common residents. The familiar forest and gravel road that led to my duplex were welcome sights.

My landlord's front door was on the opposite side of the duplex from my own front door. The place appealed to me because of its symmetry. The only way to tell whose door you're going through is by noticing the placement of the trees on the outside. I also like the isolation aspect of it. In the Oakland Hills, the properties offer great elbow room for people whose arms are 100 feet long.

Passing through the living room, I did my usual thing of waving to the painting of the collie hanging above the TV. "Hi, Crotch-smeller."

I headed straight to the kitchen and pulled out a bottle of beer. Opened the bottle above the sink. The cap bounced all over the sink making tinkling sounds and it made me think about how the moving energy of the falling bottle cap changed into sound energy. Energy isn't created or destroyed, it just changes. I proved it again when I returned the bottle opener to the drawer and slammed the drawer shut. Kchunk! Listen to that energy. I opened and closed the drawer a few more times. Kchunk! Kchunk!

I moved to the bedroom, set the beer on the dresser, picked up the photo of my ex-wife Nancy and collapsed onto the bed. Holding her picture above my head blocked the view of the ceiling and I stared at Nancy's photo for a bit, wishing she were back with me. And thankful she wasn't.

Chapter 3

Twenty-five hours and seven minutes of sleepless work and Wheat Thin crumb production later, I had completed my assignment and e-mailed the results to the powers that be. My head proposed that I should celebrate this conquest by taking two aspirin. My eyes voted for the bed. They all got what they wanted.

Two hours later, it was 8:12 p.m. and I realized I hadn't let my bladder vote. I headed for the bathroom and turned on the light.

My eyes complained.

I turned off the light.

I leaned against the mirror above the sink and reassured them that the light was off and that they could now open again.

I opened my eyes expecting the typical picture: round face, brown hair, brown eyes, long neck, but all close up since my forehead was leaning on the mirror.

But it wasn't myself I saw.

I saw a room. A room filled with cameras. Photos

were taped to the wall. I cupped my hands to the mirror and saw the room more clearly. All the cameras were pointed straight at me. But the room was dark and no one was there.

My heart pounded. "What the hell?!"

I stood up straight trying to understand what I had just seen. I was being watched? And if they watched me in here…"Oh, no."

I rushed to the bedroom mirror that ran from floor to ceiling and cupped my hands against it. More cameras and more photos taped to the walls. I thought of the time I brought a prostitute home. Not exactly the proudest moment of my life. I looked from my bedroom to the bathroom. Did it really end there? My head turned toward the living room.

There was no mirror in there. I moved into the room and looked around.

The room was empty when I first moved in…except for the painting of the collie above the TV. Luke Mc-Court, my landlord who lived in the other half of the duplex, had said he couldn't remove it. It was nailed to the house beams and would tear off part of the wall.

I collapsed onto the couch and stared at the painting. The stupid depiction of the white collie reminded me of the cheap paintings in motel rooms. I scrubbed my hands through my hair, then held them over my face. Peeking through my fingers, I peered again at the collie.

Okay. Why did Luke do this? How was taking pictures of me advantageous to him? Was that the right question? Not really. I decided to start off with questions to discern reality versus delusion. Was I actually seeing through the mirrors? Yes. Did I actually see the cameras? Yes. So far, reality was winning.

I rushed to the garage and grabbed a hammer and chisel. They felt heavy in my hands. Back in the living room, sliding the chisel between the painting and the wall, I peeled away to the truth. And there it was. A hole through the wall the size of a bullet. Through the hole looked to be a snake camera. I picked up the painting and held it to the window. The moon's light showed a small hole where the dog's dark nose should have been.

My stomach twisted around my guts. I dropped the painting to the floor and took it all in. The bathroom, the bedroom, the living room… everything I had discovered poured into me at once. I was being watched. Luke may have seen everything I had ever done. But that wasn't it. That wasn't the worst. It was my house, dammit! My house! There was no refuge there anymore.

Chapter 4

I **didn't want Luke to know I had found out**
his secret just yet, so I replaced the picture of the
collie and put back the hammer and chisel. I had to
get away. Not sure how far I'd go, I took my Anywhere
Organizer with me. It held my social security card,
one thousand Euros cash, an ATM card linked to my
emergency account that had more money than God,
an unlabeled calendar good for any year, a calculator,
pen, and my passport. Everything I needed, no matter
where I ended up.

In my Toyota, I placed the organizer in the glove
compartment, fired up the engine and drove to the
Berkeley Marina. Though it was getting close to nine
o'clock, the pier was open 24/7 and was probably
empty this time of night. I parked the car and crossed
directly onto the pier.

The pier lights seemed to go on forever, straight into
San Francisco. And San Francisco was lit up like Em-
erald City. I heard the sound of water slapping the pier
beneath me. The sour smell of the water was strong. I

was wrong about the pier being empty. A few fishermen dotted the sides of the pier. I hugged my overcoat close and walked a little faster, as though that would help leave the problems behind me.

Why did Luke do this? What did he gain? I doubted it was something sexual. Watching me was about as exciting as watching glaciers melt. Besides, there were plenty of highly sexed people in the Bay Area Luke could have rented to. Guys or girls with different partners every night, with all sorts of fetishes. I was about as unrelated from that scene as a hallmark birthday card was to a bunch of Vikings strung upside down with pythons strangling their necks. So if it wasn't sexual, what was it?

Further down the pier, it was colder and darker. I shivered and pulled my overcoat even tighter around me. Looking back, I guessed I'd walked a fourth of the 3,000-foot pier. Each time I passed a fisherman, the fisherman stared ahead, too focused on his line to notice me. But that didn't necessarily mean these fishermen ignored me as I passed. They could be watching me when my back was to them. I walked faster. I was halfway down the pier.

It was pointless trying to figure out what Luke's real motives were. I'd gain nothing from questioning his motives. Truth was, I couldn't be sure of what I saw. Yes, it all seemed real. But for all I knew it could have been the landlord-is-watching-you-behind-two-way-mirrors panic button. Just another delusion.

The wind bit harder. The stars widened their eyes.

Besides the wind whistling in my ears, my steps on the concrete were the only sound around. If anyone walked behind me, I'd hear him coming. I tried walking softer to hear better. But then there was the problem of someone matching my steps. If someone matched my steps, I wouldn't be able to tell by the sound alone whether or not someone was behind me. I turned around.

No one was there.

I rolled my eyes and continued walking west toward the end of the pier. The end was close. The pier used to be longer but parts of it broke off ages ago. In the daytime, you could still see the wooden remnants of the old pier checkered off further into the bay. But it was too dark to see the old pier now. Still, the stars were at full attention, as though the closer they examined me, the brighter the area around me became. I stopped and looked around. The cold wind blew so tough it was beginning to burn.

My heart beat faster as I realized how I had just walked myself into a corner. If anyone followed me, my only escape was a cold, wet death.

Chapter 5

If isolation didn't help me feel safe, maybe crowds would.

I trudged back to my car without incident and drove along the bay toward Oakland. I approached the Emeryville plaza known for its huge theater complex. The bookstores and restaurants were so close together, it was easy to get lost in a crowd. And it was the right time of year, too. That time between Thanksgiving and Christmas, when everyone was out shopping. I parked in the parking lot.

I passed the cell phone stores, the rug stores, and the soap and bath stores. I climbed the escalator and came upon the crowded restaurants. People surrounded me, clearly uninterested in me. I released a breath I didn't realize I'd been holding in.

I looked at all the restaurants. You got your gourmet burger, your gourmet pizza, your gourmet fish or chicken on a stick... All they needed was a gourmet pet food restaurant for those who brought their pets. Thinking about all these restaurants was a great distraction from my problems.

At the movie theater, the ticket counter was nearly desolate. When I saw the remaining showings, I understood why. The only movies that were showing soon were a foreign documentary with a name I couldn't pronounce, a Drew Barrymore chick flick, and something about giant hot dogs.

I tried the nearby bookstore. As I was already upstairs, the entrance led to the bookstore's second floor. I came to a table of books that were twenty percent off. Cookbooks, taking care of your pet, sewing tips, and how to make money off of extra real estate. I knew these would come in handy the next time I want to cook my pet while sewing a sock to hold all my extra real estate.

I looked around at the people browsing the store. From my vantage point, I could see the entire store because the indoor escalators opened like a courtyard onto the lower level. Kids were playing downstairs in the juvenile fiction area, teenagers with torn clothing hung around the graphic novel area, and prattlers clinked their coffee cups and stirred in milk and sugar at the small coffee shop inside.

I wandered back outside. Paced back and forth in front of the shops and stores. A moustached man beside me was doing the same. He looked almost like one of the fishermen I passed on the pier. Was he following me? I figured that if someone were following me, then

I should stay in one place. Anyone watching me would have to stay in one place also. Easier to spot.

Just outside the bookstore were tables for people who bought coffee. A woman sitting at one of the tables offered tarot readings. The handwritten sign in front of her said, "I can help you find your true self."

I walked up to her.

"Hi! Want a reading?" She gave me a kind smile.

"How much?"

"A half hour is $50, an hour is $75."

I felt my eyes widen.

"But I do three-card readings free of charge," the blonde-haired woman added.

I sat down, "Let's do the three-card thing. How does it work?"

"It's very simple. You pick three cards from the deck and lay them on the table." She spread the deck face down across the table.

I pointed to three. Looked for the moustached man. I saw him cheerfully greet a lady and together they walked into a Mexican restaurant. So he wasn't following me.

"That was fast," she said as she removed the cards I chose and put away the rest of the deck. "Usually my clients like to spend time touching the cards, feeling out what's right."

"Yeah, whatever." I checked out the rest of the area. No one seemed to be hanging around watching me.

The tarot reader looked to be in her late twenties, or maybe closer to my age. She wore jeans and a powder blue sweater whose sleeves were too long for her arms. Beside her was a large, half-eaten cupcake. Possibly blueberry. The three cards were placed one next to the other face down.

She pointed to each one saying, "This card represents your past, this one is your future, and this one is your overall being, your true nature."

She flipped the first one and I read the caption, "Suffering." The card had a picture of spears thrust into the body of a strange beast.

"You had a rough past," she said.

"Who hasn't?"

She smiled and said, "This card is usually reflecting a negative aspect, but what's good is that you have this card in your past. It should serve as a reminder that your life can change, and with the change can be an end to your suffering, if you're still experiencing the suffering."

I just nodded and kept checking my surroundings. Everyone seemed to have their own agenda. No one stood out.

"Here's your future," She turned over the next card. A picture of a skeleton riding a chariot had the caption "Death" underneath.

"Oooh," The woman said.

"Well, that's true," I said. "I'm not immortal." I was thankful for not being in the middle of a manic moment. I might have read too much into the cards otherwise.

"Death is not always a bad card," she explained. "It's true that it can refer to a physical death, but more often it refers to a death in your former ways, a change in your life. A new job, a new place to stay, that sort of thing."

"A new place?" I asked.

"Yes. Does that resonate with you? Are you moving soon?"

I lowered my eyes. "I suppose I am."

"What do you mean?" The woman asked.

I looked up at her. Thought about Luke taking photos of me, video footage of me, pictured him watching the time I took that prostitute home. And then I thought about how I would feel if I found out the whole thing was just one of my manic episodes. That there were no cameras and no photos. Just a stupid, ordinary painting of a collie loosened from the wall because of my paranoia. I looked at the tarot reader's sign. "I can help you find your true self," it said. My eyes fell upon the ground.

"It's nothing," I said. "What's the third card supposed to represent again?"

"The third card is your overall personality at the present," she said. She turned the card over and from my vantage point, the card was upside-down. I turned it around and saw a glowing grin with wicked eyes. A horned goat within a pentagram above the caption "The Devil."

Chapter 6

I looked at the devil card in front of me and asked, "I'm the devil?"

The tarot reader laughed and said, "The devil is a card about having fun, playing, being carefree. But it was upside down when you picked it." She held the card in front of me upside down. "So that means the opposite. You *do* care. You care about other people, and what other people think of you."

"That's not me at all."

She chuckled and pulled off a piece of her blueberry cupcake, "Then that means you don't know yourself very well." She nibbled on it and smiled.

Normally, I would have punched her, but I actually admired her for having the guts to defend her reading. "You can interpret these cards anyway you want to, right? It's whatever you want to read into it. But when I told you that wasn't me, how come you didn't say something like, 'Maybe the card means you *don't* care about others because of such and such a reason'?"

I saw a hint of a smirk in the woman's face.

"Ah, ye of little faith," She said. She picked up the three cards and joined them with the rest of the deck. "Here. Shuffle them." She extended her hand out holding the deck. Her hand looked as soft as her sweater.

I took the deck and started shuffling the cards.

"Wow! You're quite a shuffler. Where'd you learn to do that?"

"College," I said. "I took statistics and my classmates brought decks of cards to class. We'd calculate the likelihood of picking two red cards, three red cards, the same card twice. That sort of thing."

The woman didn't blink. She looked at me as though waiting for something. "And the shuffling?" She reminded.

"Oh. So several of the guys knew some fancy shuffling tricks. I picked it up from them." I placed the deck down. "There. Shuffled."

The woman spread out the deck like before. "Pick three cards again."

I smiled. I saw where this was going and it made me admire her even more. She was going to defend her reading even if it meant the odds were against her. The woman looked up at me with a smile. Her teeth were a little crooked. It made her face completely asymmetrical. Still, there was a friendliness about it that I couldn't pinpoint. Why was I sitting here with her? Oh, right. Running from somebody.

I picked out three more cards. The woman put away the rest of the deck, and placed the cards side by side on the table.

"Ready, Mr. Statistics guy?"

"Yep," I replied.

She picked up the edge of the card, but stopped. "By the way. What are the chances of picking the same card twice?"

I raised an eyebrow. "How many cards are there in a tarot deck?"

"Let's see, four suits of one through ten, and the Major Arcana,...seventy-eight."

I whistled. "Then it's one in seventy-eight. Assuming you have all the cards in your deck."

"Alright." She turned over the first card and it was the Suffering card. I tried to contain my astonishment.

She said, "Helluva coincidence, eh Mr. Statistics Guy?"

Chapter 7

I **stared at the suffering card. The odds of** getting that card a second time... Not impossible, but still. "Coincidences happen," I said at last.

"Coincidences," she said. "Okay. Now let's see the next card. What are the chances for this one?"

I smiled. There was no way it would work with the second card. "That's seventy-eight squared. So seventy-eight times seventy-eight is, say, one in six thousand."

"One in six thousand?" She nodded as though impressed. "Sounds like it would take a miracle."

I noticed the ankh shape on the back of the card. It was right side up, so the second card I picked was going to be right side up, just like last time.

She turned it over.

I didn't have to look. I knew it was going to be a different card just by the statistics. Instead I watched her face. Her mole disappeared into the dimples that formed from her defeated smile.

"I guess you're happy now, huh?" she said.

I looked at the card. It was a picture of a man dangling from one foot upside down. The caption read, "The Hanged Man."

"It just means that there isn't necessarily something paranormal or unexplainable about this stuff," I said.

"Perhaps. Or maybe that death card, that change in your life already happened. The hanged man is about suspension, you know. A period between two stages in your life. Are you moving to a new place?"

I stared at the woman for a long moment. Already happened. I couldn't live in my home anymore, yes, that already happened. But that's assuming what I saw was real. What I needed was someone to vouch for me. Someone to verify what I saw. The woman cleared her throat and straightened the cards, her eyes avoiding mine. I guess I was staring at her.

"Well let's look at the next card," she said. She placed her hand on the third card but I put my hand over hers before she could flip it.

"Could you...not turn it over?" I asked.

"Why not?"

I looked down to the table. What if I were still going through a manic moment? What would the card trigger? So far, nothing. I felt pretty level-headed, but that's how I felt before I discovered the cameras. Looking at cards that predict one's destiny was probably not a good idea for a guy with paranoid bipolar disorder. I lifted my eyes to hers and said, "There's something that concerns me."

"A virgin at tarot?" she smiled.

"Something like that."

She placed her other hand on mine, my hand sand-wiched between hers. "Let me see if you have anything to worry about."

She turned over my hand and looked at my palm. "You have a long life line." She traced the line in my palm with her finger. "And your heart line is also long but—." She moved my hand a bit closer and turned her head to get a better look, "it's very faint."

"Which means?"

"Not very stable. You're more of the one-night-stand kind of guy." She looked into my eyes and smiled. "Is that true?"

I took my hand away. "I've had my share of broken hearts. I'm not looking for a relationship anymore."

The woman looked at me with intensity. "What are you afraid of?"

I remembered Nancy. How she had to put up with my delusions. How she tried so hard to convince me it was all in my head. And how brilliant I was at twisting everything to make *her* look like the crazy one.

I looked at the tarot reader. I could trust her. Trust her eyes. She could be the one to verify what I saw. "Would you come look at my bedroom?"

She laughed, "Wow! It doesn't get any more direct than that!"

"That's not what I meant. I just…" I tried to figure out how to explain it without explaining it. "I need your help."

"Let's see what the cards say." She spread the cards out and pulled one. Placing it upright on the table, I saw a picture of a boy and girl holding hands with the words "The Lovers" below.

"Alright, Mr. Statistics Guy. I'll be happy to see your bedroom. On one condition."

"What's that?"

"Tell me your name."

"Oh." I looked away. "It's Bill."

"Okay…Bill. My name's Sophia." She shook my hand. "Let me just put the sign in my car. I'll leave my car here and you can bring me back later." She picked up the third card I didn't want to see, and looked at it. She smiled, placed it in my shirt pocket and said, "When you're ready to lose your virginity, she's right here." She tapped my shirt pocket.

Chapter 8

Patrick Sullivan listened to an old familiar country song playing in his hatchback truck.

Just because you're the prettiest girl I know, doesn't mean I'm in love with you...

Sullivan sang along, returning from a great ho-down. Kicking up his heels with the ladies had been a blast.

He drove through the Webster tube from Alameda. As usual, though the hour was late, the road was full. It was time to get off the beaten path. Sullivan turned on Seventh and headed toward Jack London Square. The street was mostly deserted except for the Cadillac-shaped vehicle driving not only the wrong direction but without headlights. Sullivan flashed his headlights as he passed them. Suddenly, he heard a screech and looked in his rear-view mirror. They had attempted a 180 and with their headlights on, their car peeled toward him.

"Oh, for crying out loud," Sullivan knew what this was all about. Gangs were known to have an initiation routine. Anyone who signals to turn on the headlights is the next victim for the new recruit. If the kid wants to join the gang, he has to shoot the guy who flashes their headlights at them.

Sullivan sped up, turned left at one corner, turned right at the next. Sure enough, they followed him.

"If there's one thing I will not tolerate…" Sullivan said. He maneuvered left and swerved his truck to the right so his truck was blocking the road. Their car stopped a short distance away and their passenger door opened. Sullivan couldn't see what the kid was holding but it didn't look like a donut.

Sullivan grabbed the double-barrel shotgun from beneath his seat, and got out of the truck so the truck was now between him and the kid. With one pump of the shotgun the kid froze. Sullivan pointed it over the top of the truck and got his clear shot. The gun pumped an explosion into the car's tire. The three-wheeled car backed up in a wobbly screech as the kid with the gun ran after them trying to get back inside.

Sullivan watched them squeal away and returned to his truck. He got on the CB radio and called in, "James 31. Seventh, near Webster. Start several units. There's been a gang-related shooting."

"10–4. Who are you?"

"James 31, off-duty. I work night shift. There's been a gang-related shooting from a Cadillac, possibly blue, with an exploded front tire."

"Uh…10–9. Did you say exploded?"

"Yeah, exploded."

"10–4. That's a Cadillac, possibly blue with an exploded tire."

"10–4." Sullivan closed the channel. He turned his radio back on and drove to work for his graveyard shift.

Chapter 9

Once at my house, Sophia entered through the garage and mudroom to the living room and sat on the couch.

"Fantastic place you have here!" She kicked off her shoes, jack-knifed her legs off the floor, and nuzzled into the corner of the couch. "Do you think I could get a beer? Or are you desperate to show me your bedroom?"

"One beer coming up," I said. I went to the kitchen, snagged two beers out, and popped the caps off into the sink. They pinged all over the sink like pachinko balls. This time, it made me think of the Brownian motion microscopic particles have when colliding with the molecules of their surroundings. I returned to the living room and offered her the beer.

"Heineken!" She said. "Nice choice." She took a drink and looked at the bottle.

I looked at the collie.

"Why are you still standing? Have a seat." She patted the place next to her.

I sat on the couch wondering if I should still reveal my fears and have her validate them.

"So, Bill. Can I ask you a question?"

"You just did."

She giggled. "Here's another. Tell me, Bill. What's your real name?" She looked at me as she took another swig from the beer.

I studied her. Is she bluffing? Is she really psychic? She burped and smiled, dramatized her innocence by over-fluttering her eyelids.

She wasn't bluffing.

"How did you know?" I asked.

She smiled wider. This was a game. "Alright, I'll tell you. You know, people do interesting things when they remember things. They look up to the left. When you told me your name, you looked up to the right. Looking up to the right means you're making something up, not trying to remember." She put the bottle down on the coffee table in front of her. "But then, anyone who has to look up to remember their name must have recently fallen off a horse and hit their head on a rock."

I nodded. Clever girl. "A woman after my heart," I said.

"Better believe it."

I drank from my beer. Thought about the bedroom mirror. All the cameras behind it. "It's Nathan," I said.

"Nathan. Now *that's* a nice name. Sit closer."

I stood up. "This isn't really why I asked you here. Could I show you something in the bedroom?"

"Well, you gotta admire a man who says what he wants." She put her beer down and followed me.

Inside the bedroom, she sat on the bed and bounced up and down. "Pretty good spring action!"

"Over here," I said pointing to the mirror. I cupped my hands and looked behind the glass. Yep. Still there.

Sophia came and cupped her hands against the glass. Her hands peeked out of her long sleeves like kittens in a mailbox.

"Uh…" Sophia said. "I don't think…"

"What do you see?"

She just looked at me like I had betrayed her in some way. "I think you should take me home, now," she said with an uneven tone. She started walking away.

I grabbed hold of her arm. "What did you see?!"

"I see a guy who makes a living posting his escapades on-line. Now let go of my arm, or so help me…"

"You see them? The cameras?"

"Of course! Why? Was I not supposed to?" Her voice got louder. But I could tell she was trying not to yell.

I let go of her arm, cupped my hands at the mirror and looked at the cameras again. "They're not mine," I said. "They're my landlord's."

"What?"

"I found them today. Just before meeting you," I said. "He's been watching me ever since I moved here, I guess. Taking photos, videotaping me…"

"Jeez!" She looked at the cameras again, then back at me. "Sorry that I thought…"

There was no need for her to apologize. I brushed it off with a wave of my hand.

"What are you going to do about it?" She asked.

"I'll call the police. See what they say," I decided. "What about you? You probably want to get home."

"I just got here!"

"I know, but you don't need to get involved in all this."

She smiled. "I know what you're trying to do."

"What?"

"You're trying to get rid of me."

"No! Believe me. I think you're gorgeous. But now is not the right time. And the truth is, I'm not a one-night-stand kind of guy."

"I know." She studied him. "I also know you're the hanged man. Suspended in a major life change." She took out a business card from her back pocket. "I'm willing to help. Call me if you need anything, okay."

"Fine." I put the card in my pocket without looking at it. "That reminds me." I pulled out the tarot card from my shirt pocket. "Here's your…" I saw the devil's grin. As though he were laughing at me. Statistically, no way that card could have been pulled.

Sophia noticed my reaction and said, "I know what I'm talking about. So call me, okay?"

I handed her the tarot card, removed her business card, and looked at her number. Same area code as mine.

"Okay," I said.

* * *

I drove Sophia back to her car and called the police. Told the guy on the other end of the line about the cameras, photos, and the painting of the collie. The guy said he'd send a team over, but not to get my hopes up. There may be little they could do to help in situations like these. After the call, I took 40th up to Broadway, turned at Pleasant Valley, and took Moraga Avenue into the hills back to my home. No. Not my home. I didn't know what to call it.

Chapter 10

❝ What time did you make your discovery, Mr. Yirmorshy?" The policeman had introduced himself as Officer Stelwarth. He and his partner had arrived, checked out the two-way mirrors and the living room and, at my request, stood outside to go over the details. Stelwarth had a firm presence and took notes in a tiny notepad. His partner was a smaller guy who talked as much as a piece of toast.

"About eight o'clock," I replied.

"What did you do afterwards?" Stelwarth asked.

I told him all that I had done after finding the painting. I told him about the pier, the Emeryville plaza where I met Sophia, and how I showed the cameras to Sophia before calling them.

The smaller officer was looking up at the stars like it was the first time he'd ever seen such things.

"What are you guys going to do?" I asked.

"For now, there isn't much we can do," Stelwarth explained. "Your landlord's equipment is on his property. Fortunately, we could see from your mirrors that the photographs hung in his rooms were of you. That's an infringement of your right to privacy. We called in a request for a search warrant. Normally, the request would be denied. But you have something going for you. The snake camera in the living room. Because it crossed his property and entered yours, he might be considered trespassing."

"Okay," I said.

"I don't want to get your hopes up," Stelwarth added, "because it's probably not enough for a search warrant. But one other thing you have going for you is that we're post 9–11. That means that getting a search warrant is a lot easier than before. The judge still has to approve it, and most judges are hard-nosed about this sort of thing, but it's worth a shot."

Stelwarth's walkie-talkie made some noise that resembled something talking. Stelwarth lifted the voice piece that dangled around the back of his neck to the front of his shirt.

"Go ahead," Stelwarth said into it.

More talking sounds emanated from the box on Stelwarth's hip. It might have been female, but I wasn't sure.

"10–4." Stelwarth turned back to me. "You heard the news."

I was astonished. Stelwarth somehow managed to understand what that box was saying. "I didn't, actually."

"It turns out Mr. Luke McCourt offered expensive camera equipment online and after getting people's credit card numbers, failed to deliver the equipment. The cards, of course, were over charged. You got your warrant."

It was a start.

"Someone is bringing it over now," he said.

While Stelwarth joined others in searching Mc-Court's place, the smaller officer stayed with me. Typically, in stressful situations like these, people advise you to do visualizations to relax. The only visualization I had was of the police finding pictures of me with the prostitute.

"Why do you think he'd do this?" I asked, distracting myself from the visualization.

"It is kind of odd," the policeman said. "Normally, voyeurs peek into women's showers and bedrooms, not men's. Did he have a lot of women friends? Or did he bring male friends home more often?"

"You're asking if he was gay?"

The policeman nodded.

"No. I mean, I don't think so."

"What do you know about him?" he asked.

"Not much," I said. "Drinks beer. Listens to classical music." I pictured him. Looked like Jack Palance without the cowboy hat. That endearing smile he had, somehow made him also look evil. And always smoking. "He smokes these foreign cigarettes. Djaras, Djarams, something like that."

Stelwarth approached and said to me, "You better come downtown. We have some questions we need to ask you."

Terrific.

Chapter 11

In the distance, Luke McCourt saw Nathan talking to a policeman. The red and yellow lights danced through the trees like a disco. With the classical music he was listening to in his car, the disco lights were surreal. Bach's inventions on harpsichord played a mathematically organized sound that kept him calm and focused.

"Nathan, I wonder if you realize what you've done." He took out a cigarette and lit it. The headlights were off. The engine was quiet. He took this opportunity to think. He could no longer go back to that place. That was certain. But what about the overall picture?

"Nathan, it seems you've forced our time sooner than I expected." He took another puff of his cigarette. The smoke swirled in his mouth, a shroud over his tongue.

"Good."

He snuffed out the cigarette, put its corpse in the car's trash, and let his car slip away into the night.

Chapter 12

The police had let me drive myself to the station. After parking my car, I met up with the officers at the front desk. They placed me in a private room. It didn't look like an interrogation room. No two-way mirror. That was a relief. It was more of a meeting room, with a long table surrounded by metal chairs. A window looked out to the rest of the police station with open horizontal blinds. Why did I have to come to the station at all? My stomach twisted the more I thought about it.

Maybe they'll understand, I thought. The loneliness of a single guy. And as George Carlin put it, sex is okay, selling is okay, so why isn't selling sex okay? But that's not how they'd see it. They'd see photos, footage, and who knows what else, of me having sex with a prostitute. There was no way the police would be "understanding" about it.

Bile came to my mouth and I swallowed my beer again. It burned going down.

The door opened and a man in black slacks, a blue button-up shirt, and a badge at his belt sat opposite me.

"How are you, Mr. Yirmorshy?" The officer said tapping a file on top of the table to line up all the documents evenly.

"Is that a joke?"

The policeman didn't respond. "My name's Detective Sullivan and I just need to ask you a few questions."

I waited.

"How long have you lived at your current residence?" Sullivan asked.

"It's running on three years now. Ever since I started working for Google."

"You work for Google?! How about that! I heard the workplace is like a resort. They got yoga there, ping pong tables, a place to speak French…"

I figured it out. Sullivan was playing good cop and later, someone playing the bad cop would come in to get me to confess.

"So do you like working there?" he asked.

"I work from home and only come in when I have to."

"Oh," Sullivan raised his eyebrows and I wondered what I had inadvertently revealed. "Must be nice. But let's get back to the case."

Now it was a "case."

He took out a notepad from his shirt pocket and clicking a pen open, asked, "Did you know Mr. McCourt before you rented the place from him?"

"No," I said slowly.

"You don't sound certain," Sullivan said.

"I just don't understand the purpose of the question."

He wrote in his notepad and asked, "Have you met any of Mr. McCourt's friends or relatives?"

"No," I said. I had this hideous image of the prostitute being Luke's sister.

Sullivan continued, "Has your family ever been famous at one time or another? Was there ever a reason people wanted to take photos of you?"

I planted my elbows on the table and put my face in my hands. "No."

"Is there any scandal you or your family are involved in?" Sullivan asked.

"What kind of scandal?"

"Mr. Yirmorshy, just tell me this. Can you think of any reason why your life might be interesting to Mr. McCourt?"

"I don't know what you're talking about! I am not the suspect here, am I? Shouldn't you be talking to Luke McCourt?"

"Mr. Yirmorshy, here's what we found in Luke Mc-Court's home."

Sullivan spread out several photographs on the table. "Do you have any idea how he got them?"

I looked at the pictures. Most of them were of myself. But not just at home. One was of me eating lunch outside my workplace, one was of my prom night, one was of me in a school play during third grade,...and one I recognized was of my mother and father during their honeymoon, before I was born.

Chapter 13

I **kept staring at the photos. How was it pos-**
sible? Wasn't it me who decided to rent the place
from Luke? But then I remembered the bar.

"Can you believe the price of beer these days?" the
stranger had asked me. He had sat next to me and ordered Coors.

"Yeah," I had said. "It's pretty steep."

"But it's not as bad as real estate," the man said.
"Have you seen the prices? Seven hundred grand, eight
hundred grand… The Bay Area ain't cheap."

"Tell me about it. I would love to get out of my
coffin-sized apartment but even renting is expensive."

"Hey! You really looking to rent?"

"Well, not really. As you said, the prices are too
steep."

" 'Cause I just got a duplex at a pretty reasonable
price, comparably speaking. And I'm looking for someone to occupy the other side. Interested?"

"How much?" I asked.

"Eleven hundred a month. It's a huge place and it's got its own garage and washing machine and everything. It's a little bit out of the way, but it's still a great place."

I liked the price. "Where is it?"

"The Oakland Hills. Why don't I give you my phone number and you can come see it sometime." The stranger had pulled out his wallet. "Here's my card. And that's me. Luke McCourt. Camera salesman at the best camera store in the Bay Area."

"Alright," I had said. "I'll call you."

That had been three years ago. Seemingly coincidental. And here the photographs in front of me to prove that it wasn't so coincidental. I told the detective how I met Luke McCourt.

"There's something else you need to see," Detective Sullivan said.

He removed a letter from the file. It was addressed to me.

"We're not sure where the letter was mailed from," Sullivan said. "The postmark says Florida, but we think it was just an out-of-the-way place to keep the location secret. At least we have the date it was mailed."

I looked at the postmark. The date was four months ago. "How come you found it in McCourt's place?"

"We think he intercepted it for some reason. Would you mind opening it?"

"Sure." I ripped it open, unfolded it and read the typed letter.

Dear Nathan,

I so look forward to meeting you face to face. You don't know who I am, but I have heard so much about you. I can't express how much joy I felt when I read your name in the Bible. The joy that comes to my heart whenever I think of you overflows, and I'm filled with a wonder that I can feel this way at all.

I suppose you must think it strange, getting a letter from some stranger. But with MEG, we'll no longer be strangers. I'm not really supposed to be sending you this, but I just couldn't resist.

You have all my love.

There was no signature. I put it down and stared into space as Sullivan picked it up to read it.

"You have no idea who this might be?" Sullivan asked.

"None," I said.

"Do you know anyone named Meg?"

I shook my head.

Sullivan looked at the letter while clicking his pen open and closed. He stopped clicking and asked, "Do you mind if we give you a copy of the letter and keep the original?"

"You can have it," I said still in a daze. Looking without seeing. It was some time before I realized Sullivan had been eyeing me with a concerned face.

"Mr. Yirmorshy, I'd like to ask you to follow me, please." Sullivan said. He got out of his chair and opened the door for me.

I stood up and slowly walked out of the room. My life was nothing like I thought it was. My entire life.

Chapter 14

"We never do this," Officer Sullivan said to me, "but there's something about this case that doesn't sit right. And since 24-hour police protection is not an option at this time, I want to show you how to protect yourself."

I followed Sullivan down the hall. We were below the first floor, and came to a thick window with a police officer behind it. The room behind the window had so many blatant security measures, I wouldn't be surprised if the police nicknamed the place "the cage."

Sullivan talked to the guy in the cage and the officer handed him two large paper targets and a gun.

"This way," Sullivan motioned with his head. "And like I said, we never do this. So if anyone asks, you're my cousin from Wisconsin."

In other words, I'm not supposed to be here. "You have a cousin in Wisconsin?"

"Now I do," Sullivan said.

We came to a basement firing range. The separate shooting areas were next to one another, and the space to get from one to the other was small. The rest of the room was large.

No one was there, as if it was available to officers but the novelty of the whole thing wore off and police didn't find much thrill in shooting anymore.

I could see large stacks of hay in the back. I guess it was the cheapest way to stop the bullets from hitting the walls.

We stopped at the last shooting area and Sullivan held up the weapon the officer from the window had handed him. "This is a Glock 22 .40 caliber, standard issue. Not my favorite, but it gets the job done." Sullivan showed me how to hold the gun, where the safety was, how to load the magazine and, if necessary, how to unload the magazine, making sure the bullet in the chamber was also removed. "You don't know how many times people have been hurt because they forgot to unload the round in the chamber."

Sullivan attached the paper target which had an outline of a man's torso. Certain spots were circled indicating lethal shots.

Sullivan hit a button and there was a satisfying whir sound as the target sped toward the back of the firing range.

"Take this and give it all you got," Sullivan said.

I took the gun. Felt heavy for such a small thing.

"First the safety," Sullivan guided.

I took the safety off.

"Then hold it with both hands just like you're doing now, and as all the movies say, 'squeeze' the trigger. Don't pull it. Just like you're completing a clenched fist."

I held it up, aimed for the heart, and fired. There was a bang and a tinkling sound on the ground.

"Good," Sullivan said. "Try blasting off an entire cartridge."

"What just fell?"

"That was the bullet casing," Sullivan explained. "See this?" He pointed to a large wooden board on my right side. It looked like an added part to the wall and had many dents in it. "The casing pops out of the gun from the side, hits this board, and falls to the ground. Now, empty the gun. Fill the guy with holes."

I began firing one bullet after the other.

"Stop, stop, stop." Sullivan interrupted the shooting. "I said empty the gun, I didn't say stop aiming. A lot of people aim their first shot, get a good one in and then fire the rest without aiming as much as they did the first shot. After each shot, aim your next one."

I took it slower and fired each bullet. At one point, I thought I had my aim just right, but my squeeze of the trigger sounded off a click. The gun was empty.

"Okay let's see how you did," Sullivan pressed the switch bringing the target back to them. I liked the whir sound. Reminded me of those street performers with whistles in their mouth pretending to be robots. They'd whistle every time they moved as if their joints were machines.

Sullivan pointed out how the target had seven holes in it. I fired ten bullets. Only two hit inside the outline of the man. None made the circled parts.

Sullivan pointed to one of the holes inside the

outline. "See that? That was your first shot. But listen carefully. I brought you down here so that you could practice shooting and get better at aiming. Your goal is not to actually hit anyone. Your goal is to shoot near them and frighten them away."

Sullivan took down the target and put up a clean one.

"This time," he said as the target whirred away from us, "I want you to hit as close to the outline as you can without actually hitting the target. Load it up."

Sullivan gave me bullets and after switching the gun's safety on, I refilled the cartridge and slid it back into the weapon.

I prepared to fire and carefully kept still as my hand clenched. It seemed different now. I wasn't just hitting a piece of paper. Now I imagined it as flesh and blood and my goal was to avoid hitting it. Each time the gun fired, the gun recoiled and I had to aim all over again. Eventually, the gun clicked empty.

Sullivan called back the target. There were eight holes outside the outline, and one hit the outline directly.

"Looks like you broadsided his head," Sullivan said. "Not good." Sullivan took the gun out of my hands and said, "Get a gun Mr. Yirmorshy, and practice at the public firing ranges. If my guess is right, you're gonna need protection. Now wait here and I'll be right back."

I watched Sullivan go. I looked at the targets I had hit. Looking at the first one, I realized how two of my shots would have seriously injured someone.

"Sir? May I ask what your business is here?"

I looked up and saw a young policeman approach. "Oh. I'm Mr. Sullivan's cousin from Wisconsin."

"Mr. Sullivan's cousin from Wisconsin," he repeated like he was interrogating me and didn't believe my story.

"Yeah, uh, he was just showing me the…"

"Relax, buddy." The officer said. "Sullivan's a good judge of character. If he thinks you're a good guy, I trust him."

The officer walked away saying, "If I had a nickel for every one of Sullivan's 'cousins'," and went to one of the firing areas and began practicing.

Sullivan marched back with a clean target and held a gun so frighteningly big, I thought it was an elephant gun, whatever that looked like.

Sullivan and the officer greeted each other with a silent nod.

"Alright," Sullivan said as he stood next to me attaching the clean target to the cable. "One last thing I want to show you. This here is a double-barrel shotgun." Sullivan hit the switch and sent the target to the distance. "The thing to keep in mind is that bullets don't make guys run, fear does. And if you want to put the fear of God in them, which do you think will do a better job at it?"

Sullivan held up the shotgun in one hand and his own Glock in the other.

"The shotgun," I said.

"Right. Problem is," Sullivan holstered his Glock,

and cocked the shotgun by pumping it with one hand, dug the holster deep into his shoulder and fired. The paper exploded leaving just a torn top left hanging. "It does a lot of damage."

I gulped.

"You fire this thing, you better damn well know how close to the target you can get before turning him into soup. Get a gun. Practice at a public firing range."

I left the station and got in my car. I turned on the engine. Thought about the duplex. Thought about what it would be like spending another night there. I turned off the engine.

Where was I going to go? I could rent a room somewhere. Couldn't sleep, though. What was the point of renting a room, then?

My stomach growled.

I reached into my back pocket and pulled out Sophia's card. Called her on my iPhone.

"Hello?" She answered.

"Did I wake you?"

"Not yet."

"Can I buy you dinfast?"

"What's that?"

"It's what you eat between dinner and breakfast."

"Cute." She gave me her address. "Come pick me up. I'll put my clothes back on. Call me when you're downstairs."

"See you in twenty minutes."

Chapter 15

Luke McCourt parked his BMW in a residential neighborhood and lit a cigarette as a Bach invention played on the radio. The house beside him stood majestic at three floors high and half a block wide. The picket fence did little to secure the place from trespassers, but Luke knew that trespassers were not a concern for the family inside. He knew about the motion-sensor lights and the double cameras positioned in each corner of the property. He knew about the window and door alarms set to go off when opened. He knew about the broken glass detectors on the windows and the alarm padding under the rug at the front door. Any secrets inside the house stayed inside the house.

Luke smiled.

He looked at his cigarette, the burning tobacco on one end, the moistened filter on the other, and made a note of all the densely-packed tobacco leaves and the fibers of the filter in between. Still, the smoke managed to slip through it all.

Luke inhaled a final cloud and the tip of the cigarette fired brighter. He exhaled, watching all the secrets of the cigarette go up in smoke.

The house was quiet. The family was, no doubt, asleep. Luke hid the dead cigarette in the ash tray, stepped out of the car, and crossed the sidewalk directly to the white picket fence.

The latch on the fence lifted easily without a squeak. Luke opened the gate, walked through, and let it slam closed behind him. The path to the front porch was made of quaint stepping stones. Luke strolled upon them, powerful lights switched on with an angry buzzing sound, and he felt as though he were in the middle of a night-lit baseball park, ready to play ball. He stepped to the door, and planted a firm finger into the doorbell.

At this time of night it would take awhile before the door was answered. Luke turned around and examined the nearby houses. A neighbor peeked through the curtains. Luke waved. The neighbor disappeared.

The front door opened and Luke turned to see the surgeon at the door wearing a bathrobe.

"Luke?" Matthew said quizzically. His eyes squinted, submitting to the glare of his own lighting system.

"I need to talk to you."

"Come in! Come in!"

But Luke had already let himself in. The surgeon turned off the alarm systems and closed the door. Luke moved directly to the kitchen.

"How are you, Matthew?" Luke picked up the tea

kettle and at the sink, fed water at its highest force down the throat of the kettle.

"I'm fine," the surgeon said, sounding uncertain as he watched Luke's actions.

Luke turned to the oven, twisted the arm of the knob until a full fire burned beneath the kettle. He crossed to the cupboard and found the box of Earl Grey.

Luke removed two mugs from a cabinet.

"Tea?" Luke asked, placing a tea bag in each of the cups.

"No, thank you. I'm trying to avoid caffeine."

"I insist," Luke said.

"I…Alright."

Luke wandered to the foot of the stairs. He looked up toward the bedrooms. "How's your wife?" The ticking of the living room clock was audible. Its sound probably went unnoticed to anyone who had lived with it day in and day out.

"She's fine."

Luke began climbing the stairs. "And your teenage daughter? She sleeps naked doesn't she?"

"How do you know tha—" Matthew grabbed Luke's sleeve. Luke looked at Matthew's hand and Matthew released his grip. "Also…uh. She's also fine."

Luke smiled as he looked at the surgeon's frightened eyes. They were much wider now. "That's wonderful, Matthew."

Luke stepped back down the stairs and returned to the oven in the kitchen. He twisted the knob to get the fire higher. Soon the kettle screamed. Without turning off the fire, Luke removed the kettle and poured its sputtering contents into the mugs.

"Something's come up." He handed a hot cup to Matthew. Matthew said nothing. He just accepted the cup and turned off the fire.

"Nathan found out he's being watched," Luke said.

"So what does that mean for me?"

"It means you have less time to finish your work because Meg will come sooner rather than later."

The surgeon nodded. "Okay," he said, looking at the floor.

"How's the progress coming?"

He nodded again. "I'll show you. Let's go to the basement."

The surgeon set down his cup and walked to a door. Luke sipped his tea as the surgeon unlocked the door and opened it revealing a staircase leading downward.

A sweet smell reminiscent of mortuaries wafted out the door. Luke heard a screeching sound. He let the surgeon lead him down to the basement. The room was enormous. On one wall, there were a few metal sinks that looked more like tubs. On another, a desk with stacks of books, a telephone, and a lamp perched like a vulture. Bookshelves empty of books but filled with jars of chemicals, plastic gloves, and surgical tools lined yet another wall.

In the center of the room lay a metal table.

Upon it was the surgeon's latest work: two bodies sewn together. One had difficulty catching a full breath, and made small bleating noises. Luke sipped his tea.

"I managed to get their blood circulation going so that they still function for a time as independent bodies. But after twenty-seven hours the one on the left died. And the one on the right is dying."

"That's quite alright," Luke said patting the surgeon on the back. "Nowhere does it say that they have to be alive."

Chapter 16

One of the only places open that time of night was Denny's. After entering the restaurant, we sat down in one of the booths. I ordered a three-egg omelet breakfast and coffee. Sophia asked for a cup of minestrone soup.

I told her all about the photographs the police found, the anonymous letter, and the mysterious mention of someone named Meg. Told her about the cop that recommended I get a gun. Sophia listened without a word. I finished the whole story by the time our food came.

"What are you going to do, now?" she asked.

"Not sure." The food looked edible. But despite my growling stomach, I didn't feel hungry.

"Why did he do that? It doesn't make sense." Sophia was referring to my landlord, Luke. She sipped the soup from a spoon. "And how old was he when your parents had their honeymoon?"

"I don't think he was even born."

"So who took the picture?"

I just shook my head. She was right. It didn't make sense.

"Tell you what," Sophia said. "Let's talk about it later. Try thinking about something else for now," Sophia said.

"Like what?"

She put her elbows on the table, hands clasped, and looked up as if she was praying. Then looked at me. "Do you still think tarot is just what you read into it? After seeing the Devil card you picked twice?"

It *was* statistically significant. About one in six thousand. I had picked Suffering as my first card, a second card, and then the Devil as my third. Normally, for the cards to be picked by chance, I'd have to pick a set of three cards about six thousand times to be sure I'd get the same sequence. Getting that same sequence was about as coincidental as a Mayor winning a raffle that he sponsored for his own town.

If tarot wasn't coincidence, then what scientific explanation was there? Unless...

Sophia placed a penny on the table. "Penny for your thoughts," she said.

"I was just thinking," I said. "Our brain is constantly releasing light in the form of brainwaves, right? Brainwaves constantly shoot out from our minds. And brainwaves are just a kind of light we can't see because their frequencies are too high."

"Never thought about it like that, but...okay. So?"

"So atoms everywhere are constantly absorbing and releasing light. Like breathing in and out."

Sophia said nothing.

"So when I look at, say the suffering card, I think of 'suffering' and all that the word means to me, and since light carries information, maybe my brain is sending those thoughts to the card using my brainwaves. And the card, which like everything else, is made up of atoms, absorbs my brainwaves."

"You lost me," Sophia said.

"Here." I moved aside my plate, took out a pen and wrote "milk" on a napkin. I placed the napkin in front of me and took a fork in one hand and a small container of cream in the other. "Suppose this is the tarot card that says 'milk'."

"Oh, yeah." Sophia played along. "*That* tarot card."

"I see it, and I think 'milk.' So my brainwaves are making this pattern in my head that says, 'milk.' And those brainwaves are released everywhere. Like this." I held the cream container to my forehead and punctured it with a fork spilling its contents all over the table.

Sophia began laughing.

"Notice that the 'milk' tarot card is absorbing my 'milk' thoughts." I carefully lifted the drenched napkin. "So now the tarot card…"

"Is as happy as a cow," Sophia laughed.

"No. It's got all the 'milk' thoughts in it." I carefully turned it over so that the word milk was hidden. "So now, if I look at the card and I can't see the word, it doesn't matter because it's releasing all these light patterns that represent 'milk.' " I squeezed different areas of the napkin. Spots of milk squished out. "And if somewhere in the back of my subconscious I really want milk as a part of my life, or milk was a major experience in my past, or I'm just thirsty, my desires or thoughts or needs of milk will match the light patterns that the card is releasing. I essentially 'see' the milk, so I choose the card."

"Wow!" Sophia said. "There's actually a point to all of this!"

"Very funny."

"I'm kidding," Sophia said with a smile. "Keep going."

"So that's probably why I picked those two cards: Suffering and the Devil. Maybe somewhere in my sub-conscious I've been thinking about suffering in my past or something…"

"What does the devil mean to you?" Sophia asked.

Didn't really want to go there. It was leaving the realm of science and entering the realm of subjectivity. But I played along. "Well, when I think of the devil, I think of evil. Horrible sins. Hell. Satan worshippers and all that."

"But that's not what the card represents," Sophia said. "It represents being at play, feeling carefree, or not caring about consequences."

I looked down at the table. Then back up at her. "Know what?"

"What?"

"With the card turned over, my subconscious may have been led to it because, generally, I don't really care what people think. And if that's what the atoms in the card were releasing, then that's probably what I sensed. Not the devil, but the carefree idea."

Sophia smiled. She sipped her soup.

"Tell me something," I said. "Do you have a favorite deck?"

"Sure," she said. "Everyone does. Mine is the Crowley deck. The one we used tonight."

"How long have you used it?"

"Fourteen years. It's the first deck I ever bought. Even though I buy others, this is the one I always use. The new ones never satisfy me."

"Great. Now notice something. If you only liked the new ones, then my theory would completely fall apart. It only works if people have looked at the cards for long periods of time, letting their ideas of the cards be absorbed by the cards. The new cards haven't been exposed to people's thoughts, so they shouldn't work as well. If you felt that only the new decks worked, then the whole absorbing-thoughts theory goes up in smoke."

Sophia smiled.

"What?" I said.

"Where's the spirit?"

"What do you mean?"

"Tarot is a kind of window to the spirit, the soul. You've completely removed the spirituality from the tarot experience."

I smiled.

"I take it you're not religious," she said.

"Correct." I looked at the light's reflection off her cheeks. "Why, are you?"

She shrugged. "Spiritual, not religious."

No spirituality was necessary for my light theory of tarot. I remembered my prom photo the police found in Luke's place. At the time of my prom, I had just learned all about the physics of light in high school. Felt like I knew it all. What was he doing with that photo?

But that wasn't the photo that troubled me most. It was the honeymoon photo. My parents. How old was Luke these days, forty? Fifty? About ten years older than me. My parents had me three years after they married. No way a seven-year-old was traipsing around Venice to take photos of my parents.

I rubbed my eyes. "I'm tired."

"Come on." Sophia put on her jacket. "It's time for you to see *my* bedroom." She gave me a wink.

Chapter 17

Where was I? My eyes squinted against the light coming from the window. But this place was…oh, yeah. Sophia's apartment. More like a voting booth with windows. I shifted in the strange bed. It was breezy under the bed covers.

Looking under the sheets, I saw I was wearing only my underwear.

How did that happen? I had driven Sophia to her apartment in downtown Berkeley. She let me in. The only rooms were the bedroom and the bathroom, and since there were no chairs I sat on the bed. She went to get me a beer, and then…and then what?

Keys jiggled at the door and after a brief battle with opening the door, in walked Sophia with a paper bag. "I'm back," she said. "I have bagels and orange juice and blueberry muffins. I didn't know what kind of bagel you liked so I got both poppy seed and plain."

"How did I get here?"

"You drove," Sophia looked at me quizzically.

"I mean, where are my clothes?"

"You don't remember last night?" Sophia asked. "You were so great! I can't believe you don't remember. How many beers did you have last night? Six? Seven?"

Think. Think. I couldn't even remember the first beer.

"Naw, I'm just kidding. I went to get you a beer and when I came back, you were out like a light."

I let out my breath. "…But I don't remember taking my clothes off," I said.

"You didn't. I took them off and put them over there."

I saw my clothes neatly folded in the corner of the room.

"I tucked you in," Sophia continued, "and even gave you a g'night kiss on the cheek."

I looked around. No couch.

"So where did you sleep?" I asked.

"Voila!" she made a graceful gesture with her arms at the foot of the bed.

"You slept on the floor?!"

"Relax," Sophia went to a small table and began unpacking the paper bag upon it. "I had plenty of padding."

Sophia pulled dishes and silverware from hidden spots around the room, like magic. Like rabbits from hats.

Sophia stopped spreading a bagel with cream cheese and looked at me. "You're not feeling weirded out from me undressing you, are you?"

"I don't think…"

"I have two brothers. I grew up with them parading about the house in their underwear or less. Believe me. I've seen it all."

I thought about what got me here in the first place. And wondered what Luke was doing right now.

"I know what's really bothering you," Sophia said climbing onto the bed. She climbed on all fours until her body was positioned above mine. "You're just sorry you didn't get to remember my goodnight kiss."

I smiled.

"This is to jog your memory." She kissed my cheek and looked at me. Then she kissed my lips. I returned the favor, and began to feel at home.

Chapter 18

Luke put out another cigarette and added it to the car's ash tray. Ashes to ashes. The parking lot's appearance worsened with the rising sun. The building was no better off: one giant white block with no windows.

Melinda had finally arrived. She walked through the parking lot toward the building. Luke knew she came to work around 6:30 a.m. Her arrival early in the day made it possible to see her alone.

Luke stepped out of the car and intercepted her at the front entrance of the building. "Melinda," He said to stop her.

"Luke?" She checked her watch as if it helped her understand his visit.

"How are you?"

Melinda looked past him at the door and glanced at the emptiness of the parking lot. "I'm fine. Are you…"

"That's a very nice business suit you're wearing." He felt her lapel, resting his knuckles on her breast. "Is it cotton?"

"I'm not sure," she said, taking a step back. "Maybe a cotton-polyester mix."

Luke smiled. "Something's come up." He told her about the police at his place, and how Nathan was now privy to Luke watching him. He mentioned his visit with the surgeon Matthew and Matthew's progress. "What's yours?"

"I've been progressing pretty well."

"Show me," Luke said.

"I…" Melinda's grip on her purse tightened.

Luke slowly lifted the purse strap off her shoulder. "Allow me to carry this for you," he said removing the purse from her hands. The purse was heavy and he knew why. Even small handguns were heavy. Luke motioned for Melinda to open the door to the building.

"Of course." After a few attempts, she managed to use her keys to open the door. She led him down several corridors, to an elevator. "By using the DNA from the specimen in Bauta, I was able to clone the eggs and fertilize them with a regular goat."

"And?" Luke asked as they boarded the elevator.

"Naturally, many of the offspring were normal." She said during the elevator's descent. "But seven have the exact traits of the specimen from Bauta."

They exited the elevator and Melinda led him to her lab. Inside, he examined the seven cages. Each cage had a young goat with two heads.

"Good," Luke said.

Chapter 19

Fully undressed, I sat upright in the afterglow of "sleeping" with Sophia in her bed, and took another bite of the blueberry muffin. Crumbs fell onto the plate that I held directly underneath my chin. Sophia had the same kind of muffin when I met her, only I thought it was a cupcake. Why did I think it had been a cupcake? I knew the difference between the two. As I pondered the way the brain mixes up pictures and words, I got distracted by Sophia getting dressed.

Sophia zipped her jeans and put on her white t-shirt. Watching her dress was just as enjoyable as when she undressed after our kiss.

But what was this going to lead to? Was Sophia expecting a commitment? The difficult times I had with my wife flashed. Especially the way I treated her when I had my delusions. I'd thought she was getting more and more distant from me just because of my sickness, but that wasn't it at all. It wasn't my sickness that made her leave. It was me. And if anything happened between Sophia and me, I'd end up treating her the same way. I was sure.

Maybe I read too much into this. For all I knew, Sophia was going to treat this like a one-night stand. After all, I didn't really love her. Is it possible that she loves me? I tried picturing her saying "I love you, Nathan."

But it wasn't Sophia that came to mind. I pictured another woman. That anonymous woman from the letter writing "I love you."

How did she put it? If she really was a 'she?' *I'm looking forward to meeting you…You don't know me but I know you…* Something like that. Those words had been written with love. Childish love, but love, nevertheless.

And what was that thing about my name being in the Bible? Everyone knew that Nathan was a biblical name, so what was the big deal?

"What's on your mind?" Sophia said. She was finishing off a bagel.

"I was just thinking about that letter yesterday."

"Oh, good," Sophia said. "I thought you were thinking twice about our lovemaking. You know. Having regrets."

"Why, do you?"

"Have regrets? Not one iota. I hope we can do this more often," she turned her back to me. "If you're up to it."

Her voice sounded casual. But I knew whatever I said next was important.

"So in the letter the police found, I think the writer was a woman." *Stupid, Nathan. Stupid. Stupid.*

Sophia's back was still turned to me, but her voice sounded genuine when she asked, "Oh, yeah? Why do you say that?"

"The way it was written sounded all lovey-dovey."

Sophia turned and nodded her head. "Okay…I can see that."

I gave her my plate.

"So how does that help explain your landlord watching you?" Sophia asked.

"Not sure." I realized how naked I felt. Literally and figuratively. A good indicator that we shouldn't get involved. Better for her that way. "And then there's that thing about my name being in the Bible. Sure Nathan is in the Bible, but does she mean my whole name is written in there somewhere?"

"It sounds pretty esoteric." Sophia began wiping the butter-knife off with a towel. "Hey!" She pointed the knife at me.

I must have shown a reaction, because she set the knife down.

"The Bible codes!"

"The what?" I asked.

"There's this New Age place where I saw this book on Bible codes. Maybe your name is somehow encoded in the Bible."

I picked up my clothes and began to get dressed. "Come on. Show me this New Age place. We're going to do some detective work!"

Chapter 20

From **Sophia's apartment on Alcatraz Av-**enue, we walked down a few blocks to Telegraph Avenue and headed toward the campus and the shops. I tried to think about McCourt and his motives. Tried to think if I ever heard him mention someone named Meg. But as we got closer to the Berkeley campus, the street got livelier and noisier. Made it difficult to concentrate. Soon we reached the bookstores. Just past the bookstores was a cacophony of vendors and street-sellers playing music at their booths. The booths lined Telegraph with people selling stickers, t-shirts, hand-made jewelry, tie-dye shirts, and artwork. The vendors emanated the sixties with their long unkempt hair and relaxed disposition. Telegraph was not just a street. It was a living being. Dancing and singing.

"I love this street," I said.

"Me too." Sophia said. "Why do you love it? You don't strike me as the sixties type."

"I'm not. I just..." I had to think about that. "There's something so pure about it. Like these people aren't trying to get ahead, they're just here to help each other out. It's something like that, something I admire but I can't put into words."

Sophia was taking her time, strolling past the different vendors. She stopped at a bumper sticker booth. One sticker said, "I am you." Another sticker said, "My other car got arrested for being high."

She moved down to a booth that had handmade jewelry. The lady selling the jewelry looked like age had taken a dark turn on her, and though she was probably only fortyish, she looked older. Much older. Random gray hairs spewed out among her black hair and lines cut across her mouth and eyes. There was a wart on her chin with two black hairs coming out of it. She sat busy winding wire around twine, making a necklace.

The booth advertised Zodiac gems. "What are these?" I asked Sophia.

"Zodiac gem stones," the lady at the booth said. "They're the very stones which your soul connects best to. They help you in your darkest times, when you need someone beside you but no one is around."

Ah. More baloney.

"What's your birthday?" She asked.

"September 13th," I said.

"September. Your birth stone is carnelian." She pulled out a tray of loose stones and picked one up. "Here," she stood handing it to me. "That's carnelian. It represents protection against evil. It also represents hope and good luck."

I studied it and felt a brief bond, however silly that

was. Probably another transfer of brainwaves. The stone was a pebble in size, really, and had a layered surface like a glass of orange juice with cream not yet stirred. I held it out to give it back.

"No, that's yours to keep," the woman said.

I stood motionless.

"Here's a list of all the different birthstones for all the different signs of the Zodiac." She handed me a small card that looked like she'd attach it to her bracelets and necklaces as an information primer.

I looked at the stone and the card, and wasn't sure what to say. Was she trying to get me to buy something for Sophia? I didn't think so. She gave me the stone altruistically. Giving without expecting something back.

"Thanks," I said at last, looking to meet her eyes.

But her eyes seemed indifferent. She nodded like it was no big deal and sat back down returning to her work.

As we continued down the street, I held up the stone, the altruism it represented, and said to Sophia, "This is why I love Telegraph Avenue."

Chapter 21

A bell jingled as Sophia opened the door to the New Age bookstore. I had to physically close the door behind me. It didn't close on its own.

The small store smelled musty. Smelled of old books and stale tea.

"Hey, Phil," Sophia said to the kid behind the counter. He must have been all of nineteen years old. At least that's what the shaggy black hair and the worn t-shirt suggested.

"Hey, Sophia! How's it going?" the kid named Phil asked.

"Great. We've got a puzzle for you."

"Ooh! I like puzzles." He clapped his hands once and rubbed them together like he was preparing to give a massage.

"Tell him, Nathan" Sophia said.

"I got a letter yesterday saying that my name was in the Bible. Any idea what that's all about? Something about Bible codes?"

"Ah! The Bible codes!" Phil nodded knowingly. "I've got two books here about them. This one's a best seller, predicts the future and all sorts of cool shit." He stepped from behind the counter, pulled a book off the shelf and gave it to me. He pulled off another book. "And this one's written by a Pulitzer-prize-winning journalist. It's more scientific about the whole thing."

I already knew which one I preferred. I took the second book he offered me and returned the first to its place on the shelf. "So what is the Bible code?"

"Beats me. I don't read 'em, I just say what other people have told me."

Terrific.

"But if your name is encoded in the Bible," Phil continued, "that's like somewhere your name is spelled out by skipping every other letter, or something like that. What is your name anyway?" He returned to his spot behind the counter.

"It's Nathan."

"Isn't that already in the Bible?" Phil asked.

The kid had a brain.

"Do you think that's all the letter meant?" I asked.

"Doesn't make sense. I mean what's the big deal? I know tons of guys named David and I don't go writing letters to them all the time saying, 'Hey, your name's in the Bible!' "

"Right," I said.

"What's your last name?"

"Yirmorshy."

"Polish, huh?" Philip asked.

"Yeah. How'd you know."

"I lived in Poland for a year." Phil looked off to the side and smiled, "Man, that was far out." He looked back at me. "So can you imagine that? 'Nathan Yirmorshy' encoded in the Bible? That'd be something, huh?"

"I'd be living a friggin' Dan Brown novel," I said.

"Hey, I won a bookplate from him." Philip nodded. "Yeah, I managed to figure out this code he had on his website and sent in my answer along with how I wanted him to sign my bookplate."

I thought it best to ignore that last comment. Didn't know what he was talking about. But apparently Sophia was interested.

"What's a bookplate?" she asked.

"Yeah, I didn't know either until I got it in the mail. It's this little sticker that has his signature on it. You can stick it on the inside part of one of his books."

I said nothing.

"Anyhow, I asked him to sign it, 'To Scissors, As if I were your friend, Dan Brown.' "

"Scissors?" Sophia asked.

"That's my pen name," Phil smiled. "Cool, huh?"

Not really.

"So then I got an e-mail from him. He wanted to make sure that's what I wanted on my bookplate. I wrote back saying that I did want it to say that, and I asked him to send it along with some vegetable soup."

"Vegetable soup?" Sophia asked.

"Yeah, but when he sent the bookplate, it came with a note that said 'sorry, no soup.' "

I was beginning to think this trip was a waste of time.

"Yeah. So then I e-mailed him saying…Now what did it say?" Phil looked down under the counter and pulled out a sheet of paper. "Ah. Here it is. I wrote 'Dan!' yada yada yada 'As for the lack of vegetable soup in your package, no problem. People don't always eat vegetable soup. I know how it is. What was I thinking?! I rarely eat soup, much less vegetable soup! The idea of you sending me soup was utterly absurd and ridiculous. I apologize.' "

Phil cleared his throat and continued, " 'Could you send me some popcorn? People always eat popcorn. They eat it in their movie houses, in their living rooms. They eat it in their front porches and outhouses. They eat it when they carry furniture to and fro, when they type newsletters and love letters, when they're participating in parades with giant, red floats. And they carry popcorn around with them everywhere they go.' "

I whispered to Sophia, "Is this supposed to be funny?"

Sophia shrugged her shoulders.

Phil continued, " 'I like to carry my popcorn next to my beeper. My beeper doesn't get much use but, boy, do I eat the popcorn! I look forward to your e-mail reply and I keep my fingers crossed for an attachment of popcorn. ON WITH THE REVOLUTION!!! —Scissors.' "

"You really sent that to Dan Brown?" Sophia asked.

"Yeah. And when he replied, his P.S. said 'This e-mail message entitles you to one large bag of popcorn should we ever meet face to face at some point in the future.' See?"

Phil showed us the page and sure enough, it was a printout of an e-mail from Dan Brown.

I shuddered. "So do you have any suggestions about what I should do with this Bible code stuff besides read your books?"

"Better than that! You don't even have to get the books. Just go to this guy." Phil pulled out a card from under the counter. I wondered what else he had behind the counter.

I looked at the card. "Rabbi Silverman?"

"Yeah. Give him a call." Phil said. "He's got this cool software that can find codes in the Bible. He comes in occasionally to see if there are any more books about it."

I remembered something else, "What about Meg?"

"You know about Meg?" Phil asked, his eyes wide. "How do you know about Meg?"

Sophia and I looked at each other.

Sophia asked, "Who is she?"

"Wait. I don't get it." Phil looked at them suspiciously. "Do you or don't you know about Meg?"

"It was in the letter," I said. "Something about no longer being strangers with Meg."

"Oh. That doesn't sound like my Meg."

"Your Meg?" Sophia asked.

"Yeah." Phil sighed. "I got this girl pregnant. It was supposed to be a casual thing. She wanted the baby. It was a baby girl, so we decided on the name Meg. Short for Megan."

Sophia smiled, "That's so sweet."

"Yeah. Sweet. Okay." Phil looked hard at Sophia. "You gotta promise me though that if you ever meet my parents, not to breathe a word of it. Cause they don't know yet and if they find out through the grapevine…It's just gonna be…Whoa!"

"Alright," Sophia said. "I promise."

"So anyway," Phil said, "I don't know which Meg you're talking about."

"Nothing biblical or anything like that?" I asked.

Phil shook his head. "Nope. Doesn't ring any bells."

I looked at the card. Rabbi Silverman. Sophia took the card from me and looked at it, too. I knew what she was thinking. Our next lead.

Chapter 22

Luke waited in the hallway. Emmanuel Perry's wife had let him in. Perry was in the middle of giving a piano lesson to some snot-nosed kid in the living room.

Luke could see the baby grand piano and the boy played horribly. It sounded like the boy was trying to make it sound bad. Luke could overhear Perry's words to the boy.

"Alright," Perry said. "That was pretty good. You got several of the notes right and there was one point where you did the legato right where you were supposed to. Good work. Now what I want you to try is…"

But before Perry could finish, his wife Katherine whispered in his ear. Perry turned, looked at Luke in the hallway, and gave an "I'll be there in a sec" wave.

"Work on this second phrase and I'll be right back," Perry told the boy. The boy began plunging his fingers into the keys.

"How are you, Luke?" Perry smiled. He shook his hand with a firm handshake.

"Fine. Just fine." Luke told Perry all about the previous night's events and included his trips to visit Melinda and Matthew. "We'll need the shipment soon. Real soon. Think you can get it?"

"Sure. No problem. Anything else you need?"

"I'm concerned about Nathan's willingness to participate. You may need to take extreme measures."

"You mean termination?"

"No. Nothing like that. You may just need to incapacitate him. There's nothing that says he has to be fully functional."

"No problem. Just give me the word and I'll take care of it."

Luke said his goodbyes and as he left he heard Perry saying to the boy, "Sounds great! Do that second phrase one more time for me."

Sullivan watched Luke get into his car. He wrote down in his notepad, "musician" under "surgeon" and "geneticist." Why was McCourt visiting these people? What did they have in common? At least the surgeon and the geneticist had their interest in biology in common, but where does the music fit in?

Sullivan called it in on his radio to dispatch. "Who lives at 6432 Oak Road?"

"One moment, I'll check."

Sullivan took a sip of his cold coffee. Police work was responsible for making him get used to cold coffee. It was the one addicting staple left in this country that was both legal and just what he needed for stake outs.

The station came back, "That would be an Emmanuel Perry and his wife Katherine. Mr. Perry was a green beret in the army."

A green beret? They specialized in weapons, including sniper.

Sullivan thanked the dispatcher, put the coffee down, and started the car to continue tailing McCourt. Whatever McCourt was planning, someone was probably going to get hurt.

Chapter 23

"Come in! Come in!" Rabbi Silverman said. He had been just as jolly on the phone as in person. It was no problem to come right over, the rabbi had said. Just knock loud. The doorbell didn't work.

His place was large but still seemed small from all the toys that covered the floor.

"How many children do you have?" Sophia asked.

"Eight," the rabbi replied.

"Eight?!"

"Yes. Five beautiful girls and three handsome boys, *baruch haShem*." He raised a finger, "And don't make a joke by mentioning that old TV show 'Eight is Enough.' It was funny the first time. Not so funny anymore. Please come with me."

We followed him through a narrow kitchen to a tiny study. Papers were strewn everywhere. Books were open and piled one on top of the other. Beside a desk were volumes of books on shelves.

"This is my office," the rabbi said. "Have a seat." He pointed to two foldout chairs next to each other. "Do you two have children?"

"Oh, no," Sophia laughed. "We're not married. We just met last night."

"And are you Jewish?" The rabbi asked Sophia.

"Well, my mother was Jewish but I'm not really religious."

The rabbi nodded and looked at me as if asking the same question.

"Same with me," I said. "My mother was Jewish but I don't practice."

The rabbi nodded and smiled and looked back and forth between Sophia and me. Then he whispered to me in a not-so-subtle manner, "She's a beautiful girl, don't you think?"

I smiled. "Yes. She is."

"Yes. She is," the rabbi repeated. Then he turned to Sophia and said, "He seems like a nice man."

Sophia and I shared a glance. She blushed. I could tell by how hot my ears were that she saw the same thing on me.

"So!" the rabbi said. "What brings you here? You said something about a Bible code."

"What are the Bible codes?" I asked.

"Many believe that the history of the universe is written in the Bible. Not just the past, but the future as well."

"So it's just a belief," I said.

"Not exactly," the rabbi said. "Isaac Newton thought that the Bible was encoded. He spent more time looking for the codes than he did studying science."

"Newton?" I asked. "Sir Isaac Newton?"

"The very same. He never found them but that was because he didn't have this." The rabbi tapped the computer. "But let's start at the beginning. Suppose you're a secret agent and you want to send a message to home base."

I scowled, not sure where this was going. "Okay."

"What would you need to do to make sure the message was sent safely?" The rabbi asked.

"Well, you'd have to have a way of making sure home base got it," I said.

"Yes, so you want to be sure it isn't intercepted by someone else," the rabbi said.

I nodded.

"Okay. Now should the message be intercepted, what steps would you take to make sure that didn't matter?" the rabbi asked.

I saw where this was going. "You'd want to make sure it was encoded."

"Fine, but supposing the enemy decodes it, sees the message, and then sends home base a different message to confuse them? How could you prevent that?"

"I'd use a key."

"A key?" Sophia asked.

"Yeah," I said. "When sending coded messages, typically the sender has a special way of letting the receiver know it was really from him. It's like he locked the message with his own personal key that only the receiver can unlock because the receiver has the same key."

"He's a smart man," the rabbi whispered to Sophia. Sophia smiled. Louder, he said, "And that is what the Bible codes are for. The codes are hidden messages that are typically events that happened after the Bible was written. And this is how God lets us know that the Bible really comes from Him."

"You're saying the Bible predicts the future?"

"I'm saying God knows the future, and that is how we know God wrote the Bible."

I rolled my eyes. "So how does the Bible reveal the future?"

"There are many different ways to put codes in the Bible. When God gave the Torah to Moses, He gave it letter by letter, not word by word. So the first Torah was like a giant search-a-word. The letters evenly spaced. If you think of the Torah like that, like a search-a-word, then you get a better idea of how the codes work. Imagine playing the search-a-word game and finding…what's your name again?"

"Nathan Yirmorshy."

"Nathan Yirmorshy every 10th letter. And then say we find crossing it…what's your name?"

"Sophia Patai."

"Sophia Patai every 15th letter. And suppose we find the current year crossing both your names diagonally. And then the city you met. Was it Berkeley?"

"Emeryville," Sophia said.

"Emeryville crossing your names and the year diagonally the other way. The chances of all those significant facts of your meeting appearing in the same vicinity of the Bible is too astronomical to be considered by random chance. If it's not a coincidence, then it must have been placed there purposefully. And who but the Divine could have known all those details about your meeting?"

I checked my watch. I didn't have any place else to be, but the internet probably had more useful information. It'd be rude to take out my phone, though.

"*Aba*! *Aba*!" A worried boy with long, curly locks of dark hair where his sideburns would be if he were older ran into the room holding a toy truck in one hand and a large battery in the other. "It broke, *Aba*." He looked to be about two years old. Four knotted fringes flailed from beneath the boy's shirt at his waist. "It broke."

"Ah, your poor truck needs a repairman, yes?" The rabbi took the truck and battery from his son's hands and easily put it back together. He flipped the switch and the wheels began to spin. After turning it off, he handed the truck to his son, "All fixed."

The boy inspected it, flipped the switch on and off himself.

"What do you say?" the rabbi asked.

"*Todah rabah*." And the kid ran off to play.

"A few questions," I said.

"Of course."

"How could a year appear as letters?"

"Ah!" The rabbi began burrowing in a pile of papers. "Every letter in the Hebrew alphabet has a numerical significance. Here it is." He pulled out a piece of paper. Looked at it. Then handed it to me.

א = 1   ב = 2   ג = 3   ד = 4   ה = 5

ו = 6   ז = 7   ח = 8   ט = 9   י = 10

כ = 20   ל = 30   מ = 40   נ = 50

ס = 60   ע = 70   פ = 80   צ = 90

ק = 100   ר = 200   ש = 300   ת = 400

Sophia excitedly said, "That's gematria, right? Hebrew numerology?"

"Eh,...in a manner of speaking. Each letter represents a number." He craned his neck and pointed out the letters on the piece of paper he had given me. "*Aleph* is one, *bet* is two, *gimel* is three, etc. But the numbers don't add up to the civil year, the year according to the Gregorian calendar. They add up to the equivalent of the Jewish year. Counting from Adam and Eve, we're already in the five thousands!"

"According to this," I said, "the highest number is..."

"*Tav*, four hundred," the rabbi said.

"It would take a lot of *tavs* to get to five thousand," I said, scanning the sheet.

"The millennia are counted separately using larger letters. The first thousand years are represented by the Hebrew letter *ALEPH*." He outstretched his arms as if to demonstrate the size of the letter. "From the years

1000 to 2000, the second thousand years, the Hebrew letter *BET* is used. So the year 1001 is written as *BET–aleph*." He had outstretched his arms again when he said *BET* and huddled over and put his hands close together when he said *aleph*.

His smile was contagious. I searched for a disinfectant.

I said, "Finding our names and the year we met may sound statistically significant, but you gotta be careful with statistics. If you torture the numbers, they'll confess. It probably isn't scientific."

"Great!" The rabbi said. "So what do you need for something to be scientifically valid."

"An experiment, for one thing," I said.

"Good, but before that. What do you need?"

Before that?

"An a priori hypothesis," the rabbi said.

Smart man.

"A what?" Sophia asked.

I told Sophia, "An a priori hypothesis is a kind of guess at what will happen in the experiment. It's only scientific, though, if it can be proved wrong. Saying 'I will fall if I jump off a cliff' is a testable guess that can be proved right or wrong. Saying 'An undetectable rabbit is spinning the Earth on its paw' is not a testable guess so it's not an a priori hypothesis."

Sophia laughed.

"Right!" the rabbi said. "So in 1994, Witztum, Rips, and Rosenberg did the Great Sages experiment. These mathematicians made the a priori hypothesis that if a computer randomly selected several historically well-known rabbis, the computer could find those names encoded in the book of Genesis. And not only their names, but near their names would be their birth or death dates encoded as well."

"And?" Sophia asked.

"And nearly all of the thirty-two names were found encoded in the Torah along with their dates."

"Thirty-two?" I asked.

"Yes."

"Why do you think the other names weren't there?" Sophia asked.

"I don't know. They found the other names in Exodus, a later book in the Torah, but not in Genesis."

"*Aba*!" An older boy, similar long locks of hair and fringes at the waist, bolted into the room holding a bendable action figure of Superman. "Yaakov won't let me play with the truck! He's had it for an hour."

"Excuse me," the rabbi said as he turned to his son. "What's the trouble?"

"Yaakov won't let me play with the truck," the boy said again. He looked about four years of age.

"Yaakov!" Rabbi Silverman called out.

"He's had it for an hour," the boy repeated, as the one named Yaakov came in.

"Yaakov," said the rabbi. "You've had the truck for a while, don't you think it fair to let Avraham have a turn?"

Yaakov looked down at the truck in his hand and said softly, "No."

"You can play with Superman," Avraham offered.

Yaakov just shook his head.

The rabbi turned to Sophia and wondered aloud, "Now what would the wise King Solomon do?" He stroked his beard. "Ah, yes! The truck, please?" He held out his hand toward Yaakov. Yaakov reluctantly gave the truck to his father. "Since neither of you will let the other have the truck all to himself," the rabbi said, "you'll have to share it." With that, he removed the battery from the truck and gave the battery to Avraham and the shell of the truck to Yaakov.

Yaakov flipped the switch a few times, saw the truck's wheels didn't spin, and grabbed the Superman action figure from Avraham while giving him the truck. Yaakov left the room.

"*Todah, Aba.*" Avraham said and also left the room.

Sophia smiled.

"Nathan!" the rabbi faced me and beamed. "You look like you have a question. Good! Tell me what's on your mind!"

"Couldn't you find anything that way? Were there any controls to this experiment? Anything that showed it was really because of the Bible and not just some coincidence?"

"Of course! A senior cryptologist of the National Security Agency didn't believe the codes were real. He tried sixty-six names and dates, and included the cities where they lived. He got the same positive effect."

"What was the P value?" I asked.

"The result of his experiment was less than 1 in

200,000 chance of it happening by coincidence."

I whistled. "The chances of getting hit by an aster-oid next year are better than that. Probability like that can't be coincidence. Are they sure they did it right?"

"The experiment was peer-reviewed twice. Each time by five different statisticians. Speaking of comput-ers, mine is all ready. Tell me what you want to search," the rabbi said.

"Try Nathan."

The rabbi paused. What was his problem?

"The difficulty is," the rabbi said, "that the Hebrew word for Nathan is 'Natan.' And since Hebrew is writ-ten without vowels, your name is written N-T-N. So the likelihood of finding a three-letter word encoded in the Torah is probably a hundred percent. I'm sure you could find it in any book."

I nodded. "Try Nathan Yirmorshy," I said.

"Great! That's N-T-N Y-R-M-R-SH-Y. In Hebrew there is a letter that has a SH sound, so that counts as one letter." The rabbi typed it into his Bible code software and let the search happen. An empty pop-up appeared on the screen with a small beep. "Well, it doesn't seem to be here."

Yep. A waste of time.

"Let me try something." The rabbi tapped the key-board and waited. "Ah! There it is!"

"What?"

"Your name! In Hebrew the consonant V can have an O sound. So here your name is spelled N-T-N Y-R-M-*V*-R-SH-Y."

```
תאליפזוובשממתילדהאתרעואלואה
ליבמהילדהאתיעישוראתיעלמואת
קרחאלהבניעשואשרילדולובארצ
כנענריקחעשואתנשירואתבניירו
אתבנתיוואתכל(נ)פשותביתוואתמ
קנהוראתכלבהמת(ח)ואתכלקניןרוא
שררכשבארצכנע(נ)וילכאלארצמפנ
יעקבאחיוכיה(י)הרכושמרבמשבת
יחדורלאיכלהא(צ)מגוריהמלשאת
אתממפנימקניה(מ)וישבעשורהרשע
ירעשוהוואאדום(ו)אלההתלדותעשוא
ביאדומבהרשעי(ר)אלהשמותבניעש
ואליפזבנעדהאש(ת)עשורעואלבנב
שמתאשתעשעשוריה(ו)רבניאליפזתימ
נאומרצפורוגעתמוקנזותמנעהית
הפילגשלאליפזבנעשורותלדלאלי
פזאתעמלקאלהבניעדהאשתעשורוא
```

The rabbi looked at the screen for a moment longer. "Ha!" He clapped his hands together once.

"What? What is it?"

"Your name is encoded every 25 letters in *Breisheet*, chapter *lamed-vav*! That's Genesis chapter thirty-six! Out of all the chapters your name could be in, that's a praiseworthy chapter!"

"Why? What happens in that chapter?" I asked.

"It's not so much what happens in that chapter that's significant. It's the number! Thirty-six! *Lamed-vav*!"

"I don't get it," I said.

"You save the world!" The rabbi exclaimed.

Chapter 24

Sullivan wrote "Truck Driver" under "Musician" in his note pad and watched Luke leave the truck depot. He didn't understand it. Why did Luke talk to a trucker? On the one hand it added up to transporting illegal shipments, but of what? Shipments of firearms that the green beret musician knew about? Drugs that the doctors could get a hold of? But on the other hand, why did Luke require a geneticist? Could the whole thing be something like a biological weapon? What were they planning?

Sullivan decided to find out. He went into the depot and found a young mechanic.

"Hi! How are you?" Sullivan beamed offering his hand to the worker.

The boyish worker shook hands out of courtesy but had a should-I-know-you look on his face.

"I know I need to talk to that guy over there," Sullivan pointed to the man Luke had been talking to, "but I can't remember his name. The guy with the gray hair."

"Hal? Hal Carter?"

"Right! Carter! Thanks a lot." Sullivan shook the young man's hand again.

"Hey, Carter!" Sullivan called out.

Carter finished closing the back door of his truck and turned around.

"My name's Sullivan. I just talked to McCourt out there and he told me to have you brief me on everything."

Carter scowled. "He did?"

"Yeah. So what do I need to know?"

Carter looked off in the distance as if he were seeking Luke. He glanced at his truck. "I need to make a delivery," he said.

"Well, do you think you could give me a lift to my work?"

He pursed his lips and said at last, "Sure. Hop in and I'll take you wherever you need to go. I'll fill you in on the way."

"Sounds great." Sullivan got into the passenger seat marveling at the height he had to climb to get inside the truck.

Carter got in the driver's seat and started the truck. "Where can I drop you off?"

Sullivan tried to think of a place that would give them enough time to talk a lot. "Is the Lawrence Hall of Science too out of the way?"

"That's perfect," Carter said. He pulled out of the depot. "You work there?"

"Yeah," Sullivan said. "I got my BA in biology and my doctorate in genetics."

"Like Melinda," Carter said. "You met her yet?"

"No, but I heard about her. She works in the lab in Emeryville, right?"

"Yup." Carter was silent for a bit. "She's real smart, know what I'm sayin'? Most girls can't tell a fan belt from a timing belt but Melinda, she's got a real head on her shoulders."

"I know what you mean," Sullivan tried to say as little as possible. He hoped the silence was uncomfortable enough for Carter to spill more information. They reached the base of the hill that held the Lawrence Hall of Science. From that point on, the road would be winding and mostly isolated.

"Did McCourt tell you about any of the other guys?"

"He mentioned Perry. Why?"

"The rest of the guys? They're good men," Carter said. "They really care about the human race, know what I mean?"

"Yeah," Sullivan replied. They were passing brown fields of grass and thick trees.

"Hold on a second. The best way to fill you in on all you need to know is if I pull over and show you something." Carter pulled over on a narrow bank. He rummaged under his seat for a bit. "Hold on. I know it's here somewhere…Ah! Here it is." He pulled out a handgun and shot Sullivan twice in the chest.

Sullivan winced at the shock of the sudden pain searing at his stomach. The majority of the burn was at the entrance wounds, and Sullivan instinctively clutched at his gut to apply pressure. The pressure reduced the pain, even if only by a bit. And it also slowed the bleeding.

Carter got out of the truck and went to the passenger door.

Think, dammit. Think! Sullivan told himself. He found it harder and harder to apply the pressure. His muscles felt tired. His arms felt heavy.

Carter opened the passenger door and pulled Sullivan out so that Sullivan fell into the grass.

A rage swelled within Sullivan and a sudden surge of energy came through. Sullivan gripped his gut tighter, knowing that if he could hold on as strong as he held now, and if Carter left him, and if someone came by soon to bring him to the hospital, he would be fine. Heck, he could even get paid leave, for awhile. That would be nice. *I can do it,* he told himself. *I can keep myself alive until someone drives by.*

He heard Carter say, "That's all you need to know," and Carter shot him in the face.

Chapter 25

Save the world? I didn't know what the rabbi was talking about. And he must have seen it in my face because he went on to explain.

"The *Talmud* says that there are thirty-six people in the world who are so righteous, it is because of their very presence that God doesn't destroy the world."

"Doesn't sound like me," I said.

"Even if the world becomes one filled with barbarians," the rabbi continued. "As long as the thirty-six are present, the world is safe. It is said that when one dies, another immediately takes his place. So there are thirty-six at all times. But should one die in an unnatural manner then the world will surely be destroyed."

"What do you mean by unnatural?"

"If someone killed him, for example."

Gulp. If Luke thinks I'm one of the thirty-six, is he interested in protecting me or bent on killing me? I'm still alive, so it seems killing me is not on the menu.

"Why thirty-six?" I asked.

"Ah! That's very interesting. Do you know what we say when we raise our glasses of wine?"

"*L'chaim?*"

"Right. 'To life!' "

"Ooh! Like that song in 'Fiddler on the Roof!' " Sophia said.

"Right! So the word 'life' in Hebrew is *chai* as in *l'chaim*. And *chai* is a two letter word whose letters add up to eighteen."

"I love *gematria*," Sophia said.

"And since these people are said to be twice as righteous as the rest of the people on Earth,…"

"Two times eighteen is thirty-six." I finished.

"Right. So these are considered double-life people. And as to the number of them, again, it's thirty-six."

"Do you think you've met any of these thirty-six righteous?" I asked.

"Most people don't believe in it. But I do. And I've met many others who believe in it, and I've met many who are very righteous. But we believers are few. Most people have trouble believing in a God who would be so cruel as to destroy the world should there be fewer than thirty-six righteous. I understand that."

It made me wonder. Not so much about the thirty-six righteous, but why I was even listening to this guy rattle off such strange ideas. Codes in the Bible, thirty-six people saving the world, it was just a bunch of hocus pocus. What mattered, though, was that whoever sent me that message probably believed in it all. So as ridiculous as these codes and thirty-six righteous were, I had to pretend to be a believer. That mentality would help me get closer to my anonymous writer. And probably closer to McCourt as well.

"What about Meg?" Sophia said.

"Who's Meg?" the rabbi asked.

"We don't know," she said. "But she was mentioned in the letter. Do the codes say anything about her?"

"No doubt," the rabbi shrugged his shoulders. "In Hebrew, Meg is a two-letter word. She'll pop up all over the place so it won't be very significant. Even if her name appears near yours, the chances are so high that I'd be more surprised if her name didn't appear there. Does she have a—"

Sophia let out a scream and collapsed to the floor.

I sank to her head and cradled it.

"Quick," I said. "Call an ambulance. It looks like she's having a seizure."

Her back was arched so much it looked like she'd snap. A guttural sound emitted from her throat and through clenched teeth she screamed out as though with tremendous difficulty, "I am!"

"*Mein gott!*" The rabbi fumbled for the phone and speed-dialed the ambulance.

"Uuungghh!" Sophia's eyes rolled to the back of her head and she began shaking uncontrollably. "That… I…am!" she shouted again. The words came out slowly. Her teeth fastened tight together.

The rabbi said into the phone, "Come ambulance! We need a quick!—I mean, we need an ambulance!"

I made sure she didn't hit her head against the floor as she continued convulsing.

"Uunggghh!" She sounded in pain. "I am…*Shekinah*," she cried and passed out.

Chapter 26

I hated hospitals. I looked around the wait-ing room of the hospital with another cup of coffee in hand. There must have been about fifteen people waiting. Most of them old. Sophia didn't strike me as someone who had needed to be taken care of. I had enough trouble as it was taking care of myself. Two people with neurological disorders went together like a meal of wine and cotton balls.

Waiting around can be tiresome. I sipped the coffee to wake me up. It did the trick.

A boy that looked to be about five years old played some handheld video game. The sounds that ema-nated from the video game sounded like he was firing a machine gun. Made me want to play it. Pinned in one of the upper corners of the room was a television broadcasting a cooking show. A well-built man wear-ing an apron was cutting a zucchini. I pictured the guy cutting his finger off and moments later rushing into the waiting room offering cooked zucchini to everyone here.

I finished my coffee and carefully placed my ninth Styrofoam cup on top of the pyramid of empty cups that balanced on the empty chair next to me. One more cup and my pyramid would be complete. An attractive, middle-aged woman in a white coat approached me. She had a stethoscope dangling around her neck.

"Mr. Yirmorshy?" She asked.

"Yes?" I stood up.

She shook my hand and introduced herself. "I examined Sophia and she seems to uh…" Her eyes averted to the pyramid of cups.

"Yes?" I coaxed.

"She probably had an epileptic seizure. It's like an electrical storm in the brain that can cause all the muscles to stiffen. Sometimes, as in the case you reported to the nurse, the muscles then go back and forth between contracting and relaxing. This will appear like a convulsion."

"That's what I guessed," I said. "So she's okay?"

"She's fine. We're just about to do an M.E.G. scan on her to…"

"What did you say?"

The doctor's eyes fluttered. "I said she's fine."

"No. You said M.E.G."

"Oh. The M.E.G. is magnetoencephalography. It's a way to record the brain's magnetic activity."

Crap. Could this be the Meg the letter was referring to?

* * *

A man in sweatpants and t-shirt ran alongside his dog up Grizzly Peak Avenue. Birds chirping in the surrounding forest filled the air. His dog was a Ridgeback and the man's shirt read, "In dog we trust." The climb was steep, but the man ran it every week. He panted less than his dog.

The run made him sweat but this early in the afternoon made the high elevation's cool temperature more tolerable for a run. His dog wasn't on a leash because the dog didn't have to be. Ridgebacks were one of the smartest breeds around, and his went to obedience school to be trained to respond to all commands.

Today was different, though. The dog ran off the road and into the woods.

The man stopped on the side of the road about to call back his dog, but ended up sneezing instead. As he wiped his nose on his sleeve, he followed the dog down to where the dog was busy pawing at the earth.

"Whatchya find, boy?"

The dog growled and tugged at something in the dirt. Stepping forward, the man had trouble registering what he saw. Was it a dead animal?

"Heel!"

The dog whimpered and sat beside his feet. The man inspected the thing in the dirt more closely, and saw a bloody shirt.

* * *

When I placed the final cup on my pyramid, Sophia walked out to the waiting room as if nothing had happened. No limp, no bandages, no snotty tissues. Like she just got up from a quick nap wearing her jeans and sweater.

"Hi," Sophia smiled through bedroom eyes.

"You ok?" I asked.

"Tired," she said. "They say I have epilepsy and I need to take this," she handed me a prescription. I read the scrawl.

"Tegretol. Doesn't ring a bell." I handed the prescription back to her.

She crumpled it up, threw it in the trash and headed toward the exit. "I don't have epilepsy," she said. "It's my sister."

I caught up to her. "I thought you only had two brothers."

We exited the hospital. The bright daylight made me squint.

"I had a twin sister who died at birth."

"Sorry," I said. Felt lame for saying it.

Sophia said "Truth is, I never knew my sister so I don't really miss her."

We walked back to my car. I started the engine and headed down Broadway back to Sophia's place.

Sophia continued as though there hadn't been any interruption in our conversation. "You know how identical twins can feel the same thing at the same time miles away?"

"I have a theory about that, but I'll tell you later. Go on," I said.

"Well, it's like I can still sense her even though she's not alive." Sophia looked out the window. "Is that strange?"

"Was her name going to be *Shekinah*?"

"What?"

"That's what you said before you passed out. You said 'I am *Shekinah*.'"

"I don't know who that is," Sophia said. "But something about that name sounds familiar."

We drove down Bancroft Avenue toward downtown Berkeley. The main street, Shattuck Avenue, was mostly a conglomeration of restaurants and movie theaters. I wasn't sure what to say. Felt uncomfortable. I hadn't had an uncomfortable silence for quite some time. The fact that I could still have them surprised me. Thought I was more mature than that.

"Oh! I have to tell you what the doctor said," I exclaimed.

I told Sophia about the M.E.G. and asked her what she thought.

"Does it make sense in the context of the letter?" she asked.

"Well, the letter said that we would no longer be strangers with MEG. Do you think the M.E.G. you saw today could somehow make people know each other?"

"Doesn't feel right to me," Sophia said. "What would be the point of having something that reads a brain's magnetic waves? It doesn't make sense."

She was right.

Sophia snapped her fingers, "I got it. So maybe it isn't a person or the hospital machine. Maybe it's a different machine!" Sophia adjusted her position in the seat so that she could face me better. "You know that two-wheeled go cart? The Segue?"

"Yeah."

"The inventor originally nicknamed it Ginger. As a kind of code. So what if Meg is the name of some invention?"

"That's a stretch."

"Well, do you have any better ideas?"

"Fine," I said. "We'll look at the international spider."

"The international spider?"

"The world-wide-web."

Sophia smiled. I took out my iPhone and handed it to her.

"How do you work this thing?" she asked.

"First, turn it on."

"Where's the on button?"

"On the top."

Sophia seemed to be struggling.

I asked, "Did you press the button?"

"Several times!"

"Don't click it. It's press and hold."

"Forget it. We're almost at my place. I have the internet," Sophia said.

"You do?" I tried picturing her room.

Didn't remember a computer.

"Yeah," Sophia said as if it was obvious. "Under my bed."

* * *

Melinda took out the aluminum pan from the kitchen oven. She took the feathery basting brush and basted the delicious looking pheasants before returning them to the oven. Paul walked into the kitchen with a handsome smile on his face.

"I just got off the phone with Luke," Paul said.

"What did he say?" Melinda asked, taking off her floral designed potholders and facing Paul.

"He's seen Nathan driving around downtown Oakland. And guess who he's with."

"Who?"

"A woman. A street worker."

Melinda sat down, struck with the implications. She looked at the white refrigerator, and read the Bible quotes on small magnets there. So the prophecies were true. She always believed it, but now she was one of the few who ever got to see her beliefs be confirmed by the unfolding of history. She felt only one thing. Pure joy.

Chapter 27

Detective Bobbie Graff had trouble parking her car on the narrow shoulder without blocking Grizzly Peak. It didn't matter much, though. There wasn't a lot of traffic. She took a cursory glance at the location. The trees served to hold up the yellow tape, "CRIME SCENE. DO NOT CROSS." Officer Stelwarth filled her in.

"Man walking his dog discovered the body a half hour ago," Stelwarth said.

"COD?" the detective asked.

"Cause of death was two shots to the chest. But we haven't found any casings, yet. Could be the killer picked them up."

"Or the vic was killed elsewhere and dumped here," she said. "ID?"

"Going to be difficult. No wallet. His hands, feet, and head have been sawed off. We only have the trunk of the body."

"At least we'll know if he's Jewish."

Stelwarth laughed. "You know, *I'm* not Jewish and *I'm*— "

"Too much information, Stelwarth" Graff said holding up her hand to stop his words.

Graff walked with Stelwarth to the body and saw the coroner examining it. It was just a stump of flesh dressed in the remains of a white button-up shirt, brown slacks, and black belt. Flies buzzed around the places where the limbs and head should have been.

"Got something," the police photographer said a few feet away.

It was a notepad. The pad was about two inches by four inches and open to an interior page with college ruled blue lines. The police photographer took a photo of it and Graff put on plastic gloves. She eased the notepad out of the loose dirt.

"Luke McCourt," she read.

Stelwarth scowled, "Lemme see?"

The detective held up the pad and Stelwarth read the page. "Shit," he said. "I know that handwriting."

I made a turn onto Alcatraz. Sophia got pretty quiet. She faced the passenger window but seemed more like she was swimming in her own thoughts. Even if Meg turned out to be the name of an invention, it didn't explain why McCourt was watching me. McCourt wasn't motivated by some perverse sexual thing. The whole thirty-six righteous thing didn't make sense, either. If he did think I was one of the thirty-six, why have a photo of my parents? Was there something in my family's past that somehow connected to him? What if he was a relative?

"I don't know why I have such strong feelings about my sister," Sophia said breaking the silence. "I didn't know her, and I tell myself that over and over but still...I think about what it might have been like with a twin sister."

I nodded, though Sophia didn't see it. She seemed to be sharing a lot of personal information with me. Like she was going to rely on me. "When I was five years old, a friend of mine got hit by a car," I said.

"Jeez," Sophia said looking at me. "And he was five, too?"

"Yeah. At the time, when we played together I was so focused on my own happiness that I didn't really care what happened to him."

"You were a kid," Sophia said.

"Yeah, but there was something else. After the incident, I noticed how the people treated me when I mentioned his death," I said. "I got more attention and I guess I just felt proud to be able to say I knew someone who died."

Sophia turned back to the window. "I don't feel proud."

"Don't you? You're talking about your sister as if you want my pity."

"What are you saying?" She looked back at me with wide eyes.

"I'm saying you don't really care about losing your sister, you're just interested in hearing me say, 'Aw, poor baby.' " I couldn't look at her. "Maybe you don't even realize it. Maybe you've somehow convinced yourself that losing your sister, someone you've never even met, is some kind of tragedy and we all have to feel sorry for you. Subconsciously, all you really want is to hear people say, 'Look at Sophia. She's just a poor victim of the world. Poor Sophia. Poor little girl.' "

Sophia was quiet for a moment and then said, "Nathan, what are you doing?"

"What do you mean?"

"You're saying things like…" she growled in frustration. "It's like you're trying to push me away, or something." I heard in her voice the tears that must have been on her face. She said, "What are you afraid of? Are you afraid of being in some committed relationship with me? Do you think I'll break your heart in the end?"

I said nothing.

She sniffed. "Who was she?"

"Who?"

"The woman whose picture you have in your bedroom. Did she leave you?"

We got to her apartment and I parked the car. Turned the engine off. Neither of us left the car. I looked at the time. Just after three o'clock. Looked down at my light-blue shirt. Picked off a piece of lint. Glanced at Sophia. She was drying her eyes and nose. I turned away.

"Nancy was my wife," I said.

Sophia said nothing.

"You're right. She did leave me." I tried to put the words together. "I'm bipolar. I have these delusions. That's why I asked you over in the first place, to confirm that the cameras weren't in my head."

Sophia said nothing.

"Anyway, I can see some pretty crazy things. And Nancy couldn't handle it. She left me to save herself from my raving delusions."

"Nathan."

I turned to look at her.

She leaned close to me, stared me in the eye and slapped her chest with each word she said. "I...am not...Nancy."

I nodded. "It's just," I averted my eyes. "I can't tell you how much I regret losing her."

"Don't regret it," Sophia said wiping her nose against the cuff of her sweater. "Be grateful of the good times you had with her. Think of her fondly, without regrets."

I sighed. "Got it. No regrets."

Chapter 28

I sat on a cushion on the floor using Sophia's bed as a table. The laptop computer was open on her bed.

I called up a search engine and typed in "Meg invention."

Most of the hits said "Meg's invention," but the ones that had Meg as the acronym M.E.G. looked promising.

I tried one. "Something about new energy and a guy named Sam Kor."

I typed "Sam Kor" in the search engine. Over 96,000 hits. I refined it to " 'Sam Kor M.E.G.' " Back down to over 1000 hits.

"That's better," I said and clicked open Sam Kor's website. "Wow. This guy's a retired captain of the U.S. Navy. Let's see…" I read aloud, "the Motionless Electromagnetic Generator…I'm an idiot!"

"What?"

"I totally forgot that the letter didn't have Meg written as a name, but had all the letters uppercase, like an acronym! This Motionless Electromagnetic Generator might be it!"

"What does it do?" Sophia asked.

I looked closely at the screen. "Hold on." I copied the patent number down on the pad of paper.

On the patent web page, I punched in the number and read the description.

"Not sure I understand all this engineering jargon, but if it's what I think it is, then it's a kind of free energy device."

Luke turned off the classical music and answered his cell phone.

"Luke, Hal here. We gotta problem."

"What is it?" Luke asked.

"Guy came to me. Said he knew you. Mentioned Melinda and Perry."

Luke listened carefully.

"He wanted me to fill him in on project MEG," Hal continued.

"What did you do?"

"I killed him."

"Good. So what's the problem? Was it clean?"

"Yeah, it was clean! Come on! This is Hal you're talking to. His head, hands, and feet are fish food by now and his trunk is underground."

"Fine. So what's the problem?"

"Found a badge. Guy was a cop."

"Damn it, Hal!" Luke said.

"He needed to die, Luke. Cop or not."

"Yes, it's just…Damn it, Hal!"

"So what do we do?"

"As of now, project MEG commences tomorrow."

"Finally," Hal sighed.

Chapter 29

My iPhone buzzed. I looked at it. "A text message from the rabbi."

"What's it say?" Sophia asked.

"Just to call him. I promised him I'd call him to let him know how you're doing."

"I'm fine."

I studied the rabbi's message. "He also says I should check my e-mail." I opened my e-mail account on Sophia's computer and saw a message sent by the rabbi.

"It's got an attachment. A pdf file." I clicked it open and frowned.

"What is it?" Sophia asked.

"I'm not sure. Some kind of search-a-word. I'll call him now."

I dialed and the rabbi answered on the first ring.

"Hi. Sophia's fine," I told him. "We're back at her place and she's in tip top shape."

"Nathan! I'm glad you called!" The rabbi sounded desperate. "You remember how Sophia said she was the *Shekinah* when she had the fit?"

"Yeah. Does that mean anything to you?"

"Absolutely! In Judaism, the *Shekinah* is the female aspect of God. The Divine Presence. Many call her the bride of God."

Huh?

"What do you think it means?" I asked him.

"I'm not sure, but I did a few searches in *Breisheet* chapter thirty-six, and I found the word *Shekinah* and you know what crosses it?"

"What?"

"Sophia. Sophia is encoded in the Bible. It's in the attachment I sent you."

I examined the open attachment.

```
דעדהלעשלעשׁאתאלייפזזרבשׁמתילל‌ה‌אתרעוא
ראבייאדרמבברהרשׁעירראלהשׁמותדבנ‌ר‌עשׁ‌ﬡ
אראוﬡשׁ‌צﬡפרלרמראשׁראﬡפאומראלרועדור
‌ﬡﬡישׁהיהאראנצצלרטשׁבלרבצובעדננעﬡשׁב
 ייד﬩‌ﬥשׁנעוצואראנאלהﬡל﬩פﬦהרחרריאל‌ﬡ
חתכלמירדדהתהרועריריועשׁﬤﬥﬥ﬩ﬤﬥ‌ﬡﬡﬦﬢﬢﬥ
```

"You saw Sophia's name?" The rabbi asked.

"I'm looking at it now."

"There's more," the rabbi said. "Sophia is the Greek word meaning Wisdom. In Hebrew wisdom is *Chochmah*. Another name for the Hebrew goddess."

I wasn't sure what to make of all this. It was so much hocus pocus. But, again, if the anonymous letter writer believed it, then it could help explain what the writer planned or expected. It could help figuring out what to do next.

"I thought there was only one God in Judaism," I said.

"There is! But God is not a He or a She. We are all made in God's image, male and female. But some believe the female aspects of God came down to Earth to be among the people. And others believe God's bride to be the Jewish people themselves."

I said nothing.

"The *Shekinah* is known as the love aspect of God, but she is also known as the divine punisher. She punished Adam and Eve and the serpent. She destroyed Sodom and Gemorrah. She drowned the Egyptians in the Red Sea, and it is said she will return for the final battle between Gog and Magog."

"Gog and Magog?"

"Ezekiel writes about a king named Gog who leads Magog, his nation, to fight in a final war. The *Talmud* refers to Gog and Magog as a part of the coming of the messiah."

My mind tried to make sense of it all. My mind was losing.

The rabbi continued, "I know this is a lot to throw at you but I feel it's important because whoever wrote you that letter may already know all of this. And if they already know it, then they'll also know that encoded in *Breisheet* thirty-six is 'Apocalypse.' "

Part 2

TEN

Chapter 30

Nuremberg, Germany
October 16, 1946

"What do they want?" Julius wondered to
himself. He lay back on the black box that functioned as his bed. The others in the cell also had a box
of their own. Julius stared at the ceiling, a cement covering held by brick walls.

"I did nothing to deserve this." Julius couldn't sleep
though it was nearly 1:00 in the morning. He continued to stare at the ceiling and wondered at how our
world created things when the need arose. We were
once cavemen and now we had ceilings. Why was he
thinking of this? It was stupid. Was this how a man
who is about to die thought?

The other men were silent. There was nothing to
say. Each of them would soon die, one by one. Except
for Hermann. But Hermann was a coward. A sissy. He
wore women's undergarments and didn't deserve to be
with the rest of us. Julius wasn't sure, however, how
Hermann had managed to get a hold of the cyanide
caplet. When they carried his body away, it was such
a show. The pictures and the newspapers accompanied

the morticians. It was all a show. But how could they do that? How could they have us be considered newsworthy when all of the Jews are doing their tricks? The Jews are the news! Not us! *Now we are the news.*

When the guards came in, Julius knew it was time. The others stood, ready to meet their fate. But Julius didn't stand. He didn't deserve this. He was not a killer, he didn't kill anyone. He was just a journalist! A journalist, for God's sake!

For God's sake! Yes, for God's sake. At least God will be ready for him. Julius knew that God would welcome him and the man who hangs him will soon be hanged. The Bolsheviks will see to that.

The guards had to physically lift Julius to his feet. He fought their grips. The others had already been hung. He was the last to be taken to the gymnasium of Landsberg Prison. Julius couldn't believe it. Death for him. A simple journalist. It was ludicrous. It was abominable. A crime itself.

As the guards led him up the wooden steps, he said to them, "And now I go to God." It was the Jews, Julius reminded himself. They were celebrating now. Celebrating my death. It was the Jews. The dirty Jews. I will not let them have their celebration! I will not!

"Heil Hitler!" Julius Streicher screamed as they pushed him to the noose. "Heil Hitler! Heil Hitler!"

When the noose was around his neck, he stared wild-eyed at the witnesses and shouted, "Purimfest 1946!" and the floor fell from beneath him.

Chapter 31

Present Day

After my conversation with the rabbi, I studied the attachment that came with his email.

I showed the encoded words to Sophia and relayed all that the rabbi had told me.

When Sophia heard about the word 'apocalypse' being encoded in Genesis thirty-six, she said, "Whatever that means, it can't be good. I'm going to see what the cards say."

She's so stuck on those cards. Did she ever make her own decisions?

"I'll see if I can find contact info for the retired captain."

I delved deeper into Captain Kor's website. There were articles about common flaws in classical physics and something called "negative entropy in open systems." I had never heard of such a thing. One of the articles listed the captain's address and telephone number.

"Here it is," I said. "And look! He's in San Francisco!"

Sophia didn't respond. She just sat on the bed flipping tarot cards.

I dialed the captain's number.

"Hello?" An old voice answered. There was a hissing sound in the background.

"Is this Retired Captain Kor?"

"Yes."

I introduced myself and asked about the motionless electromagnetic generator.

"Why don't you come over and we'll chat about it. What time's convenient for you?"

"Is now okay?"

"I think I could work you in. Do you like angel food cake?"

"What?"

"My wife just made a delicious angel food cake. You'll love it. You know how to get here?"

I could have used the online maps, but they can be as reliable as a shark protecting your sushi. So I listened to the captain and took down directions.

I ended the call and turned to Sophia. "Let's go."

"You go. The cards say I should keep focused on making money." She gathered her cards together. "I'm going to Telegraph Avenue to do some readings."

I felt a fire shake inside my head and a hardness in my gut.

"Fine," I said. With a little more force than necessary.

If it came out sounding angry, Sophia didn't seem to notice. I exhaled, relieved she didn't pick up on it.

Why did I feel rejected? Why did I take it personally? She needed to make money. She wasn't my girlfriend, we only met last night. Why did it bother me so much that she wasn't coming with me?

"Where do you want to meet when I'm done?" I asked.

Sophia took a key out of a jar of metal things.

"Here's a spare to my apartment," she said. "We'll meet here."

Score!

The autopsy for Sullivan's body was given top priority, along with any substance or DNA analysis that resulted from the autopsy. The sergeant refused to allow anyone besides the medical examiner to be present at the autopsy. He had made it clear that there was to be no personal emotions involved in processing the case. The medical examiner pressed the record button on the miniature cassette recorder and began to dictate.

"Case number 74–9437, John Doe. Caucasian male about forty-five years of age. Property belonging to Officer Patrick Casey Sullivan was found on the body, suggesting the body is Officer Sullivan. The hands, feet, and head have been removed. The remaining trunk of the body is a bit overweight, consistent with Officer Sullivan's proportions. The trunk was found to be 158 pounds putting the entire body to be about 200 pounds."

The medical examiner moved to the X-rays. "No bullets are inside the body, though there are two bullet entry wounds and no exit wounds."

He moved to the body and confirmed how it blanched when touched. Nonfixed lividity placed the time of death at under six hours. And the body was cool to the touch.

"TOD was between four to six hours ago. Sometime between nine and eleven o'clock in the morning."

He examined the bones where the limbs should have been. "Marks on the bone suggest a saw was used to cut off the limbs."

The medical examiner moved to the entry wounds and used a magnifying glass. There was something there he had never seen on a body before. A white powder.

Chapter 32

"How is it?" the retired Captain Kor asked about the angel food cake.

"It's good." And it *was* good. Damn good. I took another bite, had some longer glances at the oxygen tank that was hissing behind the captain. An air tube was fastened to Kor's nose.

"It's from a stroke I had recently," the captain explained. "All the stress from getting the M.E.G. patented took a hold on my life. So now I've learned to relax about the whole damn thing."

I heard the ticking of a clock. Looked around the living room and saw one hanging above the fire place. Kor sat in an easy chair holding a plate of crumbs, and I sat across from him on a dark green sofa finishing my own slice of cake. A worn cloth covered the sofa and easy chair. The coffee table sported stains and chipped corners. Kor had better things to do than to worry about the way his furniture looked.

"What did you say your job was?" Kor asked.

"Didn't. Computer programmer."

"Computer programmer! That's a pretty lucrative business. You could save for retirement early."

"I already have enough for retirement," I said. "So, I was wondering—"

"From computer programming?"

I blinked. "No. Investing."

"Financially savvy, then, eh? Do you have a business card."

I pulled out my card and handed it to him. "I wanted to ask—"

"So why don't you?"

I smiled at his rude question. "I *am* asking."

"No. Why don't you retire?"

"Oh. Old habits die hard, I guess."

The old man chuckled. "So what did you want to see me about?"

"What's the M.E.G.?" I asked.

"It's going to revolutionize the world," he said. "Imagine driving your electric car and never having to recharge it or change batteries. Imagine your car running forever, expense-free. And imagine having your entire home—your electric stove, your light fixtures, your television, your radio, your computer, everything electrical—using all that electricity for free. Imagine third-world countries getting the electricity they need for free. What do you say to that?"

I nodded, "Pretty good imagination."

"The motionless electromagnetic generator generates more power than you put in to it."

"That's impossible."

"Windmills do it. Solar panels do it. Hydroelectric dams do it."

"But the energy still comes from somewhere. The wind, the sun, the water. The energy comes from those things. It's not coming from nowhere."

The captain laughed. "Nowhere is an interesting place," he said.

"What do you mean?"

"Imagine a toy box. You take out all the toy trains, all the stuffed animals, all the various nick-nacks that don't belong in toy boxes, you take out the air molecules and all the atoms, what's left in the box?"

"Nothing," I said.

"Wrong."

Mrs. Evelyn Kor came into the living room and asked, "Excuse me. Is there anything else you'd like, Nathan? More angel food cake perhaps?"

"No, thanks," I said.

"It's just egg whites," she said. "No cholesterol."

"I'm fine, thanks."

"I'll have more, Ev," the captain said handing her his plate. Before she could take her hand away, he kissed it and they shared a smile.

"Actually," I said. "I'll have some more, too."

"*Now* I know you're a smart man," the captain said.

When Mrs. Kor returned to the kitchen, the captain continued, "So if it's not 'nothing' in the empty box, what is it?"

I shrugged. "Tell me."

"It's virtual particles," he said.

Okay. The captain lost some sense after the stroke. Virtual particles? I wonder if he has any "virtual friends."

"It turns out," the captain explained, "that virtual particles are popping in and out of existence. And this has been proven in the lab."

"What are virtual particles?"

"They're tiny particles that pop out of nowhere and then suddenly disappear. It's like, oh! There's a particle! And poof! Darn, the little bugger got away. The Casimir effect and the Lamb shift demonstrate this."

"The Casimir effect?" I remembered learning about it in one of my college physics courses. "Isn't that something to do with bending metal plates?"

"Exactly," Kor said. "It involves two metal plates like sheets of metal standing up parallel to each other so they're side by side like two slices of bread standing upright. The metal plates have a small gap between them. Now when the air and everything are removed from the environment, it's like the plates are in space, a complete vacuum. Nothing is around to manipulate the plates. And yet what happens? The plates move closer together! So that suggests these guys are feeling some kind of force. Roughly speaking, it's like something is pushing them together. And if there's pushing going on, then there must be something doing the pushing."

"Like what?" I asked.

"Ah! It's the power of things out of balance. That's the beauty of asymmetry! A lot of scientists like symmetry because it makes the math so much easier. But they're completely missing the, uh, are you blushing?"

"Never mind. It's nothing." Boy, my ears felt hot!

"Okay. So imagine two elephants head to head, pushing against each other." Kor pressed his fists together, as if to demonstrate. "They're pushing with equal force so that they don't move left or right. They just keep pushing. You follow?"

"Yes."

"In math, since the situation is symmetrical, the forces are insignificant because the elephants don't move. It's as if there are no forces."

I nodded.

"Now imagine standing right between the two elephants. With all that force crushing you, you wouldn't say the forces are insignificant anymore, would you?"

I chuckled. "No, I wouldn't."

"So if we have two elephants pushing against each other, all we need to do to detect the force is remove one of the elephants. Now we have a completely asymmetrical situation, and the remaining elephant charges full out crushing anything in its path."

"Okay," I said.

"And that's how the force of the virtual particles pushes the plates together. Places where space is unbalanced, asymmetrical, are where there's nothing pushing back against the virtual particles. So they're free to charge like tiny elephants from their virtual space into our space, hitting anything in their path."

"And what makes space asymmetrical?"

"Space curvature," Kor said. "Anything that bends space, like mass, will make space asymmetrical."

This actually made sense. So what if it isn't mass that causes the force of gravity? What if mass bends space, and the bending of space is what causes the force of gravity to be felt?

"So what does this have to do with free energy and the whole world-revolutionizing thing?" I asked.

"If these particles exist then they have a mass. And according to Einstein, anything that has mass has energy."

I sighed.

"What is it?"

"Even if the particles exist, how much energy could come from it?" I asked. "Moving two plates together doesn't seem like a heck of a lot."

"Remember Einstein's formula. $E=mc^2$. To find out how much energy you get, take the mass and multiply it by 90 million billion. That's how big c squared is."

I knew how big c squared is, but didn't get the connection.

"Let me put it this way," Kor said. "Einstein showed us how much energy there is in one atom. One single atom. And unfortunately, the people of Hiroshima experienced it firsthand."

Then it hit me. The significance of it. More than 140,000 people in Hiroshima had died from the atomic bomb. From one single atom. I got what I came for. I now understood the agenda. But Kor wasn't finished.

"See this coffee cup?" Kor asked lifting his cup. "If I

took the virtual particles that appeared inside this cup, it would be enough energy to destroy our planet."

McCourt's plans, the M.E.G., apocalypse. Mc-Court was planning on building a bomb. But what did any of that have to do with me?

Chapter 33

"We've got word on what the white pow-der was," Stelwarth reported to the sergeant. They were in the sergeant's office.

"Shut the door."

The sergeant had an open door policy, but not today. Not for Sullivan's case. Stelwarth closed the door.

"It was cornstarch," Stelwarth said.

"Think the perp was using gloves?"

"Makes sense. Shoots Sull—"

The sergeant looked stern.

"Shoots the victim," Stelwarth said, "picks up the casings, and removes the bullets with tweezers or something, wearing latex gloves to make sure he doesn't leave any prints. The cornstarch powder must've transferred from the gloves."

"Alright. Find McCourt. He's gotta be hiding somewhere. And get that Yimorski fella back here. See if he knows anything."

* * *

My cell phone rang. "Hold on," I said to Kor.

"Of course."

I answered it. It was the police station.

"Could you come to the station, Mr. Yirmorshy? It's urgent we talk to you. It's about Mr. McCourt."

"Be there in about an hour."

I put the iPhone away. "There's something I need to tell you." I told Kor about the two-way mirrors, the letter, the Bible codes, and everything in between. "If these people are religious fanatics, do you think they could use the M.E.G. to build a bomb?"

"Anything can be used as a weapon," Kor said. "But it's true. The M.E.G. would be powerful if used as a bomb. Even our prototype could be used for such a purpose, I imagine."

McCourt wouldn't have to look far to figure out how to make the M.E.G. All he'd have to do is go online and check out the patent. It was possible to build a device off of a patent document. But it was easier to steal the prototype. McCourt struck me to be the patient type, but not patient enough to build a machine from scratch.

"They may try to steal your prototype," I said. "Has anyone around you acted suspicious? Have you been followed recently?"

The captain laughed. Coughed. And laughed some more. "Take a look outside the window. What do you see parked across the street?"

I stepped to the window and looked. "Just a guy sitting in a Roto-Rooter van."

"Been there for three days."

"Three days?!" I asked.

Kor took a sip of his coffee. "Not always the same man, of course. Someone else sat in that van yesterday." Kor chuckled. "I like how people call me paranoid. It amuses me."

The driver didn't look like McCourt.

"Nathan, there are so many who want me dead I'm amazed I've come this far. Car companies, electric companies, certain people in the government…. But you know, assassinations these days are no longer their M.O. They just don't do it anymore. What with the internet and all the information available at everyone's fingertips, … assassinations have become embarrassing.

"So maybe those religious fanatics you mentioned have been following me. Maybe not. I'm surrounded by people interested in the M.E.G. It's hard to find Waldo in a world of tall, gangly, striped-shirt, fashion-challenged idiots."

Maybe the driver knew McCourt.

"Just a sec," I said. "I'll be back."

I walked out the front door and across Kor's front yard making a bee-line for the Roto-Rooter van. The van started up and screeched its tires against the road, peeling away. I stood in the middle of the empty street and watched the van leave. Not enough time to catch the license plate number. No telling if the driver—or anyone else inside for that matter—knew Luke. The smell of rubber lingered.

I returned to the house seeing the captain in a fit of laughter and coughing. Mrs. Kor walked in with two plates of cake and asked what was so funny.

"He scared them away, Sweetie!" Kor said. "Tell them about yesterday."

"It happened to me too," Mrs. Kor said. "I went to the van and they just drove away. I was only trying to give them a piece of cake. You know, something to eat while tracking my husband." She smiled and handed me one of the two plates.

"You're not worried about your husband?" I asked.

She shook her head. "Listen, if they wanted him dead they would have killed him a long time ago. I feel that as long as they're not hurting anyone, they can at least enjoy some angel food cake."

I looked at my slice of cake. What was Luke's obsession with watching people? What did he want from me? If there was something he wanted to do to me, why not just do it? Why not just confront me or the retired captain? What was the point of watching us? I turned to Kor. "You know, maybe that Roto-Rooter guy had nothing to do with me, but whoever sent me that letter might try to steal your prototype."

"Him and everyone else."

"Everyone else?" I asked.

"Relax," Kor said. "That problem was taken care of a long time ago. There are only two of us who know where the prototype is. Myself, and a brilliant fellow by the name of Antoine Priore. And though we are the only two who know where the prototype is, neither of us know exactly where it is."

"How is that possible?" I asked.

"Three years ago, we entrusted one man to hold onto the prototype. He sensed trouble brewing, so he had the foresight to write down the location of the prototype on a small piece of paper. But he ripped the paper in half, so each half didn't have enough information to find the prototype. He mailed each half in separate envelopes. One to Antoine Priore, and one to myself. Now there are two of us who have the information, but both of us are needed to find where it is. A few days later, the gentleman with the hidden prototype was shot in his lab and was discovered lying in a pool of blood."

I said nothing. This was all so cloak and dagger.

"It's quite a responsibility, don't you think?" Kor asked.

"What is?"

"Being the bearer of one half of the location." The captain smiled. Mrs. Kor covered her own smile with her hand.

"I can imagine."

"Do you think it's a burden?" he asked.

"Well, not if you put it in a shoebox with some old baseball cards for safekeeping."

"Nathan, ever since this stroke, I've become much more open to my surroundings. I've developed a better idea of priorities and what's important."

The captain turned to Mrs. Kor. "Could you get the envelope, my love?"

"Good," she said and left the room.

"My wife is what's important to me, now. My final days need to be with her, not with my work."

Mrs. Kor returned to the room.

"You're a good man, Nathan." Kor said. "We've only just met but I'm a good judge of character."

Mrs. Kor, still smiling, handed me the envelope.

"Don't see this as a burden," Kor said. "See this as a hand-me-down to put away—as you said—in your shoebox for safekeeping. As long as you never meet Antoine Priore, the prototype will never fall into the wrong hands and the envelope should be of no consequence in your life."

I took the envelope and felt the weight of the world between my fingertips.

Sam Kor watched his wife Ev say goodbye to the nice young man and close the front door. Sam said, "Come here and give me a hug." Ev bent over the chair and gave him a firm squeeze.

"I need to call Charlie," he said.

On the phone, Sam said, "Charlie, I found someone and he bit. He took the envelope." He read out Nathan's phone number on the business card.

Chapter 34

It was almost six p.m when I arrived at the Oakland police station. I was greeted by Officer Stelwarth. The kind of greeting you could expect from a police officer. They'll shake your hand, but all of the "good to see you" attitude is pushed away by whatever horrors they've witnessed.

"Thanks for coming in," Stelwarth said. "Follow me, please."

Stelwarth led me through a path of empty desks. Most of the police officers were gone for the day.

I wasn't taken to a private room. Instead, Stelwarth sat me down at one of the desks. I saw the gold name plate "Andrew Stelwarth" on the desk. Stelwarth sat with a hefty sigh.

"Any new info on what Luke's up to?" I asked.

"Before I tell you why I called you in, would you mind answering a few questions?"

"Shoot."

Stelwarth gave me a pointed look, then flipped through his note pad. "Could you tell me where you've been and what you've been doing ever since you came in yesterday?"

I told him about staying at Sophia's place, visiting the New Age store, the rabbi. I mentioned Sophia's seizure and how it ultimately led to the possibility of M.E.G. being the Motionless Electromagnetic Generator. I even told him about meeting Kor and discussing the free energy device. I figured, since everyone knew that free energy devices were impossible, Stelwarth would probably dismiss Kor as a nut job. No reason to hide that information. Stelwarth wouldn't be a danger to Kor.

I had to spell the names of all the people I visited so that Stelwarth could type them up on his computer. I left out the part about how the free energy device could be used as a bomb, and didn't mention the envelope. Was it illegal to hold that information back? I wasn't sure. Truth was, I had no idea if the thing really worked as a bomb. It might be just a large paper weight, for all I knew. I had no evidence one way or the other.

"You called me while I was visiting Mr. Kor," I finished.

"Fine. So the reason I called you down here is this. A few hours ago, part of Sullivan's body was found buried on Grizzly Peak."

"Sullivan's dead?!"

"Yes. Shot twice in the chest."

I sat back in the chair. Couldn't believe what I was hearing. "Any idea who did it?"

"Do you know any group of people comprised of a surgeon, geneticist, musician, truck driver?"

"Sounds like the Village People," I said and immediately regretted it. "Sorry. No, I don't."

"Any one of those, then? A surgeon, musician, or truck driver associated with Luke? Anyone?"

"I know some doctors, but no real surgeons."

Stelwarth sighed again. "We don't know who killed Officer Sullivan. No bullet shells were found, no foot prints. The path was raked clean with the shrubs."

I just met Sullivan yesterday. Now he's dead? It felt weird.

"We think that McCourt, your landlord, was involved."

"How come?"

"Sullivan's wallet was missing, but we found his note pad. It had McCourt's name and a list of people under it. We believe Sullivan was in the middle of working your case off duty when he was shot. Point is, your life may be in danger. It seems unlikely, because McCourt's been watching you all this time, he's had plenty of opportunities, but still. I advise you to be careful."

I nodded. "Who are the other people?"

"Unfortunately, he didn't write their names. Just listed them as surgeon, geneticist, musician, and truck driver. That's why I asked. Are you sure no one comes to mind?"

Now I realized the seriousness of the question. Whoever killed Sullivan probably knew Luke and these other people.

"Wait a second," I said. "Does that mean Luke isn't

the only one watching me?"

"Not necessarily. Could be McCourt knows these people, but on the side he gets his kicks watching you. Could be Luke doesn't know any of these guys and Sullivan just happened to write his name on the same page as the others."

I didn't buy that. "What about the anonymous note to me?"

Stelwarth shrugged. "Like I said. I advise you to be very careful."

It wasn't just Luke. Probably several people were watching me. But what was the point? If they wanted to steal a bomb, why follow me around? And my parents?

"What are you going to do next?" I asked.

"All of us here are saddened by the loss of Officer Sullivan," Stelwarth said. "He was a great police officer and we all want to do something about it. Your case has taken first priority now so we're going to spend 24/7 finding the killer. We're going to start with the person mentioned at the bottom of the list."

"Which one was that?"

"The 'truck driver.' We intend to question all the major truck hubs in the area."

I nodded again and looked away. If I was careful, I might be able to avoid Luke's mysterious group altogether. Problem was, I didn't know who they were. Hell, Sophia could be one of them. She wasn't, of course, but the point was I could run all I wanted and never know if I escaped them.

Time to stop running.

Chapter 35

I had to stop McCourt from following me. *It isn't bullets that get them running, its fear.* Sullivan's words hung with me as I left the police station and got into the car. What about a guy who was probably a religious fanatic and spent all his time watching me? What was he afraid of?

Potassium. I needed a lot of potassium. I twisted the ignition, shifted into gear, and drove to UC Berkeley.

Parking was impossible. But I found a pretty good place near Shattuck Avenue at the bottom of the campus.

Fire and brimstone. If that was what Luke feared, that was what Luke was going to get. No point in me trying to hide anymore. I'd just be delaying the inevitable. Whatever Luke had in mind, it was worth killing Sullivan over, and the idea of waiting in constant fear of being confronted by Luke was, well, just a waste of time.

I had a lot more important things to do with my life. The image of Sophia popped in my head. "Besides that," I told myself.

It should have been a long walk to Pimentel Hall, the chemistry building, but I found myself at the door in what seemed like no time at all. Inside, I took the stairs down to the lab. As I predicted, a class was in session. I opened the door a crack and listened in.

"If you put in 25 mL instead of 20, what do you do?" A booming voice asked.

I heard the class chant in unison, "Grumble grumble and start again."

"Right!"

Good ol' Kranz. I had to recite that very same chant when I studied chemistry at UC Berkeley. Good thing my old professor was still working here. Easier to request the potassium.

When professor Kranz finished giving the instructions, I heard the clamor of students beginning their lab experiment. I poked my head in.

"Nathan!" Kranz exclaimed. "What brings you here?"

The students lifted their heads, as if assessing me was a step needed for their lab. Apparently, I was just the right size because they returned to the measurements in front of them.

"Got a minute?"

"Come in! Come in!" Kranz walked away, waving his hand. "Step into my office."

His "office" was the corner of the room. No way the university would allow him to sit in his actual office, a separate room, while the students were working on their lab experiments.

"What brings you to our oasis?" Dr. Kranz said.

I asked to buy a jar of potassium.

"Potassium?!" Kranz smiled. "Are you going to wow friends of yours?"

"That's exactly it," I said.

"Well, I know that you're aware of all the safety precautions needed to handle the stuff, and as you can see," he unlocked and opened several cabinets, "I have my inventory fully stocked. But I cannot give you or sell you anything because that's against the law."

I said nothing.

"But sometimes my numbers of what we have can be erroneous. I might think we're fully stocked and oops! Turns out we have one less jar than I thought." He turned his back to me, watching the students.

I knew this line. One day when I was a high school student, I had a headache. I had asked the teacher for aspirin and he showed me a breath mint container filled with aspirin. He said he couldn't give me any because it was illegal for teachers to provide medical assistance. He turned his back and I took two tablets. So he had managed to help me without breaking the law.

I liberated a jar of potassium and caught sight of a spindle of magnesium ribbon.

"Uh," I said. "How well do you keep track of your magnesium."

"Again. Not so well," Kranz said keeping his back to me.

I took the spindle. From my wallet, placed a generous "donation" inside the cabinet.

"You know," Kranz said. "The environment is a fragile place. I'm a big proponent of recycle, reduce, and reuse. For example. I like reusing plastic bags that I keep in the bottom cabinet at your feet. Good for the environment."

I opened the cabinet below, took a bag, and placed the potassium and magnesium in it.

I looked around at the students. They were busy with their labs. Two students stood out, though. One looked like a young Harrison Ford, complete with rugged clothes and daring attitude. The other wore slacks, a white button-up shirt and tie. They were cleaning up, finished with the lab already.

"Well," Kranz said. "Best lock these cabinets up before one of my students gets sticky fingers."

"Thanks," I said. "Are those your latest top-of-the-class students?" I nodded to the two cleaning up.

"Billy and Charles," Kranz sighed. "One keeps asking me how to make a zombie using the puffer fish toxin, and the other keeps presenting arguments for the notion of fire being alive. You know, fire feeds, leaves waste, breathes oxygen, etc. You gotta love 'em."

I thanked Kranz again and carried my chemistry supply down to the car. Now for the hardware.

* * *

Detective Graff didn't put up a fight when her partner Detective Larry Denton told her, "I got this one."

There were dozens of truck transportation companies in Oakland. Fortunately, many of them were all on or near Maritime Street. The two of them had investigated eight of them. One detective talked to the manager while the other showed Sullivan's photo to the employees that happened to be in the area. When Denton said he "got this one," he meant he would talk to the manager.

After watching Denton go off to find the manager, Graff approached three truck drivers chatting by a soda machine. Their eyes were on her chest until they saw the badge on her belt.

"Any of you see this man before?" she asked

They scrutinized the photo she held up and each shook their head. Their eyes verified their answers. She could tell a liar by the eyes and these men weren't lying.

She heard a series of buzz sounds coming from the garage. A young mechanic was tightening the nuts on a wheel. The guy had good muscular arms and a boyish shrub of dark hair.

"Excuse me," she called out walking toward him. "Seen this man?"

The mechanic checked out the photo. "Yeah. Came here yesterday. Asked about Hal."

"Hal who?"

"Hal Carter. Truck driver."

Chapter לו

Satisfied, I walked the few blocks to where Shattuck Avenue intersected University Avenue, the giant hub of Berkeley's downtown mainly for eating and making photocopies. The store for hardware was nested between a glowing copy center and a Thailand restaurant.

I found a shabby, empty shopping cart inside the hardware store. The neon lights inside the store would have been brighter and cheery had it not been so crowded with items. The elongated aisles were narrow and stretched out tall in their own shadows. The few people there were mostly big-bellied men in jeans.

I picked out a hammer, nails, molding clay, and other tools that might come in handy. Found some tall mercury thermometers, so I grabbed a bunch. They had a portable burner that wasn't exactly a Bunsen burner, but it would do the trick.

"Can I help you find anything?" The woman wearing a standard-issue blue apron to signal she worked there looked at me with a big smile.

"No, thanks," I said. "—Actually, do you have any portable freezers that go to very low temperatures?"

"We only have one freezer." She began walking to the aisle that had it, so I followed her. "Here it is." She pointed out the box.

The box looked like it could hold a watermelon. I read the side. It advertised temperatures from zero to forty degrees below zero. Good enough. I thanked the lady, put it in my cart, and moved toward the checkout.

I came upon a variety of shovels and stopped. What frightened Luke most? Some of the shovels had pointed tips, others were rounded, some were tiny, for working in shallow soil.

No way.

I pushed my cart to the checkout line. Two people were ahead of me. At the register, a tall guy in overalls splattered with various colors of paint was pointing to a pack of screws and saying something to the cashier.

I waited a minute.

Two minutes.

I turned my head and looked at the aisle with the shovels. I had to get McCourt afraid of me enough to never follow me again, but the whole shovel thing was overkill.

No way.

Back at the register, Mr. Overalls was still having a philosophical discussion about screws with the cashier. The guy in front of me waiting for his turn shifted his weight and exhaled a deep sigh.

Three minutes.

Four minutes.

I went back to the shovels and snatched a pointed one.

Chapter 37

Detective Denton was still questioning the manager of the transportation company when Graff caught up to him.

"Where's Hal Carter?" She asked the manager.

"That's what I was just telling your partner here. The only employee that's been acting strange lately is Hal. Didn't show up for work today. And he still has one of our trucks."

"We'll need his address and phone number."

He scribbled down the information on a sticky note. "Good luck calling him. I've just been getting voice mail."

The last of my shopping was to be done at Walgreens. The store was all decked out with green and red fake foliage. The toy aisle was crowded with kids. Looked like someone was herding sheep through there.

Throngs of women filled the hygiene aisle, probably to get that soap gift set for the unfortunate husband.

I passed all the videos on sale, passed the cleanser aisle, found the food aisle. It didn't boast much, but it had exactly what I needed. With my mother's dinner table talk of her acting and how to produce some realistic special effects, I knew to get several bottles of clear corn syrup and food coloring. Nearby were some Pyrex containers. I picked a small one.

Next up was the toy aisle. I fought through the crowd and saw a cool remote-controlled corvette in the toy car area. That would come in handy. I grabbed it off the shelf and scanned the other toys. Picked up a prank cup and saucer. The packaging read, *Magnetic cup! Picks up the saucer only when you want it to! When turned on, serve the cup and saucer to your friends and watch as they struggle to get the cup off the saucer. Fool your friends!* That'll come in handy, too.

I finished my shopping with an ice chest and a few bags of ice. Necessary items that would, if nothing else, help get me out of his agenda.

Chapter 38

I opened the trunk of my car and placed the thermometers, portable burner, Pyrex bowl, toy car, and cup and saucer prank in the bag with chemicals. I carried the bag and freezer up the flight of stairs to Sophia's apartment leaving the ice chest with ice in the trunk. This was all I aimed to do. Scare him off and be done with him. Then I'd tell the police about the possible bomb thing and let them deal with that.

At the door, I remembered how Sophia didn't yet know about Sullivan's death. No need to make her worry any more than she had been. There was enough stress in her life already, what with the whole seizure thing.

I knocked on the door, even though I had the key.

Sophia heaved the door open. "You're back."

"What about my back?" I said.

She laughed. "No. You – are – back."

I set the freezer on the floor and looked for a spot to unpack the bag. A newspaper was spread open on the small table where the bagels once were. The special report headline read "30,000 Children Died Today."

"Here," Sophia said. "Let me get that out of the way." She gathered the newspaper so I could put the freezer and bag on the table.

"What was that headline about the 30,000 children?"

"Oh. Yeah. That was so sad." Sophia folded the newspaper. "I didn't want to read it. It's about the starved and dehydrated children in Africa. It said something about how they'd have to print that headline everyday to report how many die. But since it happens every day, it's not new information. So…"

"It's not news."

"Right."

I nodded and began unpacking the chemicals.

"What do you have there?" Sophia asked.

I put my hand on the biggest toy. "This is a freezer. Can freeze things to a whopping forty degrees below zero. Can you believe that?"

"Dream come true," Sophia said smirking. "And what's the wire?"

"Magnesium ribbon." I held the plug for the freezer and looked around the room.

"Over here." Sophia moved a stack of books on tarot on the floor. Behind them was an outlet.

I plugged in the freezer. It looked simple enough to work. Turning the knobs made it as cold as you liked.

"What's the stuff this potassium is in?" Sophia asked.

I turned around and saw she had opened the jar and was trying to smell the potassium. I jumped toward her. "Careful!"

Sophia looked startled. I took the jar and lid and closed it up again.

"What's wrong?" Sophia asked.

"Let's just say that whenever potassium and oxygen get together, there's bound to be a party." I placed it back on the small table beside a used butter knife. "The potassium is kept in oil so that it doesn't touch oxygen and behaves."

"Oh. So since there's oxygen in water, if you put it in water there would be a pool party?"

"Exactly."

"So how come bananas don't party?" Sophia asked.

"What?"

"Bananas are full of potassium, right?"

"Yeah, but when potassium is in its pure metal form, it's unstable. The potassium in a banana is bonded with other stuff, so it behaves."

"Like when bachelors bond to become married men, they behave."

I picked up the butter knife. "Cute."

Sophia's eyes watched me as I picked up the molding clay and pressed it around the knife.

"Really, Nathan. What're you up to?"

"Everything's going to be alright. I know just what I need to do."

"You do, huh? Then what are you doing to my knife?"

"Just need to borrow it." I rubbed the molding clay around the knife. "I've been thinking."

"About?"

"Luke and that picture he had of my parents getting married."

"Yeah?"

I placed the clay-coated knife on the table to dry. "What if he wasn't watching me, exactly. But my family. What if there's something specific to my family that he's interested in?"

"Okay. So tell me about your ancestors."

"Where to start?"

"Start with your maternal line," she said.

"Why?"

"Religion goes through the mother. And if this has something to do with religion, it's probably on your mother's side."

"Good point." I remembered my mother's pitch black hair and walked to the bathroom with a screwdriver. "Her name was Sarah Korzynski."

"Where are you going?"

"Going to get your tub faucet." I crouched at the bath tub.

"Hey! Hey! Hey! I'm gonna need that." Sophia followed me into the bathroom.

"Right now?"

She shrugged, "Well, no, but I will later."

I began taking it off the wall. "I'm just borrowing it. You'll have it back in an hour, I promise."

Sophia said nothing.

"Anyhow, I just thought of something." With the screws removed, the faucet came off easily. "My mother was an actor. Just like my grandmother."

Detective Graff stood clear of the door and knocked. The door felt solid, but not solid enough to stop a bullet should Mr. Carter decide to shoot first and ask questions later. "Mr. Carter, Oakland Police! Open up!"

No response.

She nodded to the apartment manager standing beside her and he unlocked the door for them.

"Step back, please," Graff told the manager.

Graff and Denton drew their weapons and entered low. It didn't take long to see that no one was inside. They holstered their weapons.

"Check out the bathroom," Graff said. "I got the bedroom."

A wooden crucifix hung above the bed. The blankets were missing. So was the alarm clock, assuming he had one.

"He left in a hurry," Denton called out from the bathroom. His voice reverberated off the tiles. "There's no shaving toiletries here. But he left his toothbrush and toothpaste by accident."

Graff opened the bedroom drawers. They were half empty. She wiped her fingers along the surface of the dresser. No dust lifted onto her fingers.

"No accident. He didn't leave in a hurry," she called back. "The room's too tidy. Like he cleaned up before he left. He just took what he needed without disturbing the rest."

"What guy purposely leaves his toothbrush?"

"Not sure. The only answer makes no sense."

Denton came to the bedroom. "Which is?"

Graff turned to face him. "That he won't need to brush his teeth where he's going."

Chapter 39

The faucet felt light in my hand. Until just then, it hadn't occurred to me that the women who passed down the religion in my life were both actors. "I don't know about my great grandmother, though," I said. "I know she was Jewish, but I don't know if she was an actor."

"It's a good start. What else? Where did they perform?"

I stood up and carried the faucet to the bedroom. "My mother performed in New York. My grandmother in Poland."

"Poland?"

"Yeah. Wadowice, Poland." I applied the molding clay to the faucet. The squishy clay stuck to my fingers. Kinda fun. "When I was a kid, we flew there for her funeral. It rained the whole time. And there was this scary old lady there. She gave me a candy bar." I put down the faucet and wagged a finger, imitating the lady's voice. " 'I knew your grandmother. She was a very special person. And so is your mother.' "

"Who was she?"

"I don't know. She said she knew all about the people who did acting with my grandmother." I returned my attention to the faucet and remembered loving that candy bar the lady had given me. "Oh yeah! She said 'My name is Gangsta Bar,' " I said in the same old lady voice. " 'Sounds a little like candy bar, yes? Hee, hee, hee,' "

"Gangsta?"

"I don't remember."

The molding clay now completely covered the faucet. I set it down beside the knife. I opened the bag that had the cup and saucer inside. Ripped apart the plastic wrapping and with brute strength, broke the cup and saucer. It made a satisfying cracking sound.

"What are you doing, now?" Sophia asked.

"Getting the electric magnet inside this thing." I pulled out a coil of copper around a flat piece of metal attached to a watch battery and switch. Very small. Perfect.

"Now for the car." The car had more packaging to shed. When I freed the car from all the plastic and wire twists, I used the screwdriver to open the bottom of the car. "The sensor that detects the remote control is here. Take a look. See this thing?" I showed her the bottom of the car.

"Yeah."

"If I press the button on the remote, it tells the forward function to turn on."

"Okay."

"But I don't want to turn the car on with a remote." I lifted the electric magnet. "I want to turn *this* thing on with a remote."

"Okay."

"So if I take out the sensor from the car," I removed it from the car. "And attach it to the magnet like so," I worked the wires. "Then voila!"

Sophia looked at the magnet, then at me. "Voila what?" she said.

After a quick scan of the room, I found a paperclip by a stack of mail. Turned on the magnet, and showed her how the magnet didn't pick up the paperclip.

"So you broke the magnet?" Sophia asked.

"Now watch this." I pressed down one of the buttons on the remote control and the paperclip hopped in the air to the magnet.

"Cool!" Sophia said. "But I still think making a car go around the room by remote control is cooler."

"Speaking of cooler—" I picked up the clay coated knife and with a sharp blade, cut into the clay. I traced the outline of the butter knife with the blade. Soon I had two halves of a clay mold. The clay mold held the impression of the butter knife.

I picked up a mug from the table. It read, *You're Pure Joy*. "Need this?" I asked.

"Not at the moment."

"Mind if I trash it?"

Sophia rolled her eyes. "Don't trash that cup. I got it for my birthday. If you have to trash a cup, use this one." She pulled a styrofoam cup from beneath a bedside table and handed it to me.

Above the trash can, I carefully cracked open the thermometers, and one by one, emptied their contents into the cup. The mercury swished around at the bottom of the cup. One of the only metals that was liquid at room temperature. I then poured the mercury in the mold of the knife and placed it in the freezer.

"Freezing a knife. Let me guess," Sophia said, "You're trying to make cold cuts."

I chuckled.

I sliced open the mold of the faucet and removed the faucet. Took the portable burner out of the shopping bag, plugged in the burner, and placed the magnesium ribbon in a Pyrex bowl. I placed the bowl on the burner, and waited for the magnesium to melt.

In a few minutes, when it was liquid, I poured the melted magnesium into the mold of the faucet and stuck the mold in the freezer.

"Are you done with my faucet?" Sophia asked.

"Your faucet and I had a very meaningful time together," I said returning it to the bathroom. "Thank you for parting with it for as long as you did."

"A meaningful time, huh? Just how meaningful was it?" Sophia called to me.

I screwed the faucet back in place. "It was the best of times. It was the worst of times." It startled me how accurate that description was to my current situation.

I came back to Sophia and said, "I'm beginning to get very tired but I've got a lot to do. Could you do me a favor and sleep for me?"

"Sure, no problem," she said. "Right after I get back from doing readings in San Francisco."

"San Francisco, this time?" I asked.

"Yeah. I like a little variety."

I smiled. "You know what they say. Variety's the spice of life. And if your life still needs more flavor, try paprika."

Looking at my watch, I saw that it was time.

I put on the plastic gloves, went to the freezer, and carefully removed the mercury butter knife from the mold. Left the knife in the freezer and filled the butter knife mold with more mercury. After returning the mold to the freezer, I said to Sophia, "When I'm done here, I'm going out. There's something I need to do."

"What thing?"

"I can't go into it now."

Sophia scowled and searched my eyes.

"I need to do this," I said.

She closed her eyes and nodded. She let out a sigh as I got to work molding more knives.

Chapter 40

Now for the hard part. I drove in the cold, early afternoon to Moraga Avenue in Piedmont, the city inside Oakland. A cemetery lay embedded beside Moraga Avenue. Tucked behind the cemetery was a pet cemetery. I drove through the iron gates and traced the winding contours of the hills spotted with tombstones. The green of the grass was alive, as if the sparkle in the eyes of the dead lived on in the color of the hills. I drove further. The roads got rougher. I broke through a membrane of trees meant to highlight the boundary of the cemetery. And as the layout of the cemetery changed from landscaped to forest, occasional areas of crosses made from sticks and string stuck out from the ground.

I parked the car off the road and got out. I opened the trunk, and removed the shovel, ice chest, gloves, a tarp, and a shopping bag.

I walked to a tilted gravestone, one of the older graves. The words on the handmade tombstone were barely legible. "Our beloved dog Fritz. 1970–1996."

I sighed and went to work. Digging into the dirt made my palms sweat. The backs of my hands felt frozen. I knew I wouldn't have to dig six feet, though. These graves were dug mostly by parents. Deep enough to stay below ground, but not the full six feet most graves were dug.

I stabbed the ground with the spade. The deeper I went, the more I had to stand on the rim of the blade just to get the damn thing to go into the ground. The spade soon scooped up bones with the earth. I collected the bones and put them in the shopping bag. When I had enough bones, I moved to another grave. This one was somewhat fresh. It simply said, "Scooter."

I wasn't sure what I'd become. Didn't want to dwell on it. Still, there was a part of me that was actually getting an adrenalin rush from it all. I didn't know why. And didn't want to know.

The tarp unfolded with noisy plastic crinkling sounds as I lay it on the ground beside the fresh grave. Using the spade again, I dug. The ground was easier to dig into. The dirt was loose. Still, the muscles I used in digging ached. They weren't used to this kind of exercise. Soon I came upon the corpse and had to cover my nose. It was a bloated body of what might have been a boxer.

I put on the gloves and delicately lifted the body onto the tarp. Oh, the stench!

I wrapped the dog in the tarp and the smell quickly dissipated. Put the body in the ice chest. The dog fit inside it easily.

I stood up straight. Stretched. My muscles scribbled aches across my shoulders. I pulled off my gloves and tried to erase them with a quick hand massage. A temporary fix.

I picked up the ice chest, the spade flat on top, and brought everything back to the car. Only an hour had passed but as I reflected on my actions, I thought I heard angels crying.

Chapter 41

Only 5:30 p.m. and it was already dark. The sun had set an hour ago. I drove through the cold Oakland Hills and had my car heater on high. Coming near my place, I slowed the car down to a crawl. There was the distant roar of the freeway, the crickets were yelling their heads off, but other than that, the night was quiet. The closest sound was of my car creeping on the gravel. Like crunching cereal.

I gunned the engine every so often. With the headlights on, and the sound of the engine revving, someone was bound to spot me. That was if they hadn't been following me this whole time.

I didn't pull into the garage. I let the car sit out in front of the duplex. Got out of the car and opened the trunk. Getting the ice chest out wasn't the easiest task. For a moment, I almost lost my balance. That would have been bad. A frozen dog rolling into the dust.

I brought the ice chest to the front door. Getting in was no problem. The door was busted. All I had to do was tap the door with my elbow and I was able to walk in without setting the ice chest down.

After placing the ice chest on the living room rug, I returned to the car. I was able to collect and carry the bag of chemicals, the shopping bag of dog bones, and the freezer filled with the molds of butter knives all in one trip. I walked back inside to the kitchen counter and set the freezer upon it. Wrote a little message on the side of the freezer for Luke to see.

The most difficult part was going to be the bathtub, so I decided to work there first, hoping I had enough time to finish the job.

On the ceiling above the bathtub, I attached a handkerchief like a miniature tarp. The handkerchief held the pellets of potassium. I secured it with the remote release device I made.

I hoped this would work.

I filled the tub with water and replaced the bathtub spout with the one made of magnesium. The design was slightly different, but you had to look hard to notice the difference. I was pretty sure Luke wasn't going to look hard at the bathtub spout.

The next thing was to do the placement of the dead dog, the bones, the corn syrup, and lastly the ice.

Luke answered his phone.

"It's me," Hal said. "I've been watching the house like you said, and guess who's coming to dinner?"

"I'll be right there." Luke said. "In fact, Melinda needs your help to move a few of the goats to Matthew's house. So come on over."

"What if he leaves before you get here?" Hal asked.

"Has he been there longer than fifteen minutes?"

"Yes," Hal said.

"Then he'll be there when I arrive. There are only two reasons why he'd show up. One, to pick up something he needs, which takes less than fifteen minutes. Or two, to confront me. You say it's been more than fifteen minutes? He's there to confront me. It'll take me awhile to get there, but he'll wait for me."

More than an hour later, I sat down exhausted from the work. My shirt was covered in sweat. I felt like a New Orleans taxi passenger going for a two-hour ride during the summer with a broken air conditioner.

I looked at the painting of the collie. "You must think I stink," I said.

I got up from the chair, went to the bathroom, and turned on the shower.

Luke parked his car next to Nathan's and turned off the engine. The "O Fortuna" from Carl Orff's Carmina Burana played on the radio. Luke closed his eyes and listened to the sounds of the choir singing of the sacred and the profane. The chords ripped through his heart with a passionate joy that bled to his toes and fingertips. A chill ran up his spine, the kind of chill he always got when hearing brilliant works of music.

Luke believed that this was the true test of music. If it sent a shiver up the listener's spine, it was worthy of being called brilliant. It didn't matter if it were classical or that disgusting rap. As long as it could do that, could make someone physically *feel* the music in their body, it was praiseworthy.

The piece finished. Luke turned off the radio. He sat back in his seat and let the sounds resonate in his head in the silence of the night. With a sigh of content, he opened the glove compartment and removed a .38 caliber revolver and a box of bullets. He slid a bullet into each chamber, snapped the cylinder shut, and left the car.

Chapter 42

Luke went to Nathan's front door. The door was ajar.

"Nathan! It's me, Luke," Luke pushed the door open with his foot, keeping the gun in front of him, the way his parents taught him. "I just want to talk," he said.

Luke kept his arm extended, pointing the gun into the living room as he entered it. He saw no one. He swept his arm across the perimeter of the living room, but still, no Nathan. He checked the kitchen. The kitchen was empty.

I know he's here, Luke told himself. "Nathan? I just want to talk."

Luke thrust his arm into the bedroom and switched on the light. No one was there. He moved to the bathroom. It was the last room left. He crept slowly, then pointed the gun into the bathroom. The room was too dark. He turned on the light.

Nothing.

Luke relaxed his arms and pointed the gun to the

floor. Did Nathan leave already? It looked that way. But why was the front door open?

Luke sauntered back through the house. As he passed the kitchen, he noticed some items on the kitchen table.

Those hadn't been there before, had they? Luke wondered.

He went into the kitchen and saw they were photographs. They were polaroids of Luke. One of him in Nathan's bedroom. One of him in Nathan's bathroom. All of them showing the clothes he now wore. All of them showing him holding a gun outstretched, ready to fire. All of them taken just moments ago.

So he was here, Luke realized.

He left Nathan's place and went to his own front door. The door was busted from the police entering and searching his home.

Luke pushed the door open with his foot and held his gun out in front of him. A lamp was on, and in the lamp light, Luke saw bones hanging from the ceiling, dripping with blood. The shadows of the bones swaying made it seem like there was double the number of bones. Luke wondered what possessed Nathan to do this.

He tried the light switch. It was no good. Looking up at the ceiling, Luke saw that the light fixture had been removed.

He heard the shower running. Either Nathan was there or it was a ruse to lead Luke into the bathroom into a possible trap.

He moved through the kitchen. A white box with red words scrawled on its side was on the kitchen counter. It seemed to be a kind of small refrigerator.

Was that blood? Luke asked himself.

The red words read, "Hellbound men melt steel. Don't touch!"

Luke checked the box for wires, anything that might suggest an explosive.

He saw nothing.

He carefully lifted the lid. "Butter knives?" He took one out and the sheer coldness of it made him drop it to the ground. The knife shattered into pieces. How did a knife shatter like that?

He picked up a fragment and it melted in his fingertips, metal droplets rolling right onto the floor. Luke scowled and blinked several times. A trick, he convinced himself. It had to be.

He turned his attention toward the bathroom, and kept his caution. His arms felt stiff from holding out the gun for so long. At the last minute, he pushed into the bathroom.

The shower curtain was closed and Luke wondered what he'd find behind it. It probably wouldn't be Nathan.

He pulled aside the shower curtain. Ice water? There was suddenly something dropping in the water from above. Mysterious flames appeared out of nowhere and Luke fell backwards. The flames danced upon the water making angry popping sounds. One of the flames ignited the bathtub faucet and the entire faucet exploded into a flash of light.

"What the hell is going on?!" Luke shouted, unable to see from the blinding explosion.

He used his hands to help guide himself back to the room of bones, and he felt a body topple on top of him. Was it Nathan? Luke fired in the air as he fell to the floor with the body. His eyes barely made out the dog on top of him with a grin stretched back too wide to be normal. Was it laughing? And there were white things all over him. Mary Mother of...They're maggots! Luke screamed hitting his shoulders and rubbing his fingers through his hair.

Loud popping sounds came from the window. Was Nathan shooting at him? Luke dropped his gun and ran out of his place wildly waving his arms across his body as he raced to the car. He gunned the engine, swerving along the winding road.

I walked out of the darkness. Put the remaining unused firecrackers in my pocket.

That's the last I'll see of him. Nothing like a little surrealism to scare the bejeesus out of you.

I touched the "bloody" wall and tasted it. The corn syrup with red food coloring was sweet.

Part 3

ONE

Chapter 43

Luke McCourt pulled over at a wooded shoulder, scrambled for a cigarette, and lit it with shaking hands.

What the hell? What in the hell had just happened?

He inhaled deeply on the cigarette, and exhaled watching his fear escape his lips. He relaxed his shoulders, arms, legs, and feet. He touched his chin to his chest and rolled his head to the left shoulder, then to the right shoulder. The tension in his neck was dying.

He turned off the headlights, took another drag on the cigarette and sat still, letting time pass as a plan formed. With his window open, Luke felt the chill of the air against his cheek. Its bite felt good. Clouds covered the stars and sky. The only visible light came from the glow of his cigarette when he put it to his mouth. It was nearly seven o'clock and the insect noises from the woods of the Oakland Hills screeched out.

Luke took his cell phone and dialed a number.

"You still tailing her," he asked.

"Yeah," the voice on the other end replied. "She's

still working near the Powell BART station in San Francisco. Someone just sat down with her, and from the looks of the card layout, they're getting a nine-card reading. The last client that had that layout took over an hour."

"Good."

Chapter 44

I had my cell phone back on driving to Sophia's place. As I broke into the evening's urban traffic, the phone rang.

"Nathan here."

"Nathan Yirmorshy?" a raspy voice said.

"Yes."

"This is Antoine Priore."

The man with the other half of the MEG's location. The man I was never to meet, never to speak to.

"Are you sure you should be talking to me?"

"I am dying, Mr. Yirmorshy. I've not much time left."

Terrific.

Priore continued, "I need to give you the envelope."

"Defeats the purpose, doesn't it?" I said. "They can't be together at any time."

"There is no more time left," Priore gasped. "We have reason to believe that they know where the proto-type is. You must take it and protect it."

192 | Ezra Barany

I grabbed the envelope beside me, the one Kor had given me, tore it open with my teeth and shook its contents onto the passenger seat. Unfolded the piece of paper. Not an easy task with one hand while scrunching your shoulder to hold a cell phone in place. I made a mental note to get a new Bluetooth to replace my broken one. Looked at the unfolded piece of paper. It was ripped in half vertically.

"Are you still there?" Priore asked.

"I'm here, I'm here." I said. The paper read, "Berkeley" and below that—

A car swerved into my lane.

"Damn scrotum kicker!" I muttered.

I braked too late. My car screeched and hit the car in front of me.

"Are you alright? What happened?" Priore's voice sounded different.

I pulled over as did the car in front of me.

"I'm fine," I said. "Just a fender bender. Where should I meet you?"

"Not me," Priore rasped. "Charlie. At Shakespeare's Books on Telegraph Avenue."

I got out of the car. "Alright. When?"

"I'll send Charlie over now."

Ahead, the man stepping out of the car looked at me and shook his head "Un-fucking-believable! A fucking cell phone."

"Okay," I said to Priore. "I gotta go." I put away the phone.

The man looked like he was in a rock band. His bleached blond hair ran down to below his shoulders.

He also had a bounce with his every step. Probably played the drums. His muscle-shirt announced "Trapped Bacon Grease," a slogan that either described his hair or was the name of his rock band.

Time to face the hot grease. I stepped out of the car and Grease studied the back of my victim, a silver Volkswagen Beetle with a twisted bumper.

"No way! You know who's gonna pay for this, don't you?" His voice was loud but without being very angry. He wore a rubber band on his wrist.

"I have insurance," I said.

"Lucky man."

I wrote down my address and insurance on a folded piece of paper from my pocket. Gave it to Grease in exchange for his information.

Grease saw the statistical science textbook in my car and said, "So you like statistics?"

I said nothing.

"Here's a statistic for you," Grease said, "When you're on the cell phone, the chances of getting into an accident are 20% higher. How do you like that statistic?"

I said nothing.

Grease got back in his car, still shaking his head.

Bygones. I had to get to Shakespeare's, but I wanted to look at the folded piece of paper one more time. Now where did it go? Wasn't it in my pocket…? Oh, for crapping out loud! I watched the Volkswagen drive off.

Chapter 45

Sophia gathered her tarot cards from the ground and tucked them in her purple backpack purse. In San Francisco, she had been using a wide stairway as her table. It made it easy for her to get a lot of visibility from people taking the Bay Area Rapid Transit system without obstructing their path and she didn't have to lug a table all the way to San Francisco.

She removed her BART ticket. The blue and white ticket with the magnetic strip confirmed in smudged black ink that she had enough money on it to get home. She zipped her backpack purse closed and weaved her arms through the purse's straps to put it on.

The gate to the BART train was a series of waist-high entrances with orange wedges blocking the way. Sophia went to one with a green indicator and placed her ticket in the front slot. The metal entrance accepted the ticket from the front and returned the ticket through a slot at the top. When she took the ticket, the orange wedges parted and she went through.

An escalator took her down to the two-track platform where trains went in one direction toward the San Francisco International Airport, or in the other direction through an underwater tunnel to get across the bay into Oakland. Underground, the station was filled with tourists returning from trying out the cable cars, and suits going home late from work, and couples who had dinner downtown, and kids who watched a movie after school. Sophia took off her purse and took out her cell phone to call Nathan and saw that the bars indicating how much of a phone signal she had were solid. Before she could dial the last number, the red LED signs hanging in the station flashed RICHMOND.

"Oh, yay!" Sophia cheered.

The Richmond train was one of the trains that went through Oakland, and this particular one shot into the station with a blast of squeaks and clack-clacks and hot air. Sophia put away her phone to be ready for boarding the train.

The doors slid open sideways and Sophia chose one of the four seats facing the doors. The other people that boarded were a kid in an army coat with jet black hair carrying a skateboard, and two tall women in overcoats holding shopping bags talking about a twist-neck embroidered dress that was on sale, and a suit puzzling over a Sudoku in the folded newspaper he held. A handsome gentleman in a brown tweed suit also boarded, approached the seat next to Sophia's and asked her, "Would I be troubling a lovely young lady such as yourself if I sat here?"

His smile radiated below cute cheeks. And there was something else about him that Sophia couldn't place. Did she know him?

"Go ahead," Sophia replied with a smile of her own.

The train doors closed and the kind man stooped over to sit down. As he did so, a small box fell from his coat pocket.

Sophia retrieved it. It was a box of cigarettes. The box was square and had a burgundy and black marble design and gold lettering.

"Djarum?" She read the box and handed it to him.

"Clove cigarettes," He replied with a twinkle in his eye. "From Indonesia."

Chapter 46

As I watched Grease driving away in his Volkswagen, I realized it was one of those moments. One of those moments when the heaviness in your gut feels like you've just swallowed a sandbag.

I got in my car, and tried to start the engine. It didn't take. Grease's car was getting farther away and I was about ready to throw in the towel. This wasn't my problem.

I watched Grease's car turn a corner. Considered checking the dialed numbers listing on my iPhone to call Priore back and tell him…Tell him what? Sorry, Antoine, but I've got better things to do than worry about people exploding into bits?

I tried the engine again. And again. The engine revved up at the third twist of the key. I sensed a kinship with the car, as if it was trying to say, "Come on! Let's do this thing!"

I put the car in gear and shifted into traffic. After a few turns and lane changes, I managed to spot Grease's car. Grease drove down Broadway, and fortunately,

Broadway was so well lit at night that I could tell which car was the silver Volkswagen Beetle.

I tapped on the horn as I got directly behind Grease. He slowed down, as if not sure who was honking at him or why. Then Grease seemed to figure it out because he pulled over sharply next to a used car lot and got out of the car.

I pulled up behind him.

He came to my window and asked, "What the hell is wrong with you?"

Now he sounded angry.

"I'm sorry, I'm sorry," I said getting out of the car. "I gave you my information on a piece of paper I need."

Grease looked baffled for a moment, then laughed clapping me on the shoulder. "Man, you are something, you know that? You are really something." He took out the piece of paper I needed and looked at both sides. "You're Nathan?" Grease handed it to me.

"Yes," I took back the piece of paper, pocketed it, and began writing my information on an old receipt.

"Okay, Nathan. My name's Vince."

I shook Vince's hand and he slid the rubber band from his wrist to my own.

"You are now officially a member of the Rubber Band," he said.

I had heard about the Rubber Band. There was probably a real band called the Rubber Band, but this was different. Local musicians all over were promoting safe sex by wearing rubber bands around their wrist as some kind of symbol.

"Thanks," I said, and gave him the receipt with my information on it.

"Yeah, stay safe, dude." Vince walked away shaking his head. "Unbelievable, man."

As he drove away a second time, I took out the piece of paper the retired captain had given me. It read "Berkeley," then under that was "106," and under that was "32–5."

Chapter 47

Sophia wasn't sure what an Indonesian looked like. "Are you from Indonesia?" She asked.

"Sorry?" the gentleman shouted over the din of the train.

Sophia repeated her question louder.

"No," he said and laughed. "New York. And you?"

"Well, my mother was born in Switzerland, and my father's parents were from Hungary, but he was born in the Bronx. They met in the Bronx, but I was born in San Francisco. I guess you could call me cosmopolitan." She said.

The gentleman smiled and asked, "And where are you just coming from, if I may be so bold?"

"Oh, yeah, no, I've got no secrets. Ask me anything you want," Sophia said waving it off with her hand. "I read tarot."

"Tar—?"

"Tarot, you never heard of tarot?"

"Please forgive my ignorance," the gentleman said with a smirk while raising an auburn eyebrow.

"Oh, no, don't worry about it. I'm just surprised, is all," Sophia said. "Tarot is a method of divination used with a certain deck of cards…Have we met before?"

"I think I would have remembered a face like yours," he said.

Sophia felt herself blush. "It's just, there's something about your face that I'm picking up, but I'm not sure what it is." Sophia studied his face closely. The cards could tell her. She opened her backpack purse. "Why don't I give you a reading!"

"Oh. Thank you very much. But I'm not a big believer in divination."

Sophia closed her purse and set it down beside her. "Yeah, neither is Nathan."

"Nathan? Is that you're boyfriend?"

"No," Sophia laughed. "Well, not yet, anyway."

The gentleman chuckled as if they just shared a secret. "So what's stopping you two?" he asked.

"It was never really a matter of whether we'd be friends enough to become boyfriend-girlfriend. We didn't really start off as friends. He just needed me to help him out with some weird thing that happened to him which I won't go into, but I'm telling you," she patted the air to emphasize her words, "it's really weird."

The gentleman listened carefully.

"Anyhow," Sophia said, "he just needed me to be there for him."

"Isn't that what loved ones do for each other?"

"I suppose. And, yeah, you're right. I guess I do like

him. I mean, he's handsome, he's smart, and he's so funny," she laughed.

"You just like him?" the gentleman asked.

"Okay, okay. I love him." She shook. "Ooh! I just got chills all over. It's one thing to feel it, but actually saying it. Announcing it. Putting it out there." She sighed. "It makes it so real."

"Does he know your feelings for him?"

"Yeah, I think it's pretty obvious." Sophia looked down at her bracelet with a stainless steel design of two hearts and fiddled with it. "But if he liked me the same way, I guess he would have told me by now."

"Not necessarily," the gentleman said. "Several years ago I was madly in love with an exotic Indian woman. She was a photographer, like myself, and we met at a photography expo. I had seen her work on tulips, and was struck most by one of her pieces. It was a stunning image of two blue tulips—just the tops—nested in a porcelain teacup. I spoke to her about it and one thing led to another, turned out we spent more time with each other than at the expo. I even managed to buy her blue tulips, and believe me, they were not easy to come by."

"Aww, that's so sweet."

"She made her feelings for me very clear. Unfortunately, I had a, oh, shall we say, family mission that wouldn't allow me the freedom to make the kind of commitment she was looking for."

"What kind of mission?"

"It's very complicated so I won't go into it, but let's

just say," he patted the air, "it's very complicated."

Sophia laughed.

"In her hotel room over tea, I explained to the best of my ability how I wanted to be with her but the reality of it was impossible. We parted that evening having made plans to meet for breakfast before she left for the airport. She even gave me her spare room key in case she was in the shower when I arrived." He smiled.

Sophia returned the smile.

"That evening, I returned to my room, and I'll tell you it was the longest evening of my life."

"Why's that?"

"For hours I debated whether or not I should commit my life to this wonderful woman, or should I stay true to the family mission. My conclusion was that my family be damned, I was going to give everything of me, body and soul, to this woman. And I couldn't wait to tell her so at breakfast."

"So what happened?" Sophia's eyes widened.

"I couldn't sleep the rest of the evening. But I didn't want to ruin her rest, so I waited for the agreed upon hour to arrive. At six o'clock, I knocked on her door. No answer."

"Oh, no."

"I tried again. Still, no answer. Perhaps she was in the shower. I used the key she gave me and opened the door. The room was empty. No clothes, no items in the bathroom. Only the two teacups from the night before. And in one of them, two blue tulips."

Sophia sighed.

"There was a note from her beside the teacups."

"What did it say?" Sophia asked.

"She apologized for missing our breakfast but chose to take an earlier flight because the idea of spending time with a man she could never have was too much for her to bear."

"And you didn't call her?"

"I had no contact information on her. I could have easily found it, but I took her leaving as a sign."

"A sign?"

"A sign to stay true to the family mission. But the point I'm trying to make here is that Nathan may soon realize just how much he needs you. Don't be surprised if he comes over one day with a ring. All you need to do is be there for him." The gentleman leaned close to her. "And does he have your cell phone number?"

Sophia laughed. "He does."

"Good." He smiled.

Sophia's fingers itched and tingled. Her tarot cards were so close, and they could help her decide what it was about that smile that seemed off. "I'm Sophia, by the way." She extended her hand. "What's your name?"

The gentleman looked up to his right. "Charles," he said, taking her hand.

Sophia felt her stomach tighten. The man had made up his name. A family mission? A photographer?

"Oh, dear," the man said holding her hand tighter. "It seems you caught me in a lie. I can always read fear in a face. Allow me to introduce myself. I am Luke McCourt."

Chapter 48

Sophia twisted her hand out of Luke Mc-Court's, grabbed her backpack purse, and ran to the opposite end of the train car. She had to get off this train as soon as possible. But the train had just left Embarcadero station, San Francisco's last stop before coursing through the Transbay Tube under the water to get to Oakland. Getting to the next stop was going to take some time.

The double sliding doors that led out from one car to the other had high resistance to opening. Sophia used her adrenaline and her whole body to open the first pair of sliding doors.

When the doors opened, the loud sound of the train cutting through the tunnel on its tracks clacked and sighed and squeaked and groaned. Sophia moved into the thin space between the cars and heaved her body into opening the second set of sliding doors.

The train car she entered had a few passengers who looked up at her. When the sliding doors closed behind her, the clacketing sound of the train muted, and the passengers returned to their reading and sleeping and chatting.

Sophia looked behind her. McCourt had stood up and was coming for her. She raced down to the next set of doors and pushed through those, and on to the next car, and on to the next. Each time, she got closer to the front of the train and each time, she noticed that McCourt was further back.

She made it to the front car and looked behind her. McCourt wasn't visible. He was probably a few doors down.

"You look like you're trying to get away from someone." A big grunt of a man looked up at her from his seat.

"As a matter of fact, I am," Sophia said.

"Tell you what." He removed his large, down jacket. "Sit beside me, hide under my jacket, and he'll get off the next station thinking that's what you did."

Sophia checked behind her. There was no sign of McCourt just yet. She stepped over the man's legs to get to the window seat next to him. He handed her the jacket, and she easily hid her entire body beneath it.

The jacket smelled of sweat and smoke and dirt and body odor. Her breathing made the area underneath heat up. She fought the urge to see where Luke was because she knew she'd be able to hear him. If suddenly the sound of the train got louder, that meant the sliding doors were opening and it meant someone was entering the train car.

But before that inevitable sound came, Sophia felt the train slow down.

"Oakland West," the driver announced over the PA.

The train came to a stop. Sophia heard the doors open.

She waited. The wait lasted five seconds, then ten, then fifteen.

"Doors are closing," the driver said. "Doors are closing."

She heard the ping sound of the automatic warning for the closing of the doors, and at last the doors closed.

Sophia peaked out from under the man's jacket. She didn't see McCourt on the train or in the next car over. She looked outside the window as the train pulled away from the station and saw McCourt on the platform looking left and right.

"Yes!" Sophia cried out. "Yes! Yes!" She turned to the man, "Thank you so much."

His phone was ringing. "No problem." He answered the phone while easing out a handgun and pressed the gun against her hip.

"Yeah, I got her," he said into the phone. "She came to the front of the train just like you said."

Chapter 49

It was hard for me to believe that getting the other half of this piece of paper would make sense of where the M.E.G. prototype was located. "Berkeley" probably indicated the place. The number 106 was anyone's guess. A room perhaps? Was it a Berkeley hotel? Something on the first floor? But then what about the 32–5? Couldn't be a date. Only 31 days in May, not 32.

I got back in my car and drove down Alcatraz Avenue, the dividing street between Oakland and Berkeley, toward Shakespeare's Books. The avenue was named Alcatraz because just about anywhere you were on that street, you could see the former prison on Alcatraz Island in the San Francisco Bay.

I turned right onto Telegraph. By some miracle, I found parking three feet away from the bookstore. There was a gray-haired man holding open the storefront's door as several people left. Was it closing? My watch read 8:03 pm.

"Wait!" I called out.

The guy saw me running toward him. He had a frightened look on his face. The man went inside and slammed the door shut, locking it with a quick turn of the bolt. Didn't blame him. It wasn't for nothing some people called the city Berzerkeley.

A bookseller on the street was packing his used wares.

"Mr. Yirmorshy?" A young voice said behind me.

I turned around and saw a college-age girl looking up at me. Her hair was straight and brown and had a curl at her shoulders. The thick eyeliner brought her eyes out so much, the twinkle in them nearly blinded me.

"Yes," I replied.

"I'm Charlie, Mr. Priore's daughter. He asked me to give this to you."

She held out the envelope. The same plain-looking envelope as I had been given.

"Wouldn't it make more sense if you hang on to that?" I asked.

"Dad was quite insistent."

I realized why. If they look for Antoine and find the envelope missing, his daughter may be next.

"But I don't understand why *I* should be the one to take it," I said.

"He didn't explain why," she said. "He only asked me to make sure you got this."

I took it from her hand. "How is your father?"

She looked a little confused. "Oh, he's fine. It was nice meeting you." She smiled and turned on her heel.

I wanted to stop her, but I wasn't sure what to say. So I let her go.

I looked at the envelope a little more. Should I even open it? The knowledge of the prototype's location would be mine. And if Luke already knew where the prototype was, I could try to intervene. Get it first.

Seemed dangerous.

Was this something I really wanted to do? How many people could be killed if Luke got hold of it? And how big of an "if" was that? There was still the chance that Luke had no idea where the prototype was. Getting the prototype and moving it to a different location might just make it easier for Luke to find. Should I just leave it where it was? Keep it a secret?

I turned over the envelope a few more times. The hell with it.

Inside was a duplicate folded piece of paper. When I unfolded it I saw what I was expecting. A rip along the left side of the piece of paper. It read, "High" and then far below that, "–26."

Chapter 50

Bobbie Graff sighed, feeling the exhaustion of the long day. Detectives Denton and Graff were cruising the Piedmont Avenue area in an unmarked police car, a Crown Victoria, just finishing their shift when they saw a parked semi truck in a residential area. The license plate matched the missing truck Hal Carter was last using.

Denton pulled over saying, "Check it out. Kit's in the trunk." He turned to her. "I'll call it in and keep an eye out."

Graff nodded and exited the car, opened the trunk, and pulled out the rectangular nylon bag. She walked over to the semi and put on latex gloves. Due to the truck's size, she removed the larger one hand jack, placed the metal jack on the semi's doorframe, and gently applied pressure. She got the air wedge from the bag. The air wedge looked like a blood pressure gauge for the arm. It even had a bulb to squeeze air into the bag. Graff inserted the air wedge into the doorframe and pumped the bulb. Once the gap between the truck and door was wide enough, she slid the four-foot long reach tool inside and unlocked the door.

Graff climbed inside. She opened the glove compartment, flipped through the papers, and didn't find what she was looking for. She looked beneath the seat on the driver's side.

There it was. A .38 caliber.

She left it for the crime scene investigators to bag and tag. After locking the truck shut, she packed her tools and returned to the Crown Vic.

"Got him," she said to Denton.

"Yeah?"

"Thirty-eight was under his seat. Wanted to check if it had bullets missing, but…"

"Good call," Denton said. "CSI's on their way. Where do you think the suspect is?"

Graff noticed a car a block ahead of them pulling up to the curb. The driver exited his car. He strode toward a two-story residence, climbed several steps to the front door, and rang the doorbell.

"Turn off the headlights," she told Denton.

Denton twisted the headlight switch off but kept the engine running to keep the heater on.

Once the driver was inside the house, Graff exited the car and opened the trunk. She pulled out her duffel bag and returned to the passenger seat. She unzipped the bag, removed a pair of binoculars, and focused on the house window.

"A lot of people," she said. She detached her badge from her belt, put it in the duffle bag while getting out a black t-shirt. "I'm getting a closer look."

Graff unbuttoned her blouse and removed her arms in the confined space.

"You sure that's a good idea?" Denton asked.

She pulled the t-shirt over her white bra, unclipped her hair and shook it out. "Right now, it's the best idea."

Graff took out a vanity mirror from her duffle bag, and tugged loose one of her shoelaces before getting out of the car. She took the sidewalk closest to the house. It was dark out. The house was lit up. She'd be hard to see from the inside of the house unless they were looking for her. Graff walked to a shadow made by the street lamp in front of the house, and crouched down to "tie her shoe." With her back to the living room window, she used the mirror to look behind her and see inside.

No good. The window was high up, so her position only gave her a clear view of the living room ceiling.

She tied her shoe and snuck to the window, standing just beneath the sill. Holding the mirror at the base of the window worked better. She began to count.

Luke McCourt let the others work on the specifics as he wandered to the living room window. He held a flame to a cigarette in his mouth and puff-started it.

"If only my father could see me now," he said to himself.

Luke had come so much further than his father ever did. But that was to be expected. Everything Luke learned, trained for, and absorbed was for this moment. And everything was now in place: the creature was ready, the plane was on time, and the hostage was acquired without incident and tied up in the basement.

Luke looked out the window and saw vapor from a car's exhaust pipe puff under a street lamp.

Luke smiled. "Someone's trying to stay warm."

Chapter 51

Standing outside Shakespeare's Books, I read the second note again. Now it all made sense. By itself, the second note was also meaningless: "High" and "–26." But when I put the halves together it read "Berkeley High" and below that, "106," and below that "32–5–26."

Berkeley High was Berkeley's major public high school. My next destination. But first, I needed to call Sophia before it got too late.

It was almost 9:00 pm. She should be home by now, and not yet asleep. While waiting for her to pick up, I looked around. A guitar player who looked like he lived on the streets was singing "Eight Days a Week." A girl similarly dressed, probably his girlfriend, was dancing with a Labrador Retriever. The dog had a tambourine around its neck and every time the girl got him to jump, the tambourine rang, making an irregular rhythm accompaniment to the song.

Sophia didn't pick up.

As soon as I hung up the cell phone, it rang. "Hello?"

"Mr. Yirmorshy? This is Detective Graff. Do you have a moment?"

"Yes, of course," I said. A gust of wind pushed down Telegraph Avenue. I buttoned my overcoat with one hand.

"We found a suspect, a trucker by the name of Harold Carter. Goes by Hal. Know him?"

"Hal Carter? Doesn't sound familiar."

"You sure?" she asked.

I polished my memory to see if anyone named Hal Carter would shine from under the grime. No one did. "I'm sure."

"Ok. We're about to make an arrest."

"How can I help?"

"Mr. Carter is having a meeting with several people as we speak. There are ten men and one woman. McCourt is one of them. Do you know of any groups like that?"

"Again. Nothing comes to mind."

"Did McCourt ever hold meetings at his place?"

I thought on that. "Not that I remember."

"How about the names Melinda and Paul Fallon? Know them?"

"No," I said. "Why? Who are they?"

"That's the residence the meeting is being held at," she explained. "Are you sure none of this means anything to you?"

I juggled the names in my head and tried thinking of groups with ten men and one woman. I once saw a ludicrous show involving several guys chasing after one woman. It was a comedy performed by the Berkeley

Repertory Theater. Pretty sure that was not what the detective was talking about. "Sorry. Nothing."

"Okay," she sighed. "Let me give you my number."

I scribbled down the detective's phone number. Based on the first three digits, I knew the number belonged to a cell phone.

"If you think of anything, give me a call," the detective added.

"Will do."

I hung up the phone. Ten men and one woman. I didn't remember seeing even a single man or woman with McCourt. Who else might know? McCourt, of course. Who else? Kor perhaps? I gave Kor a call. Got a message machine.

After the beep, I said, "Mr. Kor? I was just wondering if you're familiar with a group of ten men and one woman? Has anyone who's been following you or anything fit that description? Anyhow, if you do know of a group like that, go ahead and give a call to a detective by the name of Bobbie Graff of the Oakland Police." I left the detective's number and hung up.

Anyone else I could try? I realized that maybe I was approaching this all wrong. I was thinking in terms of the places the group might have gone to instead of the places where the group might go. Why not just check their agenda? I dialed the number of the man who held their agenda.

"Hello, Rabbi? Is this too late to be calling you?"

Chapter 52

Bobbie Graff felt the adrenaline pump inside of her. Detectives Graff and Denton were now with twenty-eight others from the Oakland Police, all donning bulletproof vests. They had the residence surrounded, but it took a long time. Too long for Graff's taste. She lost visibility of the suspects ten minutes before the police arrived. No one stood in the living room.

The two detectives were stationed to break in the front door. "Let's go, already," she muttered, her heart pounding.

Denton carried a walkie-talkie.

"On my mark," the voice of the captain in charge crackled through the speaker. "And go! Go! Go!"

The police rammed the door in and swarmed throughout the house. "Oakland Police! Everybody down! Down! Get down!"

Graff pushed through, eager to find the men she had been watching moments ago. She stormed the halls to the kitchen with cedar cabinets and marble counters, upstairs to the bedrooms with made queen beds and blue-green carpeting, and to the blue-tiled bathrooms.

"Clear," someone said in a distant room.

"Clear," sounded another officer's voice.

Where were they?

Denton caught up to Graff and said, "There's no one here. Must've left through the back door."

"Shit!"

"Don't worry. All their cars are still out front. They can't get far on foot."

Graff sighed. "They'll probably figure some way to get out of Oakland fast. Let's contact all the cabs in the area, in case they took a taxi."

Luke pressed the gun a little firmer into Sophia's back as the local hospital's free shuttle to BART pulled up.

"Alright, everyone," Luke said. "Climb in."

The men and Melinda carried their luggage on board and Luke discreetly escorted Sophia to a seat.

The driver had on a white, short-sleeved shirt and black pants. He looked at the various pieces of luggage. "All of you going to the airport?"

"That's right," Luke said cheerfully.

"Where ya flyin' to?"

"To a new beginning."

"Sounds nice."

Chapter 53

The rabbi held the phone to his ear sitting in his cluttered office. To him, however, the office had a divine organization that only he understood. This ability to see the order of the chaos. This was only further proof of the Almighty's great abilities.

"I am wide awake, Nathan," he said. "How are you?"

"Fine, I was—"

"Good," the rabbi said. Nathan was fine. That pleased the rabbi very much.

"And Sophia?" the rabbi asked.

"She's fine too. I was just—"

"Good. Good." Sophia was fine too. The rabbi was very pleased. "Now what can I do for you?"

"I was wondering if there's any mention of a group of people encoded in Genesis thirty-six. Ten men and one woman?"

"Hold on, let me open the software." The rabbi shifted the mouse over the icon and double-clicked. "So tell me Nathan. Who are these ten men and one woman?"

"Not sure," Nathan said. "I was hoping you could tell me."

"Let's see. Ten men in Hebrew is '*esereem eesheem.*' " The rabbi punched in the letters and clicked "Find Code" for *Braisheet* thirty-six. It took less than a second for the computer to display, "No result."

"It's not in here, Nathan. Let me try one woman."

The rabbi typed the Hebrew word for "one woman" and clicked "Find Code."

No result.

"I'm sorry, Nathan. It's not in here."

"Okay. Well, it was worth a shot. I'll call you if I have any other questions."

"Do that, Nathan." The rabbi said. "I always enjoy hearing from you."

The rabbi waited for Nathan to hang up, and then put the phone back in its cradle. Nathan seemed such a nice young man. And Sophia, a nice young woman. How wonderful it would be, should they want to marry. And what an honor to be the one to wed them.

The rabbi got up from the computer and went to the kitchen. He took out a half a cantaloupe from the fridge and began cutting a slice.

"Sophia" and "Nathan." "Nathan Yirmorshy." Sophia said, "I am *Shekinah*." All of those words. Encoded in *Braisheet* thirty-six. What did it all mean?

And "apocalypse?" Could Nathan have something to do with that?

The rabbi sat down, scooped out tablespoons from his slice of melon and ate them.

The *Shekinah*. Of all things to say. What could it mean? Sophia as the female presence of God? The *Shekinah* was often considered the part of god that dwelled on the earth. Some people knew her as *Chochmah*, the bride of God. *Chochmah*. The Hebrew word for "wisdom." And Sophia. Her name was Greek for "wisdom?"

The rabbi took another bite of the cantaloupe. He believed in coincidence, but coincidence seemed to take no role here.

And ten men, and one woman. Ten men. Ten men. What could that mean? Maybe nothing.

The cantaloupe was so sweet. The rabbi spent a moment taking in the flavor. The only way it could have been sweeter was if he should eat it on a hot day.

Ten men. Ten men. Ten men.

There were ten men in a *minyan*, a group of people praying to God. A communal prayer was heard only if there were at least ten men. A *minyan*. Could there be any connection?

The rabbi took another bite.

Where else were ten men mentioned in Judaism? Ten men. Ten men. Or ten....

The rabbi stood and went to the book shelves. Right away, he was able to pick out the book he wanted. The book of Esther.

The rabbi flipped to the section where the text looked strange. Instead of paragraphs, the words were written one under the other. The words were the names of the ten sons of Haman. Haman, a man considered worse than Hitler, was the enemy of the Jews. And here, in the text, was a description of the hanging of the ten sons of Haman. The way the names were placed, one on top of the other, the text resembled the gallows.

And then there were the small letters.

Over the centuries, the Hebrew had been copied not only to the letter, but also to the position and size. And throughout the centuries, among the names of the ten sons of Haman, there were letters with a smaller size than the rest, as if a word had a random letter within it made superscript. But recently, some editions made an additional letter small.

The rabbi analyzed the letters and tried making sense of it all. And then it hit him.

"Oh no," the rabbi said.

He raced to the computer and did a search for those letters in the book of Genesis thirty-six. He clicked on "Find Code." The result box popped up. Every six letters.

The rabbi stared wide-eyed at his computer screen. *"Mein Gott!"*

Chapter 54

I drove to Berkeley High School and parked next to a police station. Hugged my overcoat closer against the cold night. I padded down the abandoned sidewalk to a back gate leading into the high school.

The gate was closed.

I heard some laughter in the distance. Some stupid kids having a good time.

I looked back at the gate. It seemed easy enough to climb, but that wasn't my only obstacle. The doors leading to the classrooms were no doubt locked as well. I could try all the doors once inside and see if any were open.

I could also just forget the whole thing until tomorrow. But of course, the prototype might be stolen by then. What if it was already stolen? I'd have to track down Luke to steal it back. And the idea of chasing after Luke having just frightened him off chasing me was not a pretty option.

The kids in the distance were laughing again. Damn kids.

Wait! Kids!

I followed the voices to a darkened park across the street from the high school. Two guys and three girls, probably high school kids, were dressed in "grunge" clothes. The "grunge" look just meant they looked like they've been wearing the same clothes for seven weeks without showering.

As I approached them, there was a quick stifling of their laughter. Two of them hid bottles of beer.

That was good.

"Hi!" I said cheerfully. "I was wondering if you could help me out?"

"Help you out how?" a boy said beneath a war of scruffy black hair.

"I want to get inside the school. Do you know how I could break in without breaking anything?"

They laughed.

"Are you for reals?" one of the girls asked. She was clearly bra-less. She had long bleach-blonde hair, a jean jacket sitting beside her, and wore a t-shirt that said, "Nobody knows I'm a lesbian."

"I'm for reals," I said. I pulled out a hundred-dollar bill and held it up. "Just ask Ben, here."

The scruffy-haired boy pulled out his beer, took a sip and said, "I'll show you."

He put down his bottle.

"Follow me," he said. Then he turned to his friends, "I'll be back in a sec. Don't drink my brew."

I followed Scruff a few feet. "It's probably better if you just tell me. I don't want to get you in trouble."

"Trouble's my middle name," Scruff said.

I wondered if his other names were Dirty and Smelly. I stopped walking and looked back at the bra-less girl. Either she was happy to have seen me or she was cold. Alcohol and cold weather. Not good. A body couldn't tell if it was going into a state of hypothermia because alcohol gave the illusion that the body was warm. Oh, well. It was her death, not mine.

"Do we need to climb the gate?" I asked Scruffy.

"Yeah, but there's an easy place to do it." Scruffy looked impatient. "You coming?"

I looked back at the lesbian. The night was freezing. And the bite of the wind wasn't helping any. I tried to picture what she'd look like as an adult. Maybe wearing a business outfit. Or a lab coat. Could have a daughter of her own.

"Just a sec." I cupped my hands and called out to her, "Hey Blondie!" She and her friends turned to me. "You look good without a bra! Shows off your small boobs!"

Her friends busted up laughing but she made a defiant face and put on her jean jacket.

"Now, I'm ready," I told Scruffy.

Scruffy laughed saying, "Man, you are one messed up dude."

He didn't know the half of it.

He took me around a corner where there was a raised cement platform next to a gate. It functioned as a step, making the gate easier to climb.

Scruffy went over first like it was a puddle he had to

jump over. When I climbed over, my muscles began to do the shimmy. My hands felt like they were clasping at broken glass. My overcoat got caught at the top.

After my battle with the gate, Scruffy asked, "You okay?"

"Piece of cake."

He snorted and said, "Follow me."

We backtracked toward our original location. Scruffy brought me through a thin alley between two school buildings to a door at the end of the alley.

"This door is so old, it's the easiest to open," Scruffy said. "All you need is good credit."

Before I could ask, Scruffy whipped out a credit card that had a square piece cut out of it. The card was in the shape of a lower-case block-letter "n."

Scruffy slid the credit card through the slot between the door and its frame until he got to the latch. By sliding the cut out portion over the latch and pulling the card toward him, Scruffy was able to slide the latch sideways and open the door.

"Now THAT," Scruffy said holding up the credit card, "is a piece of cake."

"Where are the lockers?" I asked Scruffy.

"Straight down the hall and to your left. Why? Gonna break into the lockers?"

"No. I'm just getting my son's homework."

Scruffy snorted again. "You know, you're wasting

your time. Kids don't keep expensive stuff in their lockers anymore."

"Like I said," I replied.

"Right. Homework."

"I can take it from here," I said handing him the hundred-dollar bill.

"You got it." Scruffy gave me a weird handshake that I had trouble following, so Scruffy soon gave it up and left me on my own.

I followed the echo of my steps down the empty school halls. It brought back memories better forgotten. What kind of reflection on the school system was it when nerds, interested in being smarter, hated school? I found the lockers just as Scruffy had said. Standing next to locker number eighty-seven, I noticed the numbers increased along the hall. Looked at the two halves of paper Kor and Charlie had given me. "Berkeley High, 106, 32–5–26." I touched the numbers on the lockers with my fingers as I walked.

Eighty-seven. Eighty-eight. Eighty-nine...

What was the prototype going to look like? Assuming that's what this whole thing was about. For all I knew, I could've read the note wrong, or there was no prototype to begin with and I was about to find incriminating evidence of some disconnected crime. Maybe I was being framed.

In the movies, the mysterious locker always held a duffle bag full of money. Or a severed head. If I found a duffle bag, I'd be happy with the money. Not so happy with a severed head.

I found it. Locker #106. It was fastened shut with a standard dial-combination lock. I whirled the knob to the right several times, feeling the outer dial make contact with the inner dials. Satisfied the lock was ready for its combination, I continued twisting it to the right until it reached thirty-two. To the left a whole turn until the dial read five. Then right again to twenty-six. With a tug, the lock snapped open. I removed the combination lock from the locker, took a deep breath, and opened the locker.

No duffle bag.

I wasn't sure if I were disappointed or relieved.

Chapter 55

Instead, inside the locker there was something that looked like a square donut the size of a textbook made of metal. Down the center of the square was a bar made from a different-looking metal. Was this the M.E.G.? It wasn't at all what I had expected. But then, what did I expect? Something with belts, fans, and spinning things that go whir? Now the name made sense: Motionless Electromagnetic Generator. No moving parts.

Around the sides were coils of wires attached to a hairdryer.

I knew why out of all things it was attached to a hairdryer. If it was attached to a light bulb, it wouldn't be too impressive. Light bulbs don't need much power to light up. Hairdryers on the other hand require a tremendous amount of power. I lifted the hairdryer. It was light. No batteries. I turned on the hairdryer and a blast of heat hit my face. Where was the electricity coming from? Was it really coming from empty space? The vacuum?

I turned the hairdryer off. If you attached several of these things together you could probably power a car, a house, perhaps even run a power company. It looked so unimpressive that I had to imagine the possibilities to realize the tremendous significance.

Now where to put it?

I disconnected the hairdryer from the square device, and picked up the entire M.E.G. It was heavy. How was I going to carry it? I wished I had a duffle bag.

Or maybe... I looked at some of the other lockers. A few didn't have locks on them, so I opened them. Nothing but papers. I knew searching all the lockers for a backpack would be fruitless. Why would a student leave a backpack at school? Unless by accident. Checking all these lockers would waste a lot of time hoping for a happy accident.

I tucked my overcoat into my pants. Placed the M.E.G. inside my coat and buttoned up. As long as the coat stayed tucked in, the M.E.G. would stay hidden and not fall. I gave myself a once over. While my clothes weren't the most fashionable, the way the overcoat was tucked in still almost looked normal. A person had to look for the M.E.G. on me to see its outline. Otherwise, it was unnoticeable.

I closed the locker and walked out of the building. Returned to the easiest part of the gate and climbed over. This time, I cut my palm. The M.E.G. didn't fall out. I stood on the platform sucking my palm clean, getting the sting of it out.

"Sir, could you step down from there?!"

Two policemen approached me with their hands on their holsters.

Chapter 56

As I stepped down onto the sidewalk, one policeman spoke into his walkie-talkie, "We have an adult white male near the auditorium entrance. Keep checking the perimeter."

The other policeman said to me, "The silent alarm sounded inside the school. Do you have anything you want to tell us?"

I wasn't sure what to say. Was this the part where I ask for a lawyer? I might as well just announce "I'm guilty!" It would have the same effect.

"I got it, Dad!" A voice called from behind.

I saw Scruffy running toward us. He stopped next to me and said, "I managed to get into the building and get my homework."

God bless this boy.

"Do you mean to tell me that you actually broke into school?!" I shouted at Scruffy. "Do you realize that you did something so highly illegal, the police could've shot you! I was so worried about you, I've been wandering up and down the streets looking all over for you! The police saw me looking into the school and had a very good reason to think I was the one who broke in! I'm surprised they didn't shoot me!! Is that what you want? You want me to get shot?!"

Scruffy looked teary-eyed. This kid was good.

I turned to the police. "I'm sorry about that officers. I can promise you that my son here will pay dearly for it. No more computer, phone, and music privileges for the next three months. And his curfew is now nine o'clock instead of eleven."

One officer turned to the other and asked, "How do you want to handle this?"

"Just get their names and their address down."

I gave my name and address to the officer and the officer asked, "Your son's name?"

"Uh...Tr...ooble. Truble Yirmorshy."

I caught Scruffy hiding a smile.

"Truble? What kind of name is that?" the officer asked with sincere curiosity.

"It's Russian," I tried.

"Oh! Like ruble!"

"Exactly."

"Well, keep your eye on him. Otherwise *Truble* could get in *trouble*," the officer winked.

I forced a laugh, "That's clever."

The officers left and Scruffy said, "Wow! I feel sorry for your real children."

"Don't have any."

"Whatever. I forgot to mention the alarms. I figured you could use a hand to get out of that mess."

"Thanks for coming to the rescue," I said.

Scruffy started walking backwards. "Piece of cake!" He smiled and ran off.

Chapter 57

I **entered my car, undid my overcoat, and** removed the M.E.G. Placed it beside me in the passenger's seat and unstuffed my overcoat from my pants. As soon as I turned my cell phone back on, it rang.

"Nathan!" It was the rabbi. "Thank God you answered! I've been telephoning, trying to reach you. I have some news you're not going to like."

"What's wrong?"

"I was looking in the wrong book," the rabbi said. "Listen. The Book of Esther tells of a man named Haman. A man so cruel he is considered worse than Hitler. His plan was to destroy all the Jews. Kill them all."

I actually had some idea of the story of Queen Esther, but I let the rabbi continue.

"Haman had ten sons. And a daughter who committed suicide."

I felt a chill.

"And at the end of the book, the ten sons were hung. At the point of the book where they are hung, there are letters which have different sizes. The tiny letters are a *tav*, a *shin*, and a *zayin*. And there is one big letter. A *vav*. No one knew why the letters were made different sizes, but in 1946, a very strange thing happened. Eleven Nazis were scheduled to hang. One of them, a Nazi who wore women's undergarments, committed suicide. So ten were hung. The last one, Streicher, shouted out just before he was hung, 'Purimfest, 1946!' "

"Purimfest?" I asked.

"Purim is the holiday where we read the Book of Esther."

Oh, yeah. I knew that.

"Nathan, it was a mystery why Streicher shouted that out. But then the Jewish scholars studied the letters in the book of Esther. The ones with different sizes. The small ones add up to 707. *Tav* is 400, *shin* is 300, and *zayin* is 7. The way we keep track of the thousands is by putting a large number in front. So 707 with a big number one is 707 in the first thousand. And 707 with a big two is 1707 in the second thousand, and so on."

I didn't get all that, but I let the rabbi go on. Maybe he'd make his point soon.

"There was the big *vav*, Nathan. A six. In the Book of Esther. That means that the sixth time around is 5707."

"I don't get it," I admitted.

"Nathan, that's a Jewish calendar year. Its equivalent is 1946! The year 1946 was encoded in the Book of Esther! The year Streicher and the other men were hung!"

Chapter 58

"What does this have to do with me?" I asked. "Is it the ten men the police were asking me about?"

"Exactly," the rabbi answered. "For some reason, in recent editions of the Book of Esther, another letter has been made smaller. You have to understand, Nathan. It should never have happened. The text should always have stayed the same over the years. Why, then, is there this additional letter? I cannot begin to understand how it happened."

"What does it mean?" I asked.

"It means, Nathan, that with the additional letter, the encoded year is no longer 1946, but now adds up to the present."

Terrific.

"Nathan, that's not all," the rabbi said. "I looked for the present year in the Torah. In the entire Torah, there is only one place the letters show up."

"Let me guess," I said. "Genesis chapter thirty-six."

"Every sixth letter," the rabbi confirmed.

I put myself in McCourt's shoes. If McCourt saw that my name and the present year were encoded together, then whatever he had in store for me would happen soon.

And what about the other codes? Sophia, *Shekinah*, the apocalypse? Did they have anything to do with McCourt's grand plan or was it all just coincidence? Maybe the key was in the story of Esther.

"Rabbi, is there any mention of ten people hanging in Genesis thirty-six?"

"Let me check. I'll try the phrase 'they will hang.' "

I heard the sound of keys tapping at the other end of the line. A thought occurred to me. If McCourt saw that the book of Esther and the book of Genesis predicted his hanging, how would that make him feel? And how would he react?

"It's not here, Nathan," the rabbi said. "I tried the code both backwards and forwards."

"Backwards?"

"Yes. Many codes can be written as equidistant letter sequences backwards."

I thought I saw a zebra. I turned and a police car passed by. I was tired. I looked at the time. 11:23 p.m.? How did that happen?

"Rabbi? Have I been keeping you up?"

"Why? What time is—Oy! 11:25 already? And I have to be part of a minyan for the morning services tomorrow!"

"Minyan?" I remembered the phrase from somewhere.

"Yes. At least ten men are needed for a communal prayer. A minyan."

"Rabbi! Do you think that could be related to anything?"

"I don't know, Nathan."

"Well thanks for everything. I'll let you go."

"Goodnight, Nathan. And be careful."

"Be careful sleeping?"

"No. In general. Be careful."

"Oh. Right," I said. "Good night."

Without the rabbi to talk to, my surroundings became quiet. I sat in my car and stared at my cell phone hoping the insanity of the day would vanish with his voice.

Chapter 59

From the high school, I drove down Telegraph Avenue. The late night sidewalks were lit for the insomniacs and restless spirits compelled to take a stroll.

There was still traffic at this hour. The car in front of me had a bumper sticker that read, "Sleep with me. I'm a rock star. I belong to the Rubber Band."

I stopped at a stoplight and looked at the rubber band on my wrist. Looked outside. The streets felt mystical, like a dream.

I wanted to dream. Wanted to sleep. How was Sophia going to react to me returning so late? Would she be upset? Would she kick me out? Would she even care at all?

The light turned green.

I'm not the greatest at reading people, but I know one thing. Sophia expressed interest in me. Beyond sex. If anything, Sophia would welcome my return. But could she really handle me, with all my delusions? She said she wasn't Nancy. She made that very clear. I didn't want her to go through what Nancy had gone through. But I supposed it wasn't really my decision. Sophia was aware of my illness, and that was already an advantage over Nancy.

The more I thought about this, the more comfortable I felt about being with her. And the more I looked forward to seeing her again. I pictured her in nothing but a long t-shirt, welcoming me into her arms, into her bed. Her bed had soft white sheets that spread across the room and gently floated in a green mixture of seaweed and pea soup. The soup was warm to my skin.

I felt my entire body being flung to the side. Braked hard.

What happened?

I looked around, saw I was in my car, and the car was partly on the sidewalk.

Must have fallen asleep. No one seemed to be around. Even the car with the bumper sticker was long gone. The M.E.G. had fallen into the passenger side footwell. I picked it up and checked for damage. The M.E.G. was unharmed.

I couldn't die now. Couldn't take that privilege from McCourt. I reversed back onto the street, and turned onto Alcatraz Avenue toward Sophia's apartment. My eyelids weighed a ton. I had to remind myself that most sleeping accidents occurred when the driver felt the worst of the danger was over, like getting off a freeway. I rolled down the window. Let cold air hit my face. The closer I got to Sophia's apartment, the more I focused on the road.

I parked and exited the car with the M.E.G., glad to be out of that weapon of mass destruction. I put the M.E.G. in the trunk of the car and felt confident that it was safe there. A happy thought popped in my head. I didn't have to call Sophia on the intercom. I had the key.

I took out the key and looked at it. Proof of Sophia's trust and friendship.

Inside, I took the stairs to Sophia's door. With the key, I softly unlatched the lock. I turned the handle and pushed the door. Didn't budge.

Oh, yeah. The door. So much for entering quietly. I shoved the door hard making an obnoxiously loud sound.

By the hallway light, I saw that Sophia wasn't in bed. She wasn't in the room at all.

A cupcake lay on the floor. A brown cupcake with pink frosting and yellow ribbon stripes on top. I bent to pick it up.

It wasn't there.

Great time to start hallucinating. Made sense, though. I had skipped my last dose of meds. I had some in my pocket. Needed to remember to take them soon.

I tried calling Sophia's cell phone and a man answered almost shouting to overcome the loud background noise behind him.

"I'm sorry," I said. "I must have the wrong number."

"Nathan! So good of you to call!"

I recognized the voice now.

"That was quite a show you put on for me at the house, Nathan."

"Where's Sophia?" I felt a hole burning inside.

"Have a listen."

"Nathan!" Sophia's voice was frantic. "We're on a delivery plane! We've been flying for forty-five minutes and—"

"My, my. She certainly has a way of getting to the point, doesn't she, Nathan?"

McCourt's calm voice was maddening. Planes travel at about six hundred miles per hour. Forty-five minutes was what? Dammit! Think! It was what? Four hundred and fifty miles. North put them near Portland, South put them where? Near San Diego?

I gritted my teeth, and rushed to Sophia's bookshelf with the phone still to my ear. Found an atlas and opened to California. I traced a circle around San Francisco with my finger, estimating the radius.

"Where are you taking her?!" I asked. My voice broke as I spoke the words.

"To Israel, of course."

Then the line went dead.

I looked at the empty bed and felt I had come face-to-face with a fire-breathing dragon.

Part 4

TEN

Chapter 60

Bobbie Graff's cell phone jolted her out of her bed. She walked across the darkened bedroom in her extra-long Elvis Presley t-shirt grumbling over forgetting to put her cell phone on her nightstand. Retrieving the ringing phone from her duffle bag, she flipped it open.

"Graff," she said angrily.

"This is Nathan Yirmorshy. They kidnapped Sophia. Sophia Patai."

"What?"

"Luke McCourt. The ten men and one woman. They kidnapped her."

Now she remembered who this Nathan guy was. "Mr....Yimorsky, is it?"

"Yirmorshy."

"Mr. Yirmorshy. Tell me exactly what happened from the beginning."

Graff listened carefully to Mr. Yirmorshy explain his return to Sophia's apartment and the phone call from McCourt. Mr. Yirmorshy's voice wavered. His fear sounded genuine. As soon as Mr. Yirmorshy mentioned Israel, she said, "Israel? Are you sure?"

"Positive."

"Shit." She gripped the phone tighter.

"What's wrong?"

"It's out of my hands. Not only is it out of our jurisdiction, it's out of any U.S police jurisdiction."

"So what happens now?"

"I report it to the sergeant, who'll report it to the FBI, and I imagine they'll contact the Israeli authorities once McCourt makes his demands and whereabouts known."

"How long will that take?" Mr. Yirmorshy sounded as frustrated as she felt.

"It depends on when McCourt makes his demands. Could be a couple days, could be a couple months…" could be never if McCourt just ups and kills her.

"But by that time…" Mr. Yirmorshy said, practically a growl. "I'm going to Israel."

Shit.

"Mr. Yirmorshy, I was good friends with Officer Sullivan. I want so much to say, 'Good! Go to Israel! Get that son of a bitch and rip his heart out!' But what are you going to do once you get there? How are you going to find McCourt? And what will you do if by some miracle you do manage to find him?"

"I'll figure out something."

"Mr. Yirmorshy. McCourt is a dangerous man. And he's got an entire crew with him. Even if you were a marine, there'd be no way to fight them all and survive."

The line was silent.

Mr. Yirmorshy finally said, "Detective, I just want you to know, there's nothing you could have said to make me change my mind."

Mr. Yirmorshy hung up on her. She cursed, threw the phone across the room and it hit the wall with a thud.

Chapter 61

I **returned to the car and opened the glove** compartment. Saw the gun I acquired from Mc-Court when he dropped it at the duplex. That would come in handy. I checked the safety and placed the gun in my coat pocket. Grabbed my Anywhere Organizer from the glove compartment and unzipped it. Among the social security card, one thousand Euros, ATM card, the unlabeled calendar, calculator, and pen was my passport.

I lifted the plastic-coated passport from its pocket and felt its substantial thickness. Flipping through, memories of the Czech republic, Romania, Hungary, and Siberia floated in my head. Romania was like a time-traveling expedition where train tickets were chunks of cardboard with blue ink stamped on it. The train had passed through villages and I had seen hay-stacks. It was a wake up call to me about the millions of others in the world who lacked the typical luxuries of the West.

I returned the organizer to the glove compartment and drove toward the Bay Bridge. The San Francisco International Airport was probably my best bet for finding a flight to Israel.

The highway to the bridge was still busy, but the drive was smooth. I felt my eyes get heavy so I turned on the radio.

Squeeze da lemon, sip da lime, squeeze da lemon, slurp da lychee, squeeze da lemon, sip da li—

I turned off the radio.

When I approached the tollbooth, I slowed to a stop. Rolled down my window, thrust forward my waist to reach into my pocket, pulled out my wallet and found a twenty-dollar bill.

I offered it to the guy wearing a blue windbreaker. The tollbooth attendant was listening to a talk show. From what little I heard, it sounded like the caller was asking if sex with a dog was okay.

I collected my change and drove onto the bridge.

The city looked on fire at night. The Transamerica building was a pyramid of sparks among the other pyres of well-lit skyscrapers.

What was in Israel? How could bombing Israel accomplish their goals? But then again, it wasn't too surprising. When it came to terrorist activities, Israel was a favorite target.

As I reached San Francisco and continued south on the freeway, I considered the possible scenarios. A bomb goes off in Israel, Israel accuses one of its neighbors and attacks, other Arab nations combine efforts to attack Israel, the U.S. steps in to help Israel, the U.S. bombs the Arab nations and who knew what would happen next.

My eyes stung. I pinched the bundle of nerves between my eyes. I got off the freeway and followed the signs to the long-term parking.

When I found a parking space I looked beside me. The M.E.G. Was it capable of devastation? I mean, sure, it could give enough juice to run a hairdryer, but could it blow something up? It's just a power source. If McCourt and his group needed power, why didn't they just get an outlet? Worse thing that could happen was a short circuit.

Wait a minute.

A short circuit could destroy the wiring, and if there was no fuse or circuit breaker, rewiring a home could get pretty expensive. So if a short circuit destroyed the wiring, the source of the energy, what would happen if there was a short circuit with the M.E.G.? Its source of energy was "the vacuum," the fabric of space and time. Could a short circuit in the M.E.G. destroy space-time? The image of a chain reaction shredding space and all the planets and stars within it ran through my head.

Not good.

I decided not to take it with me. Better Sophia and I die alone than everyone all at once. Now where should I put it? That whole locker thing was a good idea. Train stations and airports had lockers, too. I grabbed the M.E.G. and stepped out of the car. Started walking.

An airport locker would be perfect.... I stopped. That would be perfect if the SF airport had any. Last I heard they ripped out all the lockers and replaced them with supervised storage, where everything is X-rayed. Not sure that storing a potential bomb would go over too well with the airport security.

I went back to the car and put it in the trunk. Only one person knew where my car was. Me. And if I die, they would ticket my car to kingdom come and eventually see what was inside. And either they'd save the day, or...most likely...they'd think it was junk and trash the whole thing.

I had better stay alive.

254 | Ezra Barany

Chapter 62

I **approached the nearest ticket counter** that had no lines.

"When's the next plane to Israel?" I asked a middle-aged woman who was probably very beautiful ten years ago, but now wore so much makeup she might have come from a free sample extravaganza at Macy's.

"Let me check that for you," she said sweetly. She looked at the screen. The computer screen gave a slight glow to her face, making her hypnotic stare at the computer disturbing.

"The next flight out leaves at 7:25 a.m."

I slammed my fist on the counter. Luke's plane will arrive hours ahead of mine. "Which flight gets me there the soonest?"

She scanned her screen with a trace of a pout. "There's a two-stop flight with Air Canada. After the first stop in Paris, it arrives in Tel Aviv tomorrow at 3:00 p.m."

I thanked the lady and searched for the Air Canada ticket counter. Found it and waited in line.

Detective Graff was right. Finding McCourt was going to be difficult. And I had no idea what I was going to do if I ever did find him.

A Middle-Eastern boy in front of me distracted me from my thoughts. He was with his mother. The boy looked about five-years old and shook his mother's arms like he was trying to create transverse waves. At first, she seemed oblivious at how her arm was being treated like a jump rope, but then she said, "Jimmy! Stop! It hurts Mamma's arm."

So his name was Jimmy. Strange name for a Middle-Easterner. The boy and his mother were called to the ticket counter and I was now up in front.

Jimmy.

Jimmy Jimmy Jimmy.

I looked at the ground, thought about Sophia, thought about the newspaper article and the thousands dying of thirst every day. My eyes felt heavy.

Jimmy Jimmy Jimmy.

Thought about who I was before I met Sophia. I swayed trying to control my balance and consciousness.

Jimmy crack corn and I don't care, Jimmy crack corn and I don't care, Jimmy crack corn and I don't caaaaaaaare—

"Next please," an Air Canada man said.

I went over to the counter and said, "Get me the next flight to Israel."

"Passport and credit card, please?"

I gave the man what he asked for. The man was bald and looked a bit like Ghandi. He had a name tag on that read Nehemia. Now that was one hell of a name.

"Sign here," Nehemia said.

I gave my John Hancock which actually looked more like a Stephen Hawking. I bet Sophia had gorgeous handwriting. If I ever find her and get her out of this whole thing, maybe she can sign things for me.

"Luggage?" Nehemia asked.

"I don't have any."

Nehemia looked at me for a moment. "How long are you staying?" he asked.

"As long as it takes. Just give me the damn ticket!"

Nehemia slowly processed my request. "Are you making *aliyah*?"

I knew that "making *aliyah*" was how us Jewish folk in the know said "moving to Israel."

"No, I'm just...visiting."

"Where will you be staying?"

"Why? There a hotel you can recommend?"

Nehemia made a scrawl with his pen on the boarding pass and handed it to me. "You'll need to go to gate G94. Enjoy your flight," he said.

He didn't mean it.

Chapter 63

I studied the security. The first task was to try getting the gun through. I saw an old lady dragging carry-on luggage behind her. She got into the security checkpoint line.

I stood behind her. Old ladies are never suspect. They never carried guns and probably could get away with murder. I got close to her luggage, unzipped a side pocket and smoothly lowered the gun inside. I stepped out of the line to see how granny did.

She put her purse in one of the bins, along with her cherry pumps which matched her red dress. Stockings covered her feet. One of the guards assisted her in lifting the luggage onto the conveyer, and she walked through the metal detector.

She smiled cheerfully at the guard who directed her to pick up her belongings.

"Uh, ma'am?" It was the guard screening the luggage through the X-ray. "Is this your bag?"

"Yes. My husband, rest his soul, bought it for me in Spain."

"We need to look inside. Would you open it for us please?"

She obliged with a smile. She opened the major compartment and they had her remove some items so they could see underneath. There was nothing to see. I knew they would let her go.

"How about the side pockets," one guard suggested. Uh oh.

She opened the side pocket and they peeked inside. One guard pulled out the gun as if he was lifting a dead rat by the tail.

"Oh my goodness!" The woman said.

"Ma'am, you'll have to come with us."

"It isn't mine! I'm certain it isn't mine!"

They directed her to a nearby room.

I could hear her say as she walked into the room, "I left mine at home! How did that get there?"

"Well," I muttered to myself, "that didn't work."

Chapter 64

I stood in the line leading to the security gate. Checked the time. It was after midnight. My phone rang and I answered.

"Nathan, it's Rabbi Silverman. It's there."

"What's there?"

"The phrase 'and they will hang.' It's there. I just was using modern Hebrew before. By switching to the old Hebrew, I found in chapter thirty-six the phrase 'and they will hang' nine times forwards and nine times backwards."

"Nine times?!"

"Yes. It surprises me, too. I'm not sure why it isn't ten."

That wasn't what surprised me. The fact that it showed up nine times both forwards and backwards seemed statistically impossible.

I told myself to focus. I needed to get to Israel. "Say, Rabbi? I have to go to Israel because they kidnapped Sophia."

"What?!"

"The point is I just bought a ticket but I think I've been marked by the ticket clerk for the security to hold me back and check me out. Do you have any suggestions for how I can convince them I'm not a terrorist and I just want to go to Israel?"

"*Lamah dafkah anee.*"

"What?"

"Should they stop you at the security, tell the gentlemen, '*lamah dafkah anee.*' Maybe if they see you know Hebrew, they'll think you're Israeli and let you through.

Seemed like a long shot.

The rabbi repeated the Hebrew phrase. "Say it over and over. Yell it if you have to."

The security guard motioned me to get in line for the metal detector.

"I have to go. Wish me luck."

I hung up the phone before the rabbi could reply.

"May I see your ticket and passport, please?" the guard said.

I handed him the ticket and passport.

The guard looked at it and said, "Come with me, please."

I hoped this would work. "*Lamah dafkah anee! Lamah dafkah anee!*"

"Sir, please."

"*LAMAH DAFKAH ANEE! LAMAH DAFKAH ANEE! LAMAH DAFKAH ANEE!!!*"

"Sir! You keep raising your voice like that and I'll have you held here overnight."

I shut up.

* * *

Two guards took me to a room with windows visible to everyone passing through security. They had me sit at a table and put the contents of my pockets on the table. I placed my keys, spare meds, two pens, and my organizer—the one with my passport, extra money, calculator, and social security card—onto the table.

One of the guards picked up my meds.

"Depakote?" he read off the label.

"It makes me a better man," I said.

He opened the bottle, sniffed the contents. "I'll be right back."

The other guard picked up my passport.

He asked, "What is your name, sir?"

"It's on the friggin' passport."

"Please pronounce it for me."

"Nathan Yirmorshy."

"And your age?"

"Twelve."

He sighed. "Sir, the longer you delay in answering my questions, the longer you stay here and risk missing your flight."

I told him my age.

"Cut him loose." It was another guard, probably the supervisor or whatever they call the head guard in charge.

"How come?" my interrogator asked.

The supervisor pointed at the door behind him and in walked some small woman with a pony tail and a posture so charged, she seemed to be in control of the entire airport.

"Detective Graff." The woman introduced herself without shaking any hands. "Mr. Yirmorshy is working undercover and any delay you gentlemen present in his assignment is obstruction."

Nice.

My interrogator grunted, "You're free to go then." He returned my passport.

"Gentlemen," Graff said. "May I have a word in private with Mr. Yirmorshy?"

"He's all yours," the supervisor said.

When the guards left the room, Graff said, "You couldn't take luggage? Even a gym bag would've been helpful in reducing suspicion."

Chapter 65

"How did you find me?" I asked Detective
Graff. "No, wait. Let me guess. First flight to Israel. Not many choices."

"Bingo."

"Now correct me if I'm wrong," I said, "but it almost sounded like you were getting me out of lock up back there to let me catch my flight."

"You can guess what I think about this ill-planned adventure you're going on."

"And like I said on the phone, nothing you say will make me change my mind."

"I figured as much. So take this."

She handed me a small aerosol can. Had some sort of safety mechanism to prevent accidental discharge.

"Pepper spray?" I asked.

"No way I'd be able to lend you a gun."

The can was light and tiny.

"Go get him, Mr. Yirmorshy." She turned and left.

For some reason, that was the moment I started feeling nervous.

Chapter 66

On to the gate. But first, I needed to wake myself up with a good face-washing. I found a men's restroom a short distance away from the security gate. There was an "in" side to the door and an "out."

"Fight the power!" I said aloud and went in through the out direction. "Boy, am I tired."

I splashed my eyes with cold water. The sting felt good. Looking at my face in the mirror, I wondered if it was the last time I'd see it.

I went out to the airport's bar. There was a waitress with very nice hair.

"Heineken," I said sitting at a counter. I felt my eyes trying to close.

The waitress brought one and I said, "Some advice: It doesn't matter how big the world is, every little thing you do can change it. Also, you have very nice hair."

The waitress smiled politely.

"And don't ever let your name get encoded in the book of Genesis, cause people will just follow you all over the place trying to blow up Israel. And then you have to dig up dogs and it's all very messy."

"Are you sure you haven't had too much to drink?" the waitress asked.

"This is my first one," I protested. "Why do you ask?" And that's when I realized my head was resting on the bar.

"Oh." I lifted my head. "I'm just very tired. You know what it is? I'm just tired of being chased."

"So you're a virgin?" The waitress asked.

"What? No! I'm tired of being *chased*, not chaste!" I sighed. "Say, do you know what *lamah dafkah anee* means?"

"It's Hebrew," someone said behind me. A gruff man with his sleeves rolled up. "It means 'why me?' "

" 'Why me?' " I asked.

"Yes," the man said.

"So how come 'Why me' in English has two words and *'Lamah dafkah anee'* has three?"

"*Lamah,* is why and *anee* is me," the man said.

"And *dafkah?"*

"There's no English translation for it," he said. "I guess you could say it translates into 'out of all the possibilities it had to be.' " The man said.

"So really," I said, "It means 'Why out of all the possibilities it had to be me?' "

"Exactly."

I nodded and drank more from my Heineken.

* * *

After finishing my beer, I found a seat at gate forty-seven feeling like a zombie. That is, *I* felt like a zombie. Not the seat. I wanted to sleep but it seemed like I crossed a zone where sleep wouldn't take me. Either that or the seat *was* a zombie and, let's face it, no one can fall asleep on a zombie.

Some creature sat next to me. I looked over. It resembled an old woman. She had on a thick coat, a newspaper in her lap, and bulky luggage. This lady was different from the one at the security gate. I watched her adjust her belongings. Getting comfortable seemed to be a chore for her but she finally settled in, reading the front page. The front page had an article on a recent earthquake, another on the pope, and a third about the president's latest controversial decision about healthcare. The woman must have sensed me staring at her because she turned to me and asked, "What do you think of the pope?"

"Probably plays a mean game of chess," was all I could think of saying.

The lady continued as if she was used to not understanding people. Probably hard of hearing. "They say he was a clerk for the Nazis," she whispered. "I don't think he ever really hated anyone, I think he was just doing a job that had nothing to do with the killing and atrocities."

Realizing the lady couldn't hear what I said anyway, I replied, "I bet he could win the Olympic medal in synchronized swimming."

"But you know, they say the antichrist will be a pope. Others think the antichrist will be Jewish."

"Either way, he'll be wearing a yarmulke, right?"

"But I adored the last pope," the old lady said. "Did you know, he used to be an actor in Poland. Back then, some of his best friends were Jewish."

"My mom was from Poland," I offered. "She couldn't swim worth beans, though."

"When he went to Israel, he tried visiting his old Jewish friend from Poland. What was her name?... Genka! That's it! Genka Barr."

Genka Barr! It wasn't Gangsta Bar, it was Genka Barr! That was the woman at my grandmother's funeral. She and my grandmother had acted together.

I faced the old woman and said loudly, "Who was Genka Barr?!"

"That was Pope John Paul's Jewish friend from a small theater in Poland."

"His Jewish friend?"

"He had a lot of Jewish friends," she said.

I remembered the funeral. Mostly by the colors. Everything had a pine or oak tone. The coffin was a simple pine box. The Jewish tradition was to be buried that way, the idea being that we are all equal in death, and should be buried in a manner that reflects this equality. No special treatment.

And I remembered my mother. Specifically, her sadness and how I felt ignored because all of the attention was on my grandmother, not me. Many old people attended. People I had never met before, including

Genka Barr. What did Ms. Barr say at the funeral? She knew my grandmother from acting in the same theater. And that my grandmother was a special woman. What did that mean?

I remembered the wrinkles in Ms. Barr's face. As she spoke to me, I studied them like the rings of a tree. Did her words have something to do with the pope? Was my grandmother and John Paul together before John Paul became the pope? That filled in some of the blanks. My mother didn't have a father. If John Paul were her father, what did that make me?

The possibilities made my head churn. The photos found in McCourt's place followed my mother's life and traced my own, from childhood to the present. Was I being followed as the grandson of a Jewish woman and a Christian man who later became the Pope?

I wanted to sit down. I was already sitting down. It didn't matter what really happened in the past. What mattered was that those ten men, Luke McCourt and the others, must believe I'm the perfect candidate for being the antichrist.

The lady next to me said, "I don't think Pope John Paul ever did any synchronized swimming, though."

Chapter 67

❝ Now boarding flight 3327 to Paris with a connection to Israel."

Either that was God speaking, or my flight was being announced on the PA system.

I stood up and waited in line to board. Advertisements, boarding calls, and white courtesy telephone requests for certain passengers bathed me as I waited.

I sat in my seat behind some college girl wearing a blue sweater and her hair in a pony tail. I looked out the window as the plane pulled off the ground and began its flight toward Paris.

Thought about what the old lady said. How the pope, before he was the pope, was friends with Ms. Barr. And no doubt with my grandmother, also.

I lowered the window shade shut and rested my head on the pillow expecting blessed sleep to take over. A feeling of thankfulness washed over me as I thought about what Detective Graff had done to get me through. Now I was on my way with everything I needed. Passport, money....Dammit! That guard hadn't given me back my meds!

Chapter 68

I arrived at the Israeli airport and considered my options as I waited in line to go through the customs check. My watch read 5 a.m. The flight to Paris and on to Israel had been uneventful but full of dreams.

I needed to find Sophia. And in order to do that, I needed to find McCourt. What did I know about McCourt? He took a delivery plane to Israel. If I found that plane, I might be able to find McCourt.

I was called up next in the customs line. The lady at the desk had lines that striped her mouth as though she'd been tight-lipped all her life. I showed my passport and asked the lady, "Where do I pick up deliveries that were flown in?"

"Deliveries? What kind of deliveries?" She said it so fast and with a thick accent, I barely understood her words.

"Cupcakes." Stupid response.

"Cupcakes?" Her face brightened and the whole building seemed lighter. "Like cupcakes with frosting and sprinkles?"

"Yes," I said.

"My mother used to make them all the time. She was such a good em…baker?"

I smiled and nodded.

"You make cupcakes?"

"Uh…no, I just make sure they're delivered properly. Do you know where they might be delivered?"

"Do you have the shipment receipt? It should say there."

Damn. I patted my pockets and said, "Darn, I think I misplaced it somewhere."

"There are lots of places, but your best bet would be Tel Aviv."

"And how do I get to Tel Aviv."

She looked at me like I had a balloon growing out of my ear.

"But it is here!" she said. "You're in Tel Aviv now!"

"Oh! That was fast. Thank you."

I took back the passport and decided I had better get a taxi. I walked past the baggage claim to the exit, a long hall that seemingly led to emptiness. But there was bound to be a taxi out there. Even this late at night. And I would ask the driver to take me to the nearest delivery airport. Then I could ask around, find out what flights came in recently, see if anyone saw about twelve people, mostly men, leaving the place.

I got to a final door, opened it and the last hallway led into sunny outdoors. Throngs of people seemed to greet me. But they were actually seeking the other people leaving the baggage claim. Why was it sunny? Oh, yeah. Time change. It was a little after 3 p.m.

Okay. Taxi. Taxi. Taxi. I wondered what the Hebrew word was for taxi. Probably easier just to look around.

I pushed through the crowd toward the street. Scanning the street, I saw a limousine with a driver holding a sign. The sign said, "Nathan Yirmorshy."

Chapter 69

"I'm Nathan."

"Get in," the driver commanded. He held the door open for me. He was heavy and I wondered if this was the man who killed Sullivan.

I got in the back of the limo. It was stupid, but what other choice was there?

The driver closed the door, went around to the front, hopped in, and began driving out of the airport.

"Where are you taking me?" I asked.

The driver didn't respond.

"Where's Sophia?"

No response.

"Are you taking me to her? Just tell me that much."

No response.

I looked out the window. We were on a freeway somewhere in Tel Aviv. At least, I guessed we were still in Tel Aviv. Maybe Tel Aviv was a small place. Wasn't sure. Maybe we had passed through several cities already.

It was time to scare him. Time to show that I knew more than he realized.

"You're never going to get the generator, you know," I said.

"What generator?"

The man spoke!

"The motionless electromagnetic generator," I explained. "The M.E.G."

There was silence in the front, and then chuckling. "You have it all wrong, buddy. You're talking about project MEG, right?"

So that's what they called it. *Project* MEG. "Yeah."

"MEG isn't an acronym, it's an abbreviation."

I was confused.

"MEG stands for Megiddo, as in Mount Megiddo. That's where I'm taking you."

The MEG didn't have anything to do with the generator? I had to completely twist my take on things. "So there are no plans for a bomb?"

The driver laughed. "Project MEG is much bigger than any bomb."

"So what's at this Mount Mega…"

"Mount Megiddo. In Hebrew the word for mount is 'har.' We're going to Har Megiddo."

I couldn't grasp the significance.

"Also known as Armageddon," the driver said.

Crap.

Chapter 70

The limo's air conditioner was cold. I looked out the window and saw fields interspersed with farm lands with what looked like avocado fields, orange groves, and apple orchards. Perhaps the farmlands were really *kibbutzim,* co-ops where groups of religious people worked on the land in exchange for food and shelter.

So they wanted to start Armageddon, and I was to be their antichrist. Now the motives for their actions were beginning to make sense. Well, it was complete nonsense, but there was a logic to it all the same.

"Did you kill officer Sullivan?" I asked quietly.

No response.

I leaned forward, "How about I just tell you what I think is going on, and if I'm wrong just stop me."

No response.

"My grandmother works at a theater troupe in Wadowice, Poland. The same one that the man who would be Pope John Paul worked at. Maybe they're friendly with each other, who knows? Maybe they even slept together. After all, my grandmother soon had my mother after working in the theater. How am I doing so far?"

No response.

"So someone decides to figure out who the antichrist will be so that they can assist with the second coming of the messiah. They figure it must be either someone who's Jewish or one of the popes. But seeing the possibility of a child who was the daughter of a Jew AND a soon-to-be pope, well, that just had to mean something, right?"

No response.

"But it couldn't have been you guys figuring all this out, because you were all just kids back then. So it had to be someone older than you. Someone who could train you to prepare for Armageddon."

"Our parents."

"Of course! Your parents." I leaned back and reflected on that. "That's why Luke McCourt has such a biblical first name." I leaned toward the driver, again. "Tell me, do you have a biblical name, too? What is it, David? Paul? John?"

No response.

"Obadiah?"

Nothing.

"Okay, so your parents follow the child of a Jew and a Pope, but it's a woman. That's gotta be a bit of a setback, right? The antichrist is supposed to be a guy, right?"

No response.

278 | Ezra Barany

"Well, I'll bet you anything it's supposed to be a guy. Anyhow, your parents train you guys to be good little Bible soldiers and meanwhile keep tabs on my mother. And when she had a son, your parents must have been a-whoopin' and a-hollerin'. And that's the story of why you guys think I'm the most photogenic celebrity in the world."

No response.

"Yep. That's why I'm Mr. Popular with you guys. Tell me, do you think McCourt ever got off on watching me? Did he ever sit in that hole watching me in my bedroom and whack off thinking, 'Oh! He's the antichrist! Oh yeah! Oh yeah!' " I tapped on my thigh with quick slaps. "Oh yeah! Oh! Oh!"

No response. I leaned back in my seat and looked out the window.

Chapter 71

We went for miles through uninhabited flat land. No trees and no people. And the road got more and more dusty. The sun seemed fierce here. Hard to be sure with the air conditioning on so high.

"Here we are," the driver said.

I looked out at a hill. "That's Mount Megiddo?" I was expecting some mammoth mountain.

Mount Megiddo was about three trees high. It looked like it used to be an actual mountain but a giant elephant stomped it flat. Maybe Armageddon already happened there and we missed it.

We drove up a dirt road. At the top, I saw a few parked cars and a large shipping truck. We pulled up next to the truck.

A cloud of dust made by the car drizzled down to the ground.

Dust to dust.

"Nathan! So good of you to join us!" It was Mc-Court. His smile would have looked friendlier if his teeth were smashed in.

In the distance, beyond McCourt, I saw other people building something made of wood. And was that Sophia further out? It looked like her wrists and ankles were tied and she sat on the ground.

I ran to her. She was dressed in purple and red scarves and lots of jewelry.

"Are you okay?" I asked.

"It's horrible!" She cried. "It's horrible what they made."

There was something written in red on her forehead. The words were too small to read from where I was. I squatted to get closer. Her forehead read, "Mystery, mother of harlots and abominations of earth." Her eyes looked red from crying.

"What they made?"

"In the truck," Sophia cried.

"You see," McCourt said to all the others. They had stopped their hammering and approached us, "He makes it so easy for us. Like the prophecy."

McCourt was talking about me.

"We needed him here, and behold, he has come." McCourt and the others had smiles on their faces. "Tie him up, Perry."

I felt strong hands hold my wrists behind my back as ropes bound me.

Once I was immobile, McCourt called his group aside to talk. Left alone with Sophia, I asked her, "What did you mean? About what they made."

"It's in the truck. An animal." Sophia looked at the ground. "You shouldn't have come. But I'm glad you did." She released a small smile.

"I wanted to save you so here I am."

"My hero," Sophia smiled wider.

"So you're sure your okay?"

She looked down at herself. "With what I'm wearing, I should feel like a million bucks."

"They didn't hurt you?"

"No."

I looked around. Dirt as far as the eye could see.

Sophia asked, "Do you know what they're up to? Is the M.E.G. safe."

I told Sophia the whole story of how the M.E.G. was not what they were after, and how they have plans to start Armageddon.

As soon as I said Armageddon, Sophia jolted. "Oh no," she said. "That's why they made that...that beast."

We sat in silence as the sun beat down on our heads. Sweat tickled the side of my face. The ropes burned into my wrists and ankles. I wanted to break free, scratch my itching face, and rub my aching limbs. Luke's group of merry men went back to work on building what looked to be a small stage.

Sophia looked at her shoes and wiggled her feet as best as she could.

"Do you think we'll come out of this alive?" Sophia asked quietly.

I thought about saying it'll be okay. Thought about lying to Sophia, comforting her as best as I could. Knew it was just wrong and she would see right through my lies.

"I doubt it," I said.

Sophia nodded.

A brief twister of hot wind lifted dust in the air. It swirled and settled again.

"So what's your theory on twins who feel things at the same time?" Sophia asked.

"What?" I searched my memory for what Sophia was talking about. "Oh. It's uh…You sure you want to hear this now?"

"Yeah. Tell me."

A welcome breeze kicked up and became a steady gust.

"Alright." I realized what Sophia was really asking for. "The thing is this. According to the theory, two photons—two pieces of light—could come from the same atom, travel miles away from each other, and then when you spin one, the other immediately spins too. They're somehow entangled even though they're miles apart."

I looked at Sophia. She stared off at nothing in particular, lost in another world.

"I know what you're doing."

She looked up at me.

I said, "You want me distracted so I won't worry."

"Is it working?"

"Sure! Hell, I'm a danger to pedestrians when I'm on the road wondering if the gravitational constant is actually a product of c^2 and Plank length over Plank mass. And what can I say? 'Oh, sorry I hit that man, Officer, but I was thinking that gravity is actually a combination of mass-energy and space curvature.' "

Sophia said nothing.

"Uh…which makes electricity a combination of mass-energy and magnetic permeability, so…magnets curve space…" I shook off those thoughts. "All I'm saying is that you don't need to worry about me. I'm fine. What about you?"

"Okay," she said. "Try to distract me. What's the point of that light thing."

"What's the point? The point is if identical twins come from the same source, the same egg, then maybe their thoughts and feelings—the electrical signals in the brain, which are forms of light—are shared by each sibling."

Sophia nodded, "And that's why I can sense my sister."

"It's not impossible. Energy never dies. The thoughts and feelings someone has had lives forever. Just as some of those stars above us may have died long ago? Their light continues to shine."

Sophia gave me a smile. She looked at her feet again and returned to her faraway place.

* * *

I looked at McCourt and the others. They were still at it, probably talking about who gets to keep the naked photos of me after their messiah returns. The one called Perry wiped his brow with a handkerchief. Ah, what I wouldn't give for a good brow-wiping right now.

"Do you have any regrets?" Sophia asked.

"Regrets?" I immediately thought of my wife, Nancy.

"What?" Sophia asked.

"I was just thinking about something the rabbi said," I lied.

"What did he say?"

I told her of the code in the Book of Esther, and the shrunken letters representing the present date.

Sophia said, "Nathan, as interesting as that is, that wasn't what you were thinking about when I asked if you had any regrets."

How did she do that?

I sighed and looked up at the clear sky. "I know I'm not a bad guy." I turned to Sophia. "I know that. I haven't killed anyone. I haven't robbed anyone. I haven't…" I turned back to my feet. The ropes on my ankles seemed to be burning deeper into my skin.

"There was a time just after I got married that I stopped taking my meds. I thought it would release the stress I had from work. Instead, it just got me paranoid on top of the stress." I thought back on how Nancy left for work with the face of worry growing deeper each day.

"But then, as I tried to sort it all out, a strange thing happened. I don't know what triggered it, but I suddenly went from feeling pathetic to apathetic. I no longer cared about anything anymore. It was a freeing feeling."

Sophia said nothing.

"I realized that if I stayed at home, slept in, I wouldn't feel guilty. I wasn't feeling anything, so all my fears of consequences didn't matter. All the stress in my life suddenly vanished."

Sophia said nothing.

"I realized I could even kill. And I knew the police would capture me, imprison me, and execute me, and I didn't care. I didn't care at all. I felt so free."

"So what helped stop you from committing a crime?" Sophia asked.

"The knowing," I said. "I knew the apathy wouldn't last and that later I would feel all the guilt that comes with doing bad things."

Sophia said nothing.

I hoped that was the end of it. Hoped I could get away without talking about the rest of it. But Sophia persisted.

"And?" She asked.

I sighed.

"I'm not a friendly guy," I said. "And when I get my paranoid delusions, I'm the life of the party, but not in a good way."

I thought about the way I had accused Nancy of talking about me behind my back, laughing at me, plotting against me, purposefully making my life a living hell. And it had been all in my head.

Sophia remained quiet.

"I want to go back. Back to the apathy. Back to not caring about what happens. Because when I upset people, make them angry and cry, I don't want to be bothered by it." I took a deep breath and said it. "I don't want to feel the regret."

Sophia said nothing.

"So I'm always trying. Trying to get back into that space of apathy. An impossible task, I know. But there it is."

I waited for Sophia's axe of judgment to fall. But what she said surprised me.

"There are other ways of avoiding feeling regret, you know," Sophia said. "Consider who you are. You had all those thoughts of killing and stealing because you didn't care about the consequences, and yet you didn't follow through with them. You didn't do it because deep down you're a decent person."

I didn't believe her. But what did it say about me that I chose not to believe her?

"So it bothers you that you make some people angry or sad? Who doesn't do that? I'm not exactly Miss Congenial, myself. You are who you are. And I love who you are. The question is, are *you* happy with who you are?"

I felt dizzy. Wasn't sure if it was a profound realization, or if it was from being off my meds for so long. But the rolling in my head, like feeling the effects of bungee jumping, made Sophia's words connect with me. She believed in me. Why didn't I?

Did she just say she loved me?

Chapter 72

The sun was dying. The sky bleeding. Cold air came with a relentless bite and I heard Sophia's teeth chatter.

In the past hour, Sophia had been quiet and I had settled into my own thoughts. I couldn't believe how much power was in those two little words, "any regrets?" The only other time Sophia had asked that question was after having sex.

Regrets? None being with her. Truth was I loved her. She believed in me. Made me feel like a good person. But I did have regrets.

I pictured my own funeral. What would the eulogy be like? More so, who would give it? The only person I talked to regularly was the man in the roach coach when I bought lunch from him. "Nathan Yirmorshy was a good man. I think. Not really sure. Never really talked to the guy much. But he liked his tuna sandwich with extra mayo."

How depressing. So what did I want the eulogy to be like? I suppose the real question is, how do I want to be remembered?

The large, wobbly man called Perry stayed nearby watching us, as the others moved to the truck. Probably making preparations.

Sophia and I were still able to speak without anyone overhearing.

"Do you know anything about Armageddon?" I asked her.

"I know a few things."

"Tell me."

"Why?"

I looked at Perry. "If I know what they're expecting, maybe I can use it to get us out of here."

Sophia thought a moment, then said, "Armageddon takes place between Jesus and the antichrist. It's a final battle."

"What else?"

"There's something about ten horns or trumpets? I can't remember."

"That's okay. So if I'm the antichrist, and Jesus doesn't show up, isn't there a chance they'll give up and let us go?"

"I don't know. Maybe."

I sighed, wishing I had a gun. But then I remembered Sullivan. *Bullets don't make guys run, fear does.* I closed my eyes and focused on a surge of force, power, fierceness entering my throat.

I opened my eyes and looked directly at the man guarding us. "Perry!"

Perry jumped, startled by my commanding voice.

"There is one among you who is my apprentice.

Your savior will not come. Not while a sinner as great as my apprentice is among you."

"What are you talking about?" Perry looked frightened. He probably never expected to talk to Mr. Antichrist directly.

"And know this. When your savior does not come, and the day is full again, your lives will know my curse from this day on, as will your children, and your children's children."

Perry turned his back on us, probably wondering when Luke and the others were going to return. It was a good start, but I needed to prove my paranormal powers if I wanted to really frighten him.

"Hey," I whispered to Sophia. "I'm a member of the Rubber Band!"

"What?" She asked.

"Perry!" I called out. "Do you really think these bindings can stop me? I could pinch you all the way from here."

Perry looked at me, then back toward Luke who stood several yards away.

I pulled the rubber band off my wrist, held one loop end with my pinky, and with my hand in the shape of a gun, wrapped the rest around the base of my thumb to the tip of my pointer finger.

I let the rubber band go and whispered, "Pow."

The rubber band flung at Perry's ear, hitting it with a good snap.

Perry swung around at us clutching his ear.

"Don't turn your back on me when I'm talking to you!" I said.

"How did you—?" He stepped backwards and tripped landing on his butt. He continued to move away from us, shuffling on all fours, then got back up and ran to the others.

"Nice one!" Sophia said. "I almost believed you."

"Yeah?"

"Yeah. You make quite a convincing antichrist. Your mom would've been proud."

"Thanks. We'll see whether what I said will help us or hurt us."

I looked where the others were. Smelled lighter fluid. McCourt seemed to be getting upset with Perry, yelling at him. But I couldn't make out the words. No doubt McCourt knew I wasn't serious, but at least the idea was planted in their minds. Would it help or hinder us, was the question.

Chapter 73

Our eleven captors came toward us. They each had in their hands a *shofar*, a ram's horn used in traditional Jewish holidays as a kind of trumpet. The shofars were also used in ancient times for calls to battle.

They dragged behind them a cage the size of a refrigerator turned on its side. Whatever was inside the cage made noises that sounded like a screaming child. I grit my teeth.

When the cage reached their handmade wooden structure, McCourt said, "Perry, Matthew, take it out of its cage and set it on the platform."

The two men opened the cage and carried the screaming animal out. I couldn't believe what I was seeing. This creature, this beast, had five heads. Heads of a goat. And the body looked like three bodies sewn together. The creature screamed endlessly now. Three goats sewn together. But with five heads.

And ten horns.

"Now untie them," McCourt said, looking at us.

"Sir?"

"From this point on, we cannot intervene in the prophecy." He pointed his gun at me. "We can only persuade."

Perry untied Sophia, leaving Matthew to untie me. Perry probably didn't have the desire to get near the antichrist, much less touch him. We were brought to the platform.

"Take this," McCourt demanded. He held out an ancient-looking cup to Sophia. Sophia accepted it.

"What's in it?" I asked.

"Don't know," she said. "Something white."

"Get on the beast," McCourt told Sophia.

Sophia seemed like she was actually considering it.

"Don't do it, Sophia." I said.

Sophia looked at the gun pointed at me.

"Don't do it," I said again. "That'll just bring them closer to their goal and bring us closer to our death."

Sophia alternated the cup from one hand to the other to rub her wrists and said, "I'm sorry, Nathan." She went to the creature. "It's like you said. The sooner they see their plans don't work, the sooner they'll let us go."

McCourt smiled. I didn't know what to say. Sophia gently squatted over the shrieking creature, careful not to hurt it. McCourt instructed the others to make a circle around the platform and with his gun pointed at me, kept me by his side.

"One of the seven angels who had the seven bowls came and spoke with me," McCourt recited, "saying,

'Come here. I will show you the judgment of the great prostitute who sits on many waters, with whom the kings of the earth committed sexual immorality, and those who dwell in the earth were made drunken with the wine of her sexual immorality."

I told myself to play it cool. If I showed signs of worry, they would think they were doing the right thing.

"He carried me away," McCourt continued, "in the Spirit into a wilderness. I saw a woman sitting on a scarlet-colored animal,"

"You know, your Barney isn't scarlet-colored," I said, "And Sophia isn't a prostitute."

"Full of blasphemous names," McCourt said louder. "Having seven heads and ten horns."

"Well, I count five heads, but you got the horns right. I'll give you that much," I said. My gut twisted inside. *Keep cool.*

"The woman was dressed in purple and scarlet," McCourt sounded angry now. "And decked with gold and precious stones and pearls, having in her hand a golden cup full of abominations and the impurities of the sexual immorality of the earth. And on her fore-head a name was written, 'Mystery, Babylon the great, the mother of the prostitutes and of the abominations of the Earth.' "

"Is that what it says? I thought it said 'mother of the prostates and of the abdominations,' " I said. "I think I need glasses is what it is."

McCourt grabbed my wrist with his free hand and put the gun in my mouth.

"I saw the woman drunken with the blood of the saints," McCourt said with a firm whisper, "and with the blood of the martyrs of Jesus. When I saw her, I wondered with great amazement. The angel said to me, 'Why do you wonder? I will tell you the mystery of the woman, and of the beast that carries her, which has the seven heads and the ten horns."

I was pretty sure that McCourt wasn't going to shoot, but when your mouth is full of gun, you tend not to take any chances.

"The beast that you saw was, and is not; and is about to come up out of the abyss and go into destruction. Those who dwell on the earth and whose names have not been written in the book of life from the foundation of the world will marvel when they see that the beast was, and is not, and shall be present. Here is the mind that has wisdom."

What was McCourt talking about? I knew it came from the New Testament, but couldn't make heads or tails out of it. Something inside clicked. I don't know where the courage came from. I should have been frightened. With a gun in my mouth, I should have been beyond frightened. But I realized I had to do something.

I moved away from McCourt, jerking the gun out of my mouth and said, "It is as I said! One of you is my apprentice and has sided with me. Your very presence makes this entire ritual meaningless."

McCourt punched the gun into my gut and said, "If it were true, if one of us sided with you and with the beast, then yes. This ritual would be meaningless. But you are wrong, Nathan. It is not *one* of us who sides with you."

I didn't understand until McCourt continued reciting. "The ten horns that you saw are ten kings who have received no kingdom as yet, but they receive the authority as kings, with the beast…for one hour."

I watched my plan backfire as not one, but ten men sided with Sophia. The ten men took turns bowing to the beast.

"These have one mind," McCourt said. "and they give their power and authority to the beast. These will war against the Lamb."

I guessed the "Lamb" was Jesus.

"And the Lamb will overcome them, for he is the Lord of lords, and King of kings."

As I listened, I realized these ten men probably thought they were doing the ultimate sacrifice: becoming the followers of the antichrist to call back Jesus and let Jesus kill them.

"The ten horns which you saw, and the beast, these will hate the prostitute," McCourt said.

One by one, the men spat on Sophia, and they took turns ripping off her purple and red scarves.

Sophia cried out and dropped the cup. The scarves drifted to the ground and she was completely uncovered. I burned with anger, wanting to run to her, but McCourt kept the gun at my chest.

"And will make her desolate, and will make her naked." McCourt was rapt, all of his focus on me.

Sophia covered herself with her hands as best as she could. And before I knew it, Matthew set fire to the edge of the platform. A ring of flames encircled the platform and surrounded the beast and Sophia.

"NOOO!" I cried out. Sophia jumped off the beast and traveled the platform's edge, trying to find a way out of the fire. She kept her body covered with her hands and I could hear her whimper.

"And will burn her utterly with fire. For God has put in their hearts to do what he has in mind, and to be of one mind, and to give their kingdom to the beast, until the words of God should be accomplished."

McCourt backed up into the circle of men, and the men raised their shofars and sounded them together in a cacophony of sound. This was my best chance. I ran toward the fire.

A loud pop sounded and my leg suddenly stopped working. I fell to the ground. When I saw McCourt's gun raised, I realized I'd just been shot in the leg.

I screamed with anger and pain. I took off my shirt and tried to rip off the sleeve. Needed to stop the bleeding. A sudden flare of fire heated my face. Looking up, I saw that the beast had caught fire, pushing closer the time that Sophia was going to burn alive. *Dammit!* I gritted my teeth and tried ripping the sleeve again. It tore off.

The men watched silently as I bandaged my leg. The only sound came from my moans of pain, and from

298 | Ezra Barany

Sophia's cries, and from the fire that crackled closer to Sophia.

"Where is your God now?" I screamed. "I'll tell you where! He's not coming." The pain hurt so much. "You said you were all with the beast for one hour. But it's as I said all along. One of you has been my apprentice this whole time. Not for just one hour." I expected McCourt to counter me but McCourt said nothing. "Your ritual has accomplished nothing! Let us go!"

McCourt slowly stepped toward me, and suddenly turned to the others. "Is this true?" he shouted. "Is there one of you who has cooperated with the anti-christ?" No one said anything. McCourt went up to Matthew. "Is it true?!"

"It's true," a voice said. It was the woman. "I have fallen. I have fallen for him and I know what I must do."

She stepped in the middle of the circle. Walked to me, caressed my face, and kissed my lips. "We finally meet face to face," she whispered.

She stood and went toward the fire. "He is right," she shouted. "The beast must be scarlet." She removed a knife from her skirt and stood beside the flames. She then sliced her palm, ran into the fire, and collapsed upon the creature, her hand flat on its back.

"Melinda!" one of the men cried out.

The flames popped and Sophia screamed, standing between the burning bodies and the edge of the fire ring.

While the man who cried out Melinda's name sat on the ground crying, none of the others said anything.

* * *

McCourt felt a surge within him. It was a surge of a new awareness, an epiphany. He felt overcome by the meaning of it all. Of course. He had expected Jesus to come from the heavens. But Jesus was just the body that God's spirit inhabited. God is not any one person, God is whomever He chooses to be. Or inhabit.

And McCourt felt His presence. It was stronger than ever before. And McCourt knew that he was the one destined to carry out the prophecy.

"Behold! I am here! Come to fulfill the prophecy!" McCourt picked up the knife Melinda dropped and began his attack.

Chapter 74

Isaw McCourt charge at me with a knife as I lay on the ground. It was over. Done. Endgame. McCourt kicked up dust. I turned to see if Sophia was watching, to make sure that the last thing Sophia sees wasn't the image of me being slaughtered.

Sophia's eyes had gone to the back of her head. She stood rigid. Her body was experiencing another seizure. That was good. She wouldn't witness my death. Hopefully, she wouldn't feel her own death, either.

McCourt jumped upon me. I raised my arms to stop him. Was I supposed to see my life flashing before my eyes?

His body felt heavy on top of me. He held the knife high. Before the knife cut into me, his head jerked back.

McCourt dropped the knife and clutched at his neck. His whole body seemed to be lifted until his toes just barely touched the ground.

I looked around and all the men were grasping their throats floating just above the ground, gasping, and trying hard to touch the ground with their toes to ease their breathing.

"Sophia!" I called out. But I knew she couldn't hear me. Still, I found myself whispering, "Are you doing this?"

Above the din of the crackling fire, Sophia said, "I am *Shekinah*."

Shekinah! The female aspect of God the rabbi mentioned? I looked at Sophia. Her hair caught on fire but didn't burn. She looked as though the fire was her hair.

"What does that mean? Who are you?" I asked.

"Before people, God was alone. Needing to be perfect, loving, caring, merciful. God could not be all those without humankind. He needed someone to give His love, to care for, to show mercy. So God split himself into the two aspects, the male and the female. The female presence breathed life into the stardust and now all people on earth carry the *Shekinah* within themselves. This is the loving bond between God and humanity. All of humanity is the bride of God."

"Why do you speak through Sophia?"

"We are the *Shekinah* of Sophia and Jessica, her twin sister. Together, I am two lives in one. Stronger within her than with others."

"But these men? Is this how you show your loving bond with humanity?"

"All their lives they wished to fulfill a prophecy. It is being fulfilled."

The hanging of ten men.

"Ten hang, but nine will die," *Shekinah* said.

"Why?"

"There is one among them. He is still needed in this world."

Suddenly, nine of the men were raised high off the ground. I could hear the snapping of their necks. And they stayed up there. They hung there like silent wind chimes. The last fell to the ground, the one called Perry. He shuffled to his feet and ran to the cars.

Sophia—*Shekinah*—did nothing to stop him.

As I heard Perry start one of the cars and drive away, I said, "What about Sophia? What are you going to do to her?"

"She carries the weight of more than two souls. It is out of my control."

Now I was getting angry.

"What's with the cryptic crap?! Aren't you God or a Goddess or something?" Damn, my leg was throbbing with pain. "Can't you do anything? Like, oh, I don't know, heal my frickin' leg?! How can something be out of your control?"

Sophia smiled. Or the *Shekinah* smiled. Someone was smiling and it was at my expense.

Finally she said, "Ask me that which is your true question."

I stared at my Sophia. Standing on the platform and burning bright but without injury. The flames kissed her body but her skin stayed unharmed. She looked as though she'd be okay.

"What about me?"

"You still have a choice. Your journey has presented you with a way to save lives or destroy them."

I said nothing.

"You can help yourself by helping others."

"Where do I start?"

The *Shekinah* walked off the platform toward me.

"Start with the one who loves you most."

The fire dropped to nothing and Sophia, as well as the nine men, collapsed to the earth.

Chapter 75

The cold air of the night bathed us now that the fire was gone. Sophia was unconscious but breathing. Sitting on the ground holding her in my arms, I noticed her hair and skin were unscathed. The words on her forehead were now smears of red from the sweat.

"Hold on," I whispered.

After placing her on the ground, I dragged my sorry ass across the dust. Searched the limo driver's pockets and found a clump of keys. The keys were heavy in my hands. I pocketed them and decided to pull off the man's coat. More difficult than expected. Each slight movement of my leg was searing pain. I found myself rolling around with the guy, feeling like a pig in dirt. At last, the coat came free, and I collapsed onto my back out of breath, and to still the pain. The stars watched over me. I felt empowered to keep working.

I crawled back to Sophia. Manipulated her body to get the coat on her. She was easier to move than the limo driver. Soon, Sophia had a large coat covering her torso. I sat behind her as though we were riding a sled, latched my arms under hers, and dragged her backwards with me toward the cars. I pushed to the cars with my good leg and felt the sting of the bullet wound burn in my other. The task was daunting considering the distance of the cars, but I took it in stride, keeping a pace. Five drags across with five yelps of pain, and a break to catch my breath. Then another five drags, then another.

I made it to the nearest car, a Honda. I knew that the car key would stand out, a big key, but many of the limo driver's keys were large car keys. I tried one after the other. Aargh! I tried them all a second time. No good. None worked.

Not sure why I thought the limo driver would have the keys to all the cars. Just seemed to make sense judging by how many car keys he had on his keychain. No point in doing this with each car, though. It would wipe me out.

I latched back onto Sophia, dragging her to the limousine. Once I got us both there, I tried the keys. The fourth key worked on the front passenger door, and I hoisted Sophia onto the seat. Slammed the door shut and crawled to the other side. Getting myself into the driver's seat hurt, but once I was inside, I felt more in control. I buckled Sophia in the seat, and started the engine. The car drove well, but its giant size was something I wasn't used to.

No G.P.S. in the car. I wasn't sure exactly where everything was, but I knew roughly where the big cities were. Once I got the car down Mount Megiddo I turned left and drove on the main road into what I hoped was the correct direction.

The brown hills and the trees. I felt isolated. There was no immediate signs of civilization. The further I drove, the more I had a bad feeling that I was going the wrong way. None of my surroundings looked familiar.

I took a risk and kept going. Didn't want to turn around. I reached out to hold Sophia's wrist. It was warm, and I felt a pulse. Good.

Green fields and groves passed my window. I drove for several miles before finally seeing signs of well-populated areas. The sun was rising and the reflecting stones of Israel began to shine. There were signs in English, Hebrew, and Arabic pointing to several places, the nearest city was called Haifa. That was a big city, wasn't it? I followed the road to Haifa. The road got smoother, and promised help. The road got wider, lined with homes, then buildings. I saw an old man carrying two enormous bags on his back. The bags looked heavy.

I pulled over and said, "Excuse me. Do you speak English?"

The man replied with a British accent. "I try."

"Where is the nearest hospital?"

The British guy gave me directions. He kept glancing at Sophia as he pointed out the roads to take. "Is she alright?" he asked.

"She'll be fine." I thanked him and went on my way. In five minutes I saw the hospital and followed an ambulance to where it parked a few feet beyond two large double doors. I drove straight onto the sidewalk nearly hitting the doors. The doors were automatic and, upon detecting the proximity of the limousine, opened wide. Several angry looking people rushed to the car. I opened my door and collapsed to the ground saying, "She had a seizure and I've been shot in the leg." I felt hands lifting me. Sounds of people calling out things in Hebrew passed over head. And sleep took me over.

Chapter 76

I saw Sophia's eyes flutter. When she opened them, I smiled from the chair I sat in and said, "Good afternoon."

Sophia looked around, noticing she was in a hotel room in bed without any clothes on. She sat up, pulled at the sheet from under its brown comforter, and held the sheet closer to her. "What happened?"

"You don't remember?" I asked smiling. "And you were so good, too!"

Sophia smirked, "Okay, okay. What really happened?"

"You're not going to believe it," I warned. "Here. Drink this." I stood on crutches, went to a table by the sunlit windows, and carefully handed her a cup of green tea. The crutches dug into my armpits.

Sophia drank the tea as I sat on her bedside recounting the entire previous evening. I told her about how McCourt suspected one of his group conspiring with me and how Melinda confessed to it, killing herself as a sacrifice. I told Sophia how I got shot in the leg. How she had another seizure and claimed to be *Shekinah*. I told her all that the *Shekinah* said, and how the ten men were hung by invisible ropes but one was let go. I mentioned the rabbi discovering "and they will hang" nine times both backwards and forwards in chapter thirty-six, and how it seemed to relate to the nine men dying.

I told her how I got her to the hospital as the sun was rising.

"And what happened at the hospital?" Sophia asked.

"I fell asleep through most of it, but when I woke up, they told me, 'Mr. Yirmorshy, the bullet just grazed your leg.' You know, I really like that phrase, 'grazed your leg.' It sounds like a deer gently nibbling me. But I'll tell you right now, I don't care if that bullet didn't actually get lodged inside me. That bullet did not 'graze' my leg. It chomped down on my leg with a growl, and chewed and chewed 'til it damn well ripped part of my leg off!"

Sophia laughed.

"That's what it felt like, anyway. But all they had to do was clean the wound and bandage it. And then when I asked about you—"

"You asked about me?" Sophia asked fluttering her eyes wearing a smile.

"Yes," I said.

"Aw, that's so sweet," Sophia tilted her head to the side.

"Yeah, I'm a real lollipop."

Sophia laughed again.

"Anyhow, they said you were fine, just in a deep sleep. But they asked me what happened."

"What'd you tell them?"

"I said we were in a hotel, I was about to clean my gun while you were taking a bath and had a seizure. In my haste to save you, the gun fell and even though I had removed the magazine, there was still a bullet in the chamber so the gun shot me in the leg."

"Nice." Sophia nodded. "Didn't they report it to the police?"

"I had to write a statement. That was it."

She looked surprised.

"Okay, so I had to convince them you didn't shoot me. It wasn't hard. Believe me. They got a lot more to worry about than a self-inflicted gunshot wound 'grazing' a leg."

"And how'd we get here?"

"Taxi," I said. "Say, did you know the word for taxi in Hebrew is 'taxi'?"

"No," Sophia smiled, "I didn't know that."

"It ought to be in Ripley's Believe it or Not!"

I scratched the itch caused by the bandage on my leg.

"I suppose the taxi driver didn't mind driving a naked lady," Sophia said.

"Ah!" I held up a finger and hobbled over to the table. Balancing on one foot, I held in front of me a blue, paper hospital gown. "I bring you one of our finest fashion designs, can be used as casual wear, evening wear, or even around the house." I moved best as I could as if to model the gown. "Be the envy of your friends as you fit in at any environment. Worried about spills and stains? No problem! This gown is disposable. Simply throw it away and no more stains to worry about!"

Sophia was laughing so hard, the bed sheets draped around her waist, leaving her chest bare.

"And as an extra bonus," I turned the gown around showing a slit in the gown that went all the way up to the back, "it is now much more convenient to moon your friends, family, or neighborhood antichrist."

Sophia laughed and wiped her tears away. She sat back and sighed. That smile of hers filled with crooked teeth was amazing. I felt it hit me in the heart. Now I truly understood the power and beauty of asymmetry.

I hopped over to the table, feeling a stinging reminder in my wounded leg. I put the blue gown back on the table and retrieved my crutches.

Sophia was no longer smiling. She looked like she was reflecting inward. "I remember most of last night. I remember how awful it was being dressed in strange scarves, Melinda writing those words on my forehead, and even the men spitting on me and tearing the scarves off. But you know what was the hardest part for me?"

I shook my head.

"Making that stupid decision of whether or not I should sit on that creature. Isn't that crazy?"

"Not very."

Sophia looked at me.

"You're always using the tarot deck to help you make decisions. I noticed your fingers twitching when you were deciding to sit on that creature. It was as though you were trying to find your tarot deck but they were missing from your hands."

Sophia nodded. She dwelled on that for a moment. I glanced around the room. It had a rustic theme going on. I looked at the hardwood floor, the brown drapes, TV, and minibar. Not counting the pain in my leg and aching armpits, I could spend the rest of my life here being quite comfortable.

Out the window, the view was breathtaking. Our hotel was on the side of a mountain, looking down onto a flat part of Haifa next to the Mediterranean Sea.

"Do you think?" Sophia paused a moment as if she was about to ask a delicate question. "Are you sure you weren't delirious when my seizure happened."

"All I can tell you is what I saw," I said. "What really happened?" I shrugged. Thought about the evidence. I got shot. I've got a whole hospital full of witnesses on that. Sophia got naked. The hospital and some British fella on the road could pretty much testify to that. Were there dead bodies on Mount Megiddo? The newspapers would soon mention it if there were.

I hobbled to Sophia's bed, set down my crutches and lay next to her on top of the covers. With my hands behind my head, I stared at the ceiling and thought about the *Shekinah's* words. *You can help yourself by helping others.*

Sophia extended her hand to me like she was hold-ing something. "Imaginary penny for your thoughts."

"I'm wondering what the *Shekinah* or you or what-ever voice it was in my head meant by saving the lives of others."

"Well, there are lots of ways to do that, right? Vol-unteer to help the homeless, donate blood, help cancer research by donating time or money. There's a lot you can do."

"She said my journey has shown me how to do it."

And then I realized what it was.

Captain Kor woke up. The alarm clock sounded odd. He hit the snooze button, but the alarm kept going. He realized it wasn't the alarm clock that was ringing, but the phone next to his alarm clock.

What time was it? He checked the clock. Who could be calling at 1:30 a.m.? He picked up the receiver.

Before he could put it to his ear, his wife asked, "What time is it?"

"It's too early," Kor said. "Go back to sleep."

He put the receiver to his ear and said, "Hello?"

"Hi, Kor? It's Nathan Yirmorshy."

Who the hell was Nathan Yirmorshy? Oh! Right! The rich fella. "Is something wrong?"

Nathan said, "Why do you ask?" Nathan's voice on the line sounded muffled by static. And Kor sensed a bit of hesitation.

"Not many people call so early in the morning," Kor said.

"Oh! I'm sorry! What time is it there?"

"Here?" Kor said. "Where are you?"

"Israel," Nathan said. "I forgot about the time difference."

"What are you doing in Israel?"

"You wouldn't believe me if I told you. Should I call back later?"

"No, of course not. What's on your mind?"

"I'd like to help with getting the M.E.G. out there, mass producing the thing. What do you think?"

Kor was surprised to hear those words. *It worked!* "Nathan, when you come back from Israel, call me up and we'll meet in Emeryville."

"Why? What's in Emeryville?"

"I have a confession to make," Kor said.

Chapter 77

Katherine Perry, the wife of Emmanuel
Perry, ironed the last of her husband's shirts and
placed it among the others. She looked at the pile and
felt the worry return, so she dug for the first shirt and
started to iron it again. She knew he wasn't coming
back. She could hear it in his voice, in his words, and
yet his voice had been so positive.

"If everything goes okay, we'll be together again and
in the happiest of all places," he had said.

She hated the sound of that.

Katherine flipped the shirt over and began ironing
the cuffs. She knew where he was talking about. She
hoped she was wrong but deep in her heart, she knew.
And for them to meet there? They would both have to
be dead.

The front door opened. Katherine rushed to the
door and saw the best gift God had given her.

"Manny!" she cried as she rushed into his arms.
"Thank goodness you're alright." She looked up at
him and saw the sadness in his eyes. "It didn't go as

planned?" she asked.

"No," was all he managed to say.

"Come. Sit down." Katherine took off his coat and led him to the couch in the piano room. "I'll get you some tea."

She moved to the kitchen, half-worried that he wasn't going to be there when she returned. But it was a silly worry and she knew it. She put on the kettle and worked at getting a teabag ready. Piano music began playing from the living room. He was playing Chopin's "Storm." He always played that piece when he was in a bad mood, which wasn't very often.

Katherine knew it helped him to bang out the chords and let his fists fly against the keys with the rage that the piece expressed. She turned off the kettle before it could screech. It was time to let Manny release his pain. Katherine waited and listened for the piece to play out until the end.

But there was an interruption in the music. The music stopped. Katherine listened very carefully. What was that sound? Was he crying?

Katherine picked up the envelope that was addressed to both of them. She took it to the living room.

Manny quickly dried his eyes as Katherine said, "Manny, dear, look who sent us a photo."

He took the card in his plump hands and removed it from the envelope while looking at the return address. "It's from Harold?" he asked in a broken voice.

"Yes," she said sitting next to him.

"I remember when he was still trying to play that

children's Russian dance piece on the piano. Do you remember that?" He asked with a smile on his face.

"I remember."

Manny read the card and said, "The Horowitz prize for best performance?"

"He won, Manny." She put her arms around his shoulders and squeezed them. "He won first place."

Manny smiled.

"See the good you do?" she asked.

Manny looked at her as if she said something more important than she realized. He held her and wept in her arms.

Chapter 78

Two days after our ordeal in Israel, I was back in the San Francisco Bay Area. I had called Kor earlier and he told me where we should meet. I had to cross railroad tracks and pot-hole stricken roads to get to the isolated address in Emeryville. The place was a warehouse made of metal and concrete.

Kor and his wife were already waiting at the entrance. His wife had one hand on the back of his wheelchair. I approached them and Kor extended his hand, "Good to see you again," he said.

"Likewise," I said.

"As I said before, I never played much of a role in the actual invention of the M.E.G., but I do play a role in getting the information about it out there. You might say I'm the advertiser promoting it."

"I don't understand. The prototype was supposed to be guarded like a well-kept secret, right?"

"One of my hair-brained schemes, I'm afraid. You see, I'm using several methods of promoting the M.E.G.

I have a website, I speak with prospective investors, and I also added some drama to the whole thing."

"Drama?"

"Come inside and you'll see what I mean."

Mrs. Kor wheeled him to the door and I followed. Kor unlocked the door and opened it. Inside, the whole place was one big room.

And I saw box after box piled one on top of another. There must have been hundreds, no, thousands of boxes. Each one advertising its contents: "Motionless Electromagnetic Generator."

"We've just started the mass production stage," Kor said.

I stared at all the boxes of M.E.G.s. What was special about the prototype?

"The prototype," I said.

"It's in a glass case at the home of one of the inventors."

"And the one in the locker?"

"Put there by the Berkeley High School physics teacher. You met her. She gave you the second envelope," Kor said.

I remembered the young woman, "She was a physics teacher?" I asked.

"My friend's daughter, as a matter of fact," Kor said.

"Mr. Priore's daughter."

"Afraid not. Antoine Priore is just a personal hero of mine. Like I said. I added some drama."

"So her real father?"

"Lives in Pittsburg and is doing quite well."

I shook my head. It didn't make sense. "Why all the intrigue? The envelopes? Hiding the so-called prototype in a locker?"

"It was a gimmick I was trying out," Kor said apologetically. "I hoped that anyone who had great experience with handling financial matters might become interested in backing the M.E.G. if it somehow became a part of their life."

I felt anger rising within me. I was used. But at the same time, it didn't change the amazing significance of the M.E.G. I took a deep breath and let it go.

It took more than one deep breath.

They were patient with me, and waited for my next words.

"I'd like to buy them all from you."

"All of them?!" Kor looked stunned.

"And more, when you make them."

"What are you going to use them for, if you don't mind my asking?"

"I'm gonna save the world," I said.

I returned to my car and began my trip back to Berkeley. Kor and his wife had been pleased when I explained how their M.E.G.s would be put to use. We worked out the details in completing the purchase and delivery.

There was one last thing to do.

Chapter 79

Sophia lay on her comfortable bed in her Berkeley apartment. She reflected on all that happened to her and felt something missing from the apartment. Her thin arm flopped beside her. Nothing was there. And that's what was missing. She missed Nathan. She loved him.

But did he love her? Her gut said he did. But there was that time when she asked if he had any regrets over their lovemaking, and he seemed to blow it off. What did he mean by ignoring the question? Maybe he was just freaked out for some reason. Sophia noticed that it was always easier to tell if a guy loved her when she wasn't interested. For some reason, whenever she actually loved the guy, figuring out how the guy felt became the hardest mystery to solve.

But Nathan loved her. She was almost sure of it. So the next question was, what should she do about it? Sophia grabbed the Crowley tarot deck and it felt heavy and plastic and superficial. Then she put the deck back down. She didn't need the deck to make decisions anymore.

There was a knock on the door.

"Yeah?" Sophia called out.

"It's me. Nathan."

"Just the man I wanted to see," Sophia said, and smiled to herself as she reached for the lock.

I heard the door unlatch so I quickly put the small jewelry box in my pocket. I watched the door being open with a mighty heave.

"Hi, Sophia," I kissed her on the cheek.

"Is that all?" Sophia asked. Suddenly her eyes bulged.

"What?"

Using a great Mae West accent she asked, "Is that a jewelry box in your pocket or are you just glad to see me?"

I smiled. "I have something I need to tell you."

"Tell me or ask me?" Sophia said.

This was going to be harder than I thought. "Have a seat." I pointed to the bed and sat down next to her. "When I first met you, everything you said encouraged me, made me feel good, and I felt like as long as I was with you, I knew I would be a good person."

Sophia looked at me with deep eyes.

"But you took me to a part of myself I never knew existed." I tried to figure out how to say this. "You helped me to…care about others."

I took her hand.

"I realize now that all I felt for you initially stemmed from the need of being told I was a good person. But you helped me to realize I don't need to hear that from anyone except myself."

Sophia's eyes began to drift. Looked like she knew what was coming next.

"I'll be leaving the country soon. If I asked you to be with me, I think I would just be asking for someone to always be there to validate me. I need to practice giving myself validation, right now. But I want you to have this."

I took out the jewelry box from my pocket and handed it to her. "A parting gift. As an expression of how I feel about our time together."

Sophia nodded without opening the box. Tears fell from her eyes and she hugged me.

I held her back to look into her eyes, my hands on her shoulders. "I'll see you again. I promise." From looking at her eyes, it seemed to me that she believed my truthful words. "And who knows what the future holds, right?"

"Who knows?" She gave me a smile.

I gave her a kiss and embedded its memory in my heart as a code waiting to be unlocked.

Chapter 80

After driving away from Sophia's apartment in the early afternoon, I pulled over to the curb. Interrupted the trip to my duplex. I looked out through the car window. Other cars passed me, probably wondering why I pulled over. I picked up my phone. Had one more call to make.

"Hi, Rabbi? It's me, Nathan."

"Nathan! Are you all right?"

"I'm fine. Listen," I said. "The Torah mentioned an apocalypse."

"Yes," the rabbi said. "The word was encoded in *Breisheet.*"

I told him all that happened. The entire evening on Mount Megiddo, Sophia's seizure, the *Shekinah's* words, everything. When I told the rabbi about Sophia speaking as the *Shekinah*, he said something in Hebrew I didn't understand. It sounded like he was expressing his shock. I explained all else that happened that evening.

"It's incredible, Nathan."

"Yeah. I was wondering if you knew why the Bible said there'd be an apocalypse, and yet one didn't happen."

"One moment," the rabbi said. "I have my computer on. Let me try checking something."

I heard him typing. Soon, the rabbi said, "Nathan, I don't know what to say."

"You don't know?"

"No, what I mean is, these things are easier to find after the fact."

"What things?" I asked.

"Here it is. Right in front of me. Crossing over the word apocalypse is the phrase, 'was averted.' "

I sighed.

"What is it, Nathan."

"It's just…It shows that anyone can read whatever they want into the Bible."

Were the codes really there? I thought about the statistical study the rabbi mentioned. Wondered if it was done right.

"Nathan, do you know the story of the manna from heaven?"

"Sure. While the Israelites were wandering through the desert, God fed them manna."

"Exactly. Well, the midrash says that the *taiim*—the taste—of the manna was what anyone wanted it to be. Should they want it to taste like strawberries, it would taste like strawberries. Should they want it to taste like Sugar Snaps cereal, it would taste like Sugar Snaps cereal."

"Sugar Snaps?"

"Nathan, the ones who looked for the *taiim* enjoyed the manna. The ones who didn't look for the *taiim* found it to be tasteless."

"So?"

"So the Torah is the same. We can find all the inconsistencies, and problems with it to our hearts content. But should we want to improve ourselves, then we must search for the goodness of the Torah. The *taiim*. The question is, Nathan, what goodness will *you* take from God's words? "

I looked outside. Cars drove by.

"Thank you, Rabbi." I hung up and pulled off the curb to continue on my way to the duplex.

The rabbi placed the phone back in its cradle and sat still, reflecting on everything Nathan just told him.

"*Baruch HaShem.*"

He pulled a set of keys from his pocket and unlocked the metal cabinet at his feet. The bolt popped out and he opened the drawer. In the back of the drawer, he reached in and felt for the catch. When the catch released, the back of the drawer sprung open, allowing him to pull the drawer a centimeter further and reveal a hidden back section to the drawer. Inside was a single manila file. He pulled it out and opened it. A piece of paper numbered from one to thirty-six had the names of thirty-five men. The last one, number thirty-six was still blank.

He thought about Nathan and his adventure in Israel, and Nathan's encounter with the *Shekinah*. But most of all, the rabbi thought about what Nathan had said. The *Shekinah* spoke through Sophia, a woman of two souls: her sister and herself. Double *chai*. Double eighteen.

Beside number thirty-six, the Rabbi wrote "Sophia Patai."

Epilogue

Five months later

Sophia lugged the brown bag of groceries into her apartment building. She set the bag down by the row of metal mailboxes, opened her mailbox, and flipped through the mail.

"Junk, junk, junk, bill, junk, bill, junk, and junk."

She tossed the junk mail into the blue recycling box, grabbed her bag of groceries off the floor, and snatched her rolled up newspaper that lay atop the mailboxes.

After climbing the flight of stairs, she juggled the groceries, mail, and newspaper while putting all her weight against the door to open it. The door finally gave way and she let her momentum propel her and everything in her hands onto the bed. Some oranges rolled out of the tipped-over bag and off the bed onto the floor.

She bent over to pick up the oranges and her eye got a hold of one of the newspaper's headings: "Thousands of Lives Saved by New Invention."

Sophia glanced briefly at the first paragraph of the article. It mentioned Nathan's name! She sat down and twisted the ring on her finger as she read the article.

BADUKROM, Ghana (AP) — Thousands of lives are saved everyday with a new invention that provides free energy to desalinate water. Nathan Yirmorshy, co-coordinator of Project MEG, has demonstrated that a device called the Motionless Electromagnetic Generator (M.E.G.) has the ability to provide the electricity necessary to purify water for drinking.

The M.E.G. was patented in the US in 2002. Don Hammel, a volunteer for Project M.E.G. told us that the M.E.G.s are free energy devices that extract energy from the vacuum, which is empty space. This idea of energy from the vacuum, Hammel said, has been buried in the scientific literature for decades but has never been put to practical use until recently. Hammel explained that this project was Mr. Yirmorshy's baby and considering how it has saved the lives of some 112,000 Africans daily, Hammel considers Yirmorshy to be one of the finest humanitarians with vision of our time. When asking Nathan Yirmorshy for comment he only said, "Cupcakes."

Sophia laughed through her tears of joy. She looked at the ring Nathan gave her. The royal blue sapphires, her birthstone, sparkled and glittered and promised. It was an expression of how he felt about their time together. She took the ring off to look at the inscription again. Inside the ring she read the words, "No regrets."

Fact

Sir Isaac Newton spent more time searching for codes and prophecies in the Bible than he did studying science. Most of the letter in the prologue was taken directly from Newton's writings.

The Bible codes phenomenon was not established firmly in the realm of science until 1994 when Doron Witztum, Eliyahu Rips, and Yoav Rosenberg published "Equidistant Letter Sequences in the Book of Genesis" in *Statistical Science*. The paper has been met with controversy, personal attacks, and ridicule. Responses claiming to be scientific scrutiny against the experiment have been published in many places, including Statistical Science. For example, one criticism was the "wiggle room" possible in the spellings of names used in the experiment. When looking for "Johnathan" to see if it is encoded in the Bible, for instance, one might do a search for "Johnathan," "Johnny," "John," and "Jon." If only "Jon" appears, then the name is technically found encoded in the Bible. Opponents offered a list of different spellings Witztum, Rips, and Rosenberg could have used in their experiment. When Witztum, Rips, and Rosenberg tried the alternate spellings suggested by their opponents, their results *improved.*

The Motionless Electromagnetic Generator uses recent discoveries in physics to be an effective alternate energy source. Again, controversy, personal attacks, and ridicule have been directed at the inventors. People have said the inventors claim to have built a perpetual motion machine. Incidentally, perpetual motion is not impossible. In fact, it is the definition of Newton's first law of motion. What people mean when they say perpetual motion is impossible, however, is that energy cannot be made from nothing, which is true. But the inventors don't claim that the Motionless Electromagnetic Generator makes energy from nothing; they claim it makes energy from the fabric of spacetime. Considering that the shape of spacetime has the ability to pull planets into orbit, spacetime is not the same as "nothing." Information on how the Motionless Electromagnetic Generator works can be seen in "Explanation of the Motionless Electromagnetic Generator with O(3) Electrodynamics," Foundations of Physics Letters, 14(1), and "Explanation of the Motionless Electromagnetic Generator with the Sachs Theory of Electrodynamics," Foundations of Physics Letters, 14(8).

Lastly, the correspondence with author Dan Brown mentioned in the book is an actual correspondence I had with him. I look forward to the popcorn.

Appendix

TEN

Introduction to the Essays

Ever since the paper on the Genesis codes by Doron Witztum, Eliyahu Rips, and Yoav Rosenberg was published in *Statistical Science* in 1994, a flurry of magazines, websites, and books – including this one – have sensationalized the phenomenon. I've asked Mr. Witztum permission to reprint his public statement to emphasize that the equidistant letter sequences – the letter skipping codes – cannot be used as a method for predicting the future. Imagine finding encoded words, similar to pulling a bunch of words out of a hat, and getting, "Ezra Barany," "banana slug," "cheese ravioli," "eats with licorice." Does that mean I'll one day see a banana slug while eating cheese ravioli with licorice for dessert? Does it mean a banana slug will one day see me while it's eating ravioli and licorice? I sure hope it doesn't mean I'll one day eat a banana slug with licorice. Trying to determine the future by examining a bunch of encoded words is impossible. In my opinion, the only conclusion one can reach from the Genesis code experiment done by Witztum,'

Rips, and Rosenberg is that the author of the book of Genesis was prescient. And when I first learned of the Torah Codes in Aish HaTorah's Discovery seminar in Jerusalem, realizing the author had to be prescient was significant enough to have me rethink my relationship with Judaism. I hope it does the same for you.

I've included an excerpt from Jeffrey Satinover's book *Cracking the Bible Code* as a historical primer on how the Bible codes went from being an intriguing phenomenon to a rigorously scrutinized study. In the excerpt, Satinover mentions an Aaron code. Eliyahu Rips, Professor of Mathematics, did a search for the number of times the encoded name "Aaron" came up within Leviticus 1:1-13, a passage about the burnt offering performed by Aaron's sons. Based on the number of times the letters that spell "Aaron" come up within the passage, and based on a random distribution of those letters, the expected number of encoded "Aaron"s was 8.3. In other words, the name "Aaron" was expected to appear encoded about 8 times within the passage. *The name appeared 25 times.* To confirm the results were significant, Rips tried a control experiment using jumbled versions of the letters that spelled Aaron's name. The control experiment had insignificant results. He also tried searching different texts of the same length. Again, insignificant results. Only Leviticus 1:1-13 had the statistically significant result. A cryptologist calculated the odds of this happening at 1 in 2,166,818.

Other essays in the Appendix address the *Shekinah*. The *Shekinah* is, in my mind, a concept too often ignored. I felt it imperative to compile a collection of essays that would help clarify the role *Shekinah* takes in Judaism. Rabbi Shefa Gold's beautiful and personal expression of the *Shekinah* in her essay "*Shechina* and *Mishkan*" is a heartfelt articulation of how we can feel God's presence in our lives if we provide a dwelling place for God within us. "God: Some Feminist Questions" by Dr. Judith Plaskow is a vital perspective on how so much more must be done in Judaism to honor women. Dr. Zvi Bellin's essay powerfully illustrates one of the moments he felt the *Shekinah* in his life, and I found it significant that he portrays God as having the aspect of presence, and not as having a gender. Tania Schweig's essay beautifully reveals the *Shekinah* as the electric energy you and I feel when we communicate and search for truth together. I hope you will enjoy these essays, not as a complete look at what the *Shekinah* means in Judaism, but as a stepping stone to further investigate what Judaism means to you.

The Bible Code Emerges

Excerpt from Chapter 8
of *Cracking the Bible Code*

Jeffrey Satinover, M.D.

I was skeptical when I first became aware of the Torah codes. But when I saw how the advent of technology allowed a careful study of the validity of the codes, I realized I needed to learn more about them. I discovered Jeffrey Satinover's book Cracking the Bible Code. *Satinover's book gave me the insight I needed to understand the history of codes in general and the role they played in Judaism specifically. As a result, I crafted the rabbi character in my story to provide evidence in support of the Torah codes, and give the reader context for the codes. ~EB*

For millennia, the codes in the Torah could never have been more than a sidelight. They were simply too hard to find, and they were extraordinarily difficult to confirm. Indeed, the very idea of *statistical* confirmation is relatively new (and it remains confusing to many still). When, in the thirteenth century, Rabbenu Bachya had remarked that "if the eyes of your heart will be opened, you will see that [the encoded date of the primordial new moon] is not by chance," he was conceptually far ahead of his time in even addressing the possibility that it might be. But he did not have the mathematical tools to justify his claim. It only *seemed* to him to be true. The skeptic would—and should—try to burst the bubble. The eyes of the heart always see what they want to see. Jeremiah himself pointed out that "the heart is deceitful above all things" (Jeremiah 17:9).

What precipitated a dramatic new era in the ancient story of the codes was not simply the discovery of the never before identified "Aaron" code in Leviticus (discussed in Chapter Three); it was the application of formal statistical analyses to the codes—and the unexpected results. Therein lay the confluence of generations of intellectual, spiritual, and scientific endeavors. The claim that codes existed in the Torah lay at the very heart of kabbalah, the ancient Jewish tradition. Out of this tradition, as we have seen, developed the art of cryptology, and as the crucial element for cryptology's further development there emerged mathematical statistics. In time, the success in the making and breaking of codes became a life-and-death matter for nations—and by the twentieth century, for the entire world. Such pressures force-bred the development of computers. With all these elements in place, it became possible for the first time ever to reexamine the ancient mystery. Before Eliyahu Rips's work on the "Aaron" phenomenon, no code in the Torah had ever been approached in that way—nor could have been.

At about the same time, other Israeli scientists had become aware of the phenomenon and were beginning their own investigations. Mostly the investigations were cooperative, but as in any scientific endeavor, competition began to arise as well—all to the good, since structured adversarial debate between qualified disputants is both the emotional fuel for scientific advance and the best insurance of intellectual rigor. (Your work had better be good because your highly qualified opponent has a big investment in proving it isn't.)

But this precipitated another kind of debate: between religion and science. Even at this early stage, some religious voices were beginning to express concern that in such an approach to the sacred Torah, science was treading where it ought not. It was a reaction that would arise repeatedly, among both believers and skeptics. This dichotomy is the modern form of Cartesian duality, a kind of mental and psychological "keeping kosher"—not with separate plates for meat and milk, but with separate mental repositories for science and faith, matter and spirit, head and heart. But to keep science apart from religion is to keep hope and wish uncontaminated by solid evidence. In any event, the first of Maimonidies' thirteen principles of the Jewish faith states, "*Know* there is God...," don't just believe it. How does one do that without evidence?

By the late 1980's, the challenge as to whether the codes research was "kosher" had been put to respected rabbinical authorities. Had an ancient gateway, theretofore tightly sealed, been opened wide to yet another level of meaning in the Torah, or was the gate an illusion? Should the gate be opened using so cold and profane a key as statistics, in principle a "skeleton key," which anyone could use on anything? Should it be opened *at all*? Assuming the work proved scientifically valid, just what *were* its religious implications? What if the research failed? What would that prove, or seem to? What effect might be expected on the spiritual well-being of those involved in the research, not to mention those not closely involved—and unable to form an independent assessment?

These were serious concerns with potentially serious consequences. Not too long ago, a young Jewish couple considering a return to Orthodoxy put off the bris of their newborn son—the ritual circumcision that brings the child into the Covenant of Abraham—pending the publication of a refereed scientific paper on the codes. When such a paper was published (see Chapter Twelve), they proceeded with the bris. This scenario had to have been a thoughtful rabbi's worst nightmare for dozens of reasons. The most obvious of these is the question, What would they do if the paper was later rebutted?

But in the eighties, these storms were as yet no more than mild crosscurrents to Eliyahu Rips's careful, dispassionate process of testing and probing the solidity of the growing number of findings. As the head began to discern the outlines of what the heart had long envisioned, specific parameters of the codes phenomenon began to take shape—parameters that could be sharply defined and measured. Accordingly, the search process was refined. The research began to grow more focused, and therefore increasingly subject to rigorous scrutiny and quantitative assessment. Unstructured exploration slowly gave way to a-priori hypothesis formation, controlled testing, and statistical analysis. The phenomenon began to look genuine, possibly, even to those with scientific—not just religious—training. It was now worth examining, even if still too imprecise for formal publication and peer review. [...]

A growing number of scientists, rabbis, astonished secularists, and curious visitors from all over the world were beginning to peek over the shoulders of the growing number of scientific experts now seriously studying the "poetic exaggerations" of the sages. Dr. Moshe Katz, a bioengineer at the Technion in Haifa, Israel's equivalent of MIT, began to pursue the phenomenon at first in concert with Rips and later independently. Controversy began to brew, with highly qualified scientists and nonscientists, religionists and secularists, lining up on both sides of the question, Can these findings possibly be real? Opinions were rarely moderate. Either the material was unequivocal proof not only of divine authorship, but of any theological principle you wish (all at the same time); or else it was utter nonsense. That Eliyahu Rips was on the former side of the debate, however, was a bit disconcerting.

By now, it was the mid-1980s. A physics student in Israel who had just completed his master's thesis on general relativity had also left his secular life behind to become a *baal t'shuva*. The term means literally a "master of repentance" and refers to those who return to a strict observance of the ancient faith. He, too, had come to learn of the codes in the Torah, and the more he learned, the more he became convinced they were genuine. He carefully consulted with the senior rabbis who were his teachers and guides as to how he should best pursue this material—or whether he should pursue it at all. They gave him their blessing, and with that he turned his considerable intellectual gifts to the daunting task of placing codes on a rock-solid scientific foundation. In short order, Doron Witztum would become the preeminent codes researcher in the world, ratcheting up the technique to a yet higher level of sophistication and power; generating evidence of its validity that began to reach high-level scientific publishing circles.

Jeffrey Satinover, M.D., is a practicing psychiatrist and former William James Lecturer in Psychology and Religion at Harvard. He holds degrees from M.I.T., the Harvard Graduate School of Education, Yale University, the University of Texas, and recently completed a Ph.D. in physics (summa cum laude) at the University of Nice, France. He lives with his family in Connecticut.

Public Statement

By Doron Witztum
Jerusalem June 4, 1997

One of the only researchers of the Torah codes to have his study published in a scientific journal, Doron Witztum clarifies the value of the Torah codes with caution, and presents his thoughts in a manner that helps establish credibility for them. Even though my main character, Nathan Yirmorshy, did not go the next step toward evaluating the veracity and integrity of the codes himself, I wrote this novel to invite the reader to take that step. An excellent place to start is by reading Doron Witztum's own perspective. ~EB

A. **People often ask why, over the last 12** years, I have spent so much time in the field of hidden codes in the Torah, instead of my original field of interest-modern physics and general relativity. The discovery we have made concerning hidden patterns in the Torah is ultimately much more far-reaching and significant. The repercussions of our discovery touch on the very nature of human existence. It can be looked at as the same feeling Robinson Crusoe had when he first discovered the tracks in the sand, that he wasn't alone on the island.

We have called this press conference as the researchers who did the original research on the topic of hidden codes. We will be focusing on three issues:

1) How, using standard scientific and statistical tools, we found that details of ancient and modern history are encoded in the original Hebrew text of the Torah.

2) To discuss the many books and works that have been published related to this field that have no scientific basis, and are therefore meaningless

3) As the researchers, we will explain why it is impossible to use codes to predict the future.

B. A brief overview of the development of codes research

1. According to mystical sources in Jewish tradition, the Torah can be read and understood on many levels, including the level of a "hidden text." It is composed of words spelled out by skipping equal numbers of letters through the original Hebrew text.

We call this phenomenon ELS- Equidistant Letter Sequences. The problem with measuring the significance of what we find is that ELSs will certainly appear in any text, and any word may appear many times at many skip distances.

2. Twelve years ago, I developed a method to see if this hidden text could be scientifically and objectively validated. The idea is as follows: It is a natural property of any text that words that are conceptually related are likely to appear in the same area of the text. Therefore we decided to see if the ELSs of related words also tend to appear in the same area of the text of the Torah. In order for the convergence of two ELSs to be considered successful, we developed two criteria. a) A close proximity of two ELSs b) That the ELSs that appear are ELSs with a relatively short skip distances between the letters, compared to other ELSs of that word.

3. Professor Eliyahu Rips developed the mathematical system for measuring the statistical significance of the results. Yoav Rosenberg took Eliyahu's ideas and developed an appropriate computer program to carry out these experiments.

4. In 1986, an extensive experiment was conducted which checked the overall tendency of convergence of a large list of pairs of words: names of famous personalities and their dates of birth and death. The experiment succeeded. A paper describing the results was sent to a scientific publication, and this became the beginning point of a rigorous six year process of review and analysis until it was finally published. Several referees checked the work and asked for further testing. One of these involved re-running the experiment with a completely fresh set of data, and also checking other control texts. This was done and the research passed all tests with very highly significant results. The article was finally published by *Statistical Science* in 1994.

5. Harold Gans, formerly a senior cryptologic mathematician at the U.S. Department of Defense, conducted an independent experiment to test the phenomenon that we discovered, using a different set of data. His experiment also succeeded with highly significant results. He sent his paper for publication to a scientific journal. Their response was "This phenomenon has already been scientifically established, so your work is just another example of the phenomenon."

6. We have conducted seven other experiments that are available as pre-prints.

7. At present, I am completing a book that gives a true view of this fantastic phenomenon, and that will describe not only the ten experiments I mentioned, but also many other successful experiments which reveal a vast spectrum of subjects, ancient and modern.

C. Our comments on the book of Michael Drosnin, and other similar books that have been published

1. On the one hand, we are happy to see publicity for the phenomenon of Torah codes. 2. On the other hand, there is a danger that the entire credibility of codes research will be destroyed. Mr. Drosnin's work employs no scientific methodology. No distinction is made between statistically valid codes, and accidental appearances, which can be found in any book. For example, Drosnin's "code" of the comet Shoemaker Levy crashing into Jupiter is statistically meaningless. Such a code can be found by accident in 1 out of any 3 books checked!

2. What is the danger of research done with no scientific parameters? For example, we know that the field of health involves systematic rigorous testing of new medicines. If someone freely distributes a medicine that has undergone no scientific testing, there are two areas of damage: 1) The credibility of useful and helpful medicines will be severely compromised. 2) People may end up using useless medicines in place of helpful ones.

In codes research, we are dealing with a similar situation: 1) The credibility of serious codes research will be compromised by amateurs whose "discoveries" are scientifically meaningless; 2) People will exploit the Torah to present all kinds of counterfeit proofs, by finding "hidden messages", that bolster their ideology.

We have a very important and valuable phenomenon that has been discovered. It's a scientific discovery that can really help us get a better understanding of the nature of our existence. Rather than have it watered down with people's personal exploitation or misunderstanding, we should be investing more in serious research and understanding of the phenomenon.

In summary, one who wishes to show legitimate examples of Torah codes should at least follow two basic rules: A. Use mathematical tools that can provide a level of statistical measurement between the minimal occurrences of ELSs. B. Use an objectively chosen list of words to look for:

I will now show an example of what I mean by an objective list. This example has never been shown before publicly:

The process is to take one central word, find its minimal occurrence in the text, and then construct a tableau based on it. In this case, our topic is the death camp Auschwitz. We take an objectively chosen list of related words. In this case, we are looking for the names of the subcamps that comprised the Auschwitz complex. We make a tableau based on the words "of Auschwitz." With our tableau set, the computer will systematically look throughout the text for a minimal occurrence of each of the sub-camps. Any one of these words can appear anywhere in the text of Genesis. We find something very unexpected that they consistently appear in the area of the words "of Auschwitz."

D. The Future: Mr. Drosnin's book is based on a false claim. It is impossible to use Torah codes to predict the future.

I myself as the original researcher of the phenomenon of Torah codes, investigated thoroughly the question of predicting the future. I reached the conclusion that it is impossible. I saw this through experimentation and also as a simple point of logic. There are several reasons why it's impossible. I will give the most basic reason. In general, we always have difficulty understanding a text where we don't have any syntax or punctuation. In the plain Hebrew text of the Torah, without punctuation, I could easily read the ten commandments as telling me to steal and murder. There's a verse that describes Moses being commanded to bring incense. I could easily read it as a commandment to use drugs. All we have is a few isolated encoded words of a hidden text.

Maybe we're missing some very critical words. It's literally impossible to learn a coherent story out of the juxtaposition of a few words that may be somehow related. Additionally, just like there is a code that Rabin will be assassinated, I also found a code saying that Churchill will be assassinated!

Even regarding past events, there are ELSs of words that appear near each other that have no relation to each other. It is therefore unwise, and one could say irresponsible, to make "predictions" based on ELSs of words appearing near each other.

In summary, we see that predicting the future is impossible. We see that by publicizing books and works of examples of codes that have no scientific basis, it ruins the integrity of serious research. And finally, we see that the scientific phenomenon of Torah codes is a real one, and is one that deserves serious attention.

Doron Witztum was a post-graduate physics student before Torah codes captured his attention in the mid-1980s when he became friends with Professor Rips. He and Professor Rips worked together systematizing a way of examining the Torah code phenomenon to formally test the hypothesis of whether or not they occur by chance. The result of their joint work was eventually published in *Statistical Science* in 1994. Since then, Doron has dedicated his professional efforts to the development of advanced techniques for detecting and testing the Torah code hypothesis.

Shechina and Mishkan

Rabbi Shefa Gold

The rabbi in my story described the Shekinah *as Divine Presence. Nathan and Sophia got to experience that firsthand. In* Shechina and Mishkan, *Shefa Gold explains the connection between the Divine Presence and the dwelling place within us, so the reader may have their own experience. ~EB*

The Book of Exodus, mapping our people's journey to Freedom, culminates in the building of the *Mishkan* (the portable sanctuary that we carried through the wilderness). *Va'asuli Mikdash v'shochanti b'tocham.* "Build for me a holy place so that I might dwell within." This commandment is the one that I hear, the one that guides me each day as I journey to Freedom. *Mishkan* means "dwelling place". *Shochanti* means "I will dwell." And from the same root, *Shechina*... "She who dwells within us."

God will take us out of *Mitzrayim*, the narrow place, the place of separation... in order to "be your God" which means to be in connection and to know the Oneness of all. How do we know that oneness? How do we come into connection? By building a holy place, by making a space in our hearts, relationships, communities, world… for God's Presence, for *Shechina*. Without that holy place, that innerness… we are back in slavery, disconnected from the whole.

I make my heart into a *Mishkan,* a dwelling place for God, by cultivating an inner life, by listening into the silence, by being vulnerable to the beauty that transforms, by learning the power of wilderness, by clearing away the ashes of the past, by honoring the Holy of Holies at my core. From within, *Shechina* whispers.

I make my relationships into a *Mishkan,* a dwelling place for God, by stepping back in awe of my beloved, and trusting the space between us as holy, by stepping forward in service, by taking responsibility for my own triggers, by acknowledging the mystery of Love, by paying attention to the details of kindness. From the space between, *Shechina* speaks.

I make my community into a *Mishkan,* a dwelling place for God, by honoring differences while celebrating our shared humanity, by making room for expression, by not being afraid of conflict, by having faith in the process of collaboration, by laughing together, by learning from our mistakes and inspiring each other with visions. From among us *Shechina* sings.

I make my World into a *Mishkan,* a dwelling place for God, by trusting my heart, honoring my relationships, building communities, by knowing and living the interconnectedness of all Being, by enjoying each miraculous moment in unconditional gratefulness for the journey of Life, by spreading joy whenever I can, by keeping my heart open in compassion, by awakening the light at the core of darkness. From that innerness, *Shechina* shines.

Shechina isn't somebody "other." She lives whenever I build that holy place, whenever I make space for Her, whenever "I" get out of the way. She whispers, speaks, sings, shines whenever I am still enough to listen or transparent enough to channel Her Light.

Shechina isn't some goddess outside us. She is the force that underlies and unifies all that is. When she touches me, I can only surrender to her power. In Her absence (my forgetfulness), I am inconsolable. When *Shechina* is hidden, I am enslaved, held captive on the surface of this world, a victim of circumstance. When *Shechina* reveals Herself, each moment unfolds in infinite, intricate beauty; each molecule vibrates in exquisite harmony; and darkness itself shines.

When *Shechina* is at home in my heart, my relationships, my community, my world… then this _is_ The Promised Land flowing with milk from the Source of Nurture and honey from the sweetness of some unnamable essence.

It is the *Mishkan* that gives us access to the *Shechina*. And Her Presence opens the door to the infinite, right here at the heart of this finite world. She shows us the vastness, the eternal soul that still shines in each moment, even through the ravages of change, even through our dying. To experience that radiance, that light of *Shechina*, is to know Freedom.

It is the *Mishkan* that gives us access to the *Shechina*. And we must build the *Mishkan* by being generous, by paying attention to the details of spiritual practice, by forgiving the past and opening completely to the Divine flow, by bringing to this project, a highly-refined sense of beauty, creativity and adventure.

Shechina longs for us as we long for Her. "Build for me a holy place," she calls, "so that I might dwell within."

Rabbi Shefa Gold is a leader in Aleph: the Alliance for Jewish Renewal and received her ordination both from the Reconstructionist Rabbinical College and from Rabbi Zalman Schachter-Shalomi. She is the director of C-DEEP, The Center for Devotional, Energy and Ecstatic Practice in Jemez Springs, New Mexico. Shefa composes and performs spiritual music, has produced ten albums, and her liturgies have been published in several new prayerbooks. She teaches workshops and retreats on the theory and art of Chanting, Devotional Healing, Spiritual Community Building, Meditation, and trains Chant Leaders in Kol Zimra, a two year program for rabbis, cantors and lay leaders. She is also on the faculty of the Institute for Jewish Spirituality. Shefa combines her grounding in Judaism with a background in Buddhist, Christian, Islamic, and Native American spiritual traditions to make her uniquely qualified as a spiritual bridge celebrating the shared path of devotion. She is the author of *Torah Journeys: The Inner Path to the Promised*

Land, and *In the Fever of Love: An Illumination of the Song of Songs* published by Ben Yehuda Press.

For information about how to order CD's and about Shefa's teaching schedule, visit her website: www. rabbishefagold.com.

God: Some Feminist Questions

Why female pronouns for God may not be enough.

Judith Plaskow

In The Torah Codes *the* Shekinah *shows up as Her own character, sharing my vision to provide the female aspect of God in support of reconnecting Jewish women to Judaism. Dr. Judith Plaskow makes the point that female pronouns might not satisfy women's need to feel more connected to Judaism, and that Jewish women need to find the contemporary language for the living presence of God today.*
~EB

An extraordinary passage in *Pesikta Rabbati* (21.6) describes the many guises in which the one God has appeared to the children of Israel. God spoke to the Israelites on Mount Sinai not "face to face" (Deuteronomy 5:4) but "face after face." "To one he appeared standing, and to one seated; to one as a young man and to one as an old man." Showing them a plurality of aspects, each appropriate to some part of the divine message, God revealed a threatening face and a severe face, an angry face and a joyous face, a laughing face and a friendly face.

This midrash at once points the way out of the feminist dilemma of God-language and simultaneously illustrates its most trying aspect. It acknowledges the legitimacy, indeed the necessity, of plural ways of perceiving and speaking about the one God. It asserts that multiple images of God are not contradictions of monotheism but ways in which limited human beings apprehend and respond to the all-embracing divine reality. And yet, while the passage authorizes theological and liturgical inventiveness, the many faces of God it describes are only male ones. God is an old man or a young man, a man of war or a man of wisdom, but never a woman.

This unyielding maleness of the dominant Jewish image of God is not the end of the feminist critique of God-language, but it is its beginning. The absence of female metaphors for God witnesses to and perpetuates the devaluation of femaleness in the Jewish tradition. The God-language of a religious community is drawn from the qualities and roles the community most values, and exclusively male imagery exalts and upholds maleness as the human standard. It belies the biblical insight that God created human beings, male and female, in God's image. It denigrates women's lives and experiences as resources for knowing the sacred.

Transforming Meaning, Not Just Old Terms

As this language has become increasingly alienating to large numbers of women, those committed to shaping a living Jewish spirituality and theology have looked for ways to change it. They have sought a richer and wider range of images for speaking about and to the sacred. The *Pesikta Rabbati* passage seems to suggest that of those who saw God on Sinai "face after face," it was only the men who recorded and passed down their experiences. Feminists have taken on the task of recovering and forging a female language for God, female not simply in its metaphors but in its mode of religious apprehension and expression.

But if feminist attempts to find a new vocabulary for God began in the concern with gender, they have not resulted in a uniform response to the oppressiveness of traditional language. Rather feminist explorations of God-language have gradually opened up deeper dimensions of the problem of God. Early feminist efforts to make God a mother and give her a womb, to praise her as birthgiver and nourisher, performed important functions. They validated women's sexuality and power as part of the sacred. They pressed worshippers to confront the maleness of a supposedly sex-neutral liturgy. Yet at the same time, these efforts often left intact images of dominance and power that were still deeply troubling. If the hand that drowned the Egyptians in the Red Sea was a female hand, did that make it any more a hand feminists wanted to worship?

The issue of the maleness of God-language has thus ineluctably moved to the question of the nature of the God feminists want to pray to. Where do Jewish women find God in our experience, and what do we find there? What images most powerfully evoke and express the reality of God in our lives?

The Guises of the Empowering Other

While these questions lend themselves to unanimity even less than the issue of gender, there is a theme that seems to sound strongly through a range of feminist discussions of God-language: the need to articulate a new understanding of divine power. If the traditional God is a deity outside and above humanity, exercising power over us, women's coming to power in community has generated a counter-image of the power of God as empowerment. Many Jewish feminist arguments about and experiments with God-language can be understood to revolve around the issue of how to express this new image and experience of power in a way that is Jewishly/feministly authentic.

For some Jewish feminists, for example, it is non-personal imagery for God that most effectively captures a conception of divine power as that which moves through everything. Metaphors for God as source and fountain of life evoke the deity that is the wellspring of our action without tying us to gendered language that channels and confines. For other feminists, the question of divine power lends new interest to the continuing debate about viability of the image of *Shekinah* in a feminist Judaism. This image, which at first seemed to promise such a clear Jewish way to incorporate female language into theology and liturgy, also has been resisted by many feminists as part of a system that links femaleness to immanence, physicality, and evil. In the context of the quest for new metaphors for power, however, this image of deity provides an interesting resource for feminist thinking about a God who dwells in the world and in the power of human relation.

For still other feminists, it is incorporation of the names of goddesses into feminist liturgy that best conveys multiple images of female power, images that may have had power to our foremothers and that thus connect us in community to them. Use of these images does not constitute polytheism any more than do the multiple images of *Pesikta Rabbati*. Rather, these images fill out the traditional record, exploring and recovering faces of God that have been forgotten or expunged.

The Old/New Search for the Ineffable

These forays into new imagery are experimental and tentative, and there are many Jews for whom some or all of them will seem shocking or foreign. Yet if we attend to the roots and intention of these lively experiments, we can find in feminist experience a potentially powerful resource for the revivification of Jewish religious language. The feminist experience is one of finding in community both a sense of personal identity and power, and the power and knowledge of God. This experience may not be so different from that of the early Israelites who found together in community both a new national identity and connection with the God who gave it.

From a feminist perspective, the problem with traditional Jewish God-language is that the initial experience of empowered community found expression in images that established hierarchy within the Jewish community and that marginalized or excluded half of its members. The challenge to women as we seek to name the God we have experienced "face after face," is to find a language that carries through the experience of divine power in community and that evokes the living presence of God in the whole Jewish people.

Dr. Judith Plaskow is a professor of religious studies at Manhattan College. She is the author of the landmark work *Standing Again at Sinai: Judaism from a Feminist Perspective*, and the author or editor of four other books, including *The Coming of Lilith: Essays on Feminism, Judaism, and Sexual Ethics, 1972-2003*. Dr. Plaskow has lectured widely on feminist theology in the United States and Europe. She co-founded *The Journal of Feminist Studies in Religion* and co-edited it for its first ten years. She is Past President of the American Academy of Religion. Her books are available now at Amazon.com.

The Power of Presence

Zvi Bellin, Ph.D.

While The Torah Codes *increases awareness of the* Shekinah, *the* Shekinah *that makes Her appearance in the novel is not the same* Shekinah *in which every Jew believes. Zvi Bellin, for example, presents the* Shekinah *as a divine connection between two people from different worlds.* ~EB

❝You are a black panther, not a computer." Cowering in a large blue plush chair, she said these first words to me in a hushed tone with the point of an elongated ashen finger. I inhaled, waited, wondering if I had permission to come closer and learn more. At 43-years old, Nnedi was a patient in a mental hospital. She spent most of her days locked in a ward, wearing an oversized faded violet sweat suit, and nodding on and off from psychotropic medications. She spoke with a West African accent, perhaps Nigerian, perhaps Ghanaian. Her skin was dark chocolate, though with several crimson blemishes which she picked into her skin with her own nails. Her hair was shaved short, and her eyes shown a deep brown.

I met Nnedi when I interned as a Psychiatric Chaplain for a summer in 2006. When I was not leading psycho-spiritual groups for patients, I was tasked to visit various wards to connect with patients individually. The healing work of a chaplain can be very raw. I had no needles, or herbs, no medicines or machines. The only thing I carried was my own story and my own presence, and these, I have learned, are enough to make space for change. That morning, Nnedi and I gazed into each other's eyes wondering if there was a connection to be made.

I asked her if she wanted to chat with me for a while. She pointed to the chair next to her, inviting me to sit, and answered, "You are a black panther. I see it in your eyes. You are good." I took the seat, curiosity brewing within me. We held gentle conversation about the program on television that was playing in the day room, and deepened into the details of her life before she came to the hospital. Estranged from her family, she had been living on the streets, alone and sick. She was unsure of what her diagnosis was, or if she had any long-term health problems. Nnedi was arrested while she was wandering the streets, seemingly in a rage, shouting and attempting to undress herself in public. She did not know how long she had been in the mental institution, though seemed content to have shelter, food, and the occasional conversation.

What I saw before me was a strong, though delicate woman. Able to survive on rough urban streets, and probably a victim of multiple traumas throughout her life, without medication Nnedi teetered on the brink of sanity. I later learned from her files that she was HIV positive, though refused to acknowledge this. She had a daughter, though was in no state to play the role of mother. On intake, Nnedi reported being beaten throughout her life, she talked about men attempting to murder her, and multiple sexual assaults. Nnedi was a case of how the harshness of the word could absolutely break a person. Where does healing for a person like Nnedi begin?

"Ha, ha! You are a black panther! Not a computer" She shouted this time, leaning closer and sitting on the edge of her chair. Her bold smile revealed more than pearly white teeth; it demonstrated a commitment to her aliveness. Her joy was contagious, and I found myself smiling too, a hearty chuckle bubbling forth from my belly. "Nnedi," I asked, "What does it mean that I am a black panther and not a computer?" Her eyes lit up with hope and wisdom, as if finally, someone inquired what she had been longing to talk about.

"A black panther is an animal," she began matter-of-factly. "It is of nature. You are of the Earth, of this planet. You have a good heart and you care. You sit and listen. A computer does not care. It only asks question after question, and then goes away. It just analyzes."

My body was flooded with warmth and respect for Nnedi, as she acknowledged the subtle natural medicine we had been sharing. My time for our visit was coming to its end, though I asked one last question.

"Nnedi, who is a computer?" I inquired in a gentle tone.

She peered around slowly, from side to side, scanning the entire room. She looked back into my eyes, and said softly with complete conviction, "The doctors. They only want to give me medicine and then leave. They don't really care."

My heart broke and I was also amazed. From the depths of her insanity she was teaching me and all those who would listen a lesson about true healing. I asked Nnedi if I could visit with her again. Her response was to take my hand and hold it softly against her cheek. I thanked her for sharing time with me and humbly walked away.

What is Shekinah? It is the lingering presence of comfort that exists when you place your hand on your heart and take a deep breath. Shekinah is the vehicle of presence that allows two people who come from different lands, generations, and stories to connect, communicate and bring each other valuable lessons and healing. My story above is about how Nnedi and I brought simple presence forward in our exchange. In the Rabbinic text, *Ethics of the Fathers* (Chapter 3:3), we are taught that when two people study Torah together the Shekinah rests. To me this means that certain kinds of relationships allow the transcendent spirit of the world, which cannot regularly relate to this world, a place to rest and become felt. With the presence of Shekinah we tangibly manifest God in our relationships between self, other, and world.

There is no need for fancy tools or ancient theories to make this happen. Nnedi and I approached each other with curiosity, respect, and willingness. We wanted to learn from one another, we wanted to see the other as valuable and worthy of connection. We were so very different, though the same physical matter, and in the Jewish perspective of Shekinah, this unites us and creates the capacity for love. During my summer as a chaplain, I learned about the power of my own presence. By simply showing up to a situation, with my unique story, I create the potential for real change. That change can be positive, negative, or neutral. In the Jewish story, the ability of presence to transform the world is possible because an aspect of God, the Shekinah, still lingers and hovers, still caresses and imbibes the face of the Earth.

Dr. Zvi Bellin holds a Ph.D. in Pastoral Counseling and is a Nationally Certified Counselor. Through his work with Nehirim: GLBT Jewish Culture and Spirituality (www.nehirim.com) and Moishe House (www.moishehouse.org), Zvi has directed intimate retreats for Jewish communities that are both spiritually uplifting and intellectually stimulating. His teaching style follows the tradition of blending Torah study with contemplative Jewish practice. Zvi has studied extensively with teachers spanning various Jewish denominations, including, Rabbi David Zeller, Miriam Ribner, Rabbi Zvi Miller, and Rabbi Jeff Roth. For more information visit www.meaningthroughbeing.com.

Shekinah

Tania Schweig

Tania Schweig presents an interpretation of the Shekinah *that is different from the one described in* The Torah Codes, *and is similar to Zvi Bellin's. Tania's* Shekinah *brings sparks and fire, a portrayal embodied in Nathan's vision of Her. As you read Tania's words, you'll notice that her expression of defining the* Shekinah *comes straight from the heart. ~EB*

Shekinah.
I pause. No thoughts. Just an instinct to put hand on belly, close eyes, breathe in.

Shekinah.
I remember.
I'm 21, or so. It's summer in Jerusalem, my first. I've come from Berkeley, cynicism in tow. I've come to visit a friend for late night talks, irreverent arguments. I don't buy this religious phase she's in. Friday night arrives after a flurry of shopping and cooking and

cleaning. We light candles and exit the house, opening the door into the fresh quiet. All artificial noise has stopped. And it feels as though all artifice has stopped with it. Dressed in flowing skirts we walk through the newly silenced streets. What is that feeling? Like the lightness of the head after a haircut or the blissful vitality after the fever has broken: the senses are heightened, alert to the exquisite beauty of the falling light, sated by the perfection of what is. I feel in love with something. My heart expands, upwards and outwards. The quiet has a softness, a roundness. There is space in this quiet and there is potential. We sing into the quiet: L'cha Dodi, Likrat Kala, Come with me my beloved, to welcome the Bride! Why does it actually feel like a wedding? How is it possible that even the paved sidewalk can be part of this joy?

Shekinah.

I imagine. I imagine one of those awesome Torah conversations that starts with a simple contradiction in the text. We push and pull and dig. Argument that rises above the self. Argument for the sake of Truth. Together we peel away layers. You say something and I pause. My eyes open on the inside. We must have gotten there, we must have exposed the shining core! It flickers in and out, because that electric spark between two minds can only stay so long, but we both know in that small moment that it was real: This living Torah! This living Torah!

Again.

Shekinah.

And what can I say? Do you know that when the Shekinah actually rested in the Holy of Holies that the two angels on the ark would face each other? Were there sparks then? I imagine them, staring at each other, these angels of gold. Staring at each other. The energy of their seeing like electrons jumping back and forth, back and forth.

The Shekinah is Presence, God's very Presence here with us, on this earth, in our passionate conversations in search of truth. In our moments of open and receptive quiet. They say that the Shekinah is in exile, just like us. She'll be back when we've made things right. But there are glimpses and traces... and for us impoverished souls even a glimpse can ignite.

Or.

Could it be that the Holy of Holies is still here? In the space between two faces, two faces genuinely gazing towards each other? Electric Shekinah sparks dancing and rising between and above.

Tania Smith Schweig has a B.A. in Sociology from U.C. Berkeley and a Masters and Credential in Special Education from USF. She spent a year in intensive Torah study at Pardes Institute in Jerusalem and continues her Jewish education through weekly engagement with traditional and philosophical texts. Tania helped create the resource program at Oakland Hebrew Day School where she works as a learning specialist. She is also a mother of five and writer of personal essays on Jewish topics. Tania's essay entitled "Back to the Future" explores the ways in which Shabbat observance reveals the deep relevance of Torah life in today's complex world. It is archived at http://www.kqed.org/a/perspectives/R911200735

Acknowledgments

You've all read the trite phrase in hundreds of acknowledgments, "This book could not
have been completed without the help of the following
people." But in my case, it's true, so there's no avoiding
the statement. I want to thank the contributors, Doron
Witztum, Rabbi Shefa Gold, Dr. Judith Plaskow, Dr.
Zvi Bellins, and Tania Schweig for transforming my
book from a thumping good read to a thumping good
discussion builder.

Thanks also goes to my proof readers which
include my bride Beth Barany, my critique group
buddies Julie Moorro, Mary Newton (a.k.a. Meredith
Ironside), Allerton Steele (a.k.a. William Brasse), and
family members: my father-in-law Martin Reisberg,
my parents Bella and Ron Barany, my cousin Derri
Pollack, and others. If it weren't for them, all of my
sentences would be very, very, very difficult as it would
be to, like, read hard.

I also wish to honor the emotional and financial
support I received from my parents, Kate Gong, and

others. You can see the names of all the wonderful people who contributed financially to the completion of this book at www.TheTorahCodes.com.

Thanks also goes to software company Research Systems at www.Research-Systems.com, for providing me their Bible code program "CodeFinder" which was used to generate the Bible code images for this book. And a warm thanks to Heather Smith who did the cover design. Her patience with me was an accomplishment in itself.

Lastly, the contents of the story *The Torah Codes* in no way reflect the opinions of the contributors. Any errors or exaggerations of Judeo-Christian tenets are my own.

About the Author

Ezra Barany has been fascinated by codes and puzzles ever since he was a little tot. He started writing suspense and thriller stories in college and got seriously interested in the Bible Codes while attending Aish HaTorah's Discovery Seminar in Jerusalem. *The Torah Codes* is Ezra's first novel. Ezra has been a high school physics teacher, fiction writing teacher, songwriting teacher, ESL teacher to French children and pop performer. In his free time, he writes mushy love songs inspired by his wife and book coach Beth Barany.

Ezra now lives in the San Francisco Bay Area, where he is working on his next book. He is available for presentations and select readings. To inquire about an appearance, please contact Ezra@TheTorahCodes.com.

Breinigsville, PA USA
22 March 2011
258162BV00001B/1/P